CANTERBURY WOODS

GC FISHER

Printed and bound in Great Britain by Clays Ltd, Elcograf S.p.A

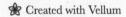 Created with Vellum

FOREWORD

Lockdown has been hard on a whole range of people, for so many different reasons. It caused me to look much closer to home, to look at people around me and question my own assumptions about who was okay and who was not. I wanted to find out who was giving help and who needed it. Throughout this story I have touched on a number of issues, all of which justify significantly greater exploration but I hope that this fictional story will help you to start your own discussions.

ACKNOWLEDGMENTS

Thanks to all of those who have kindly read the manuscript and those who have provided insights into the worlds I have touched on. Trauma and PTSD Victoria Hamilton; homelessness John, ex servicemen and servicewomen Jan; police matters Steve Swain; story editor Rachael Morris; story editor Raoul Morris.

Story readers and thank you so much for the encouragement: Andy Briggs, Anita Lewton, Alexandra Peers, Anne Gately, Anne Westcott, Avril Roundtree, Carla Morris, Carmilla Cardina, Caroline Morris, Catherine Droubaix, Christina Coleman, Corrie Jeffreys, Damian Morris, Edward Hillier, Fiona Boyd Stokes, Gill Wilson, Gillian Whyte Fagundes, Hugh Horsford, Jane Kagon, Jean Hogg, Jean Stanton, Jenny Kos, Jenny Richardson, John Richardson, Kim Horsford, Marcella Finnegan, Maria Sheehy, Matthew Scott, Melise Nevin, Nathalie Milliken, Richard Nevin, Ruth Kelly, Sally Fegan-Wyles, Sandra Gray, Susan Mulhall, Wendy Taylor, William Fegan.

Would you like to keep up to date? Join the mailing list:
https://www.gcfisherauthor.com/contact

CHAPTER 1

THE WORLD RETURNS TO A
NEW KIND OF NORMAL

Things had got better, but Maeve had to accept that it would never be the same as before. Maeve had taken to walking the woods further away from home, in the stretch from Canterbury towards Fordwich. It meant a short cycle first, but this area, touching the old military base, was a lot less manicured than the ancient Blean forest, so generally less frequented and much quieter.

Maeve got out of the house early, not too early, but early enough to miss the pre-work runners, and hopefully to be well on her way before the dog walkers, and the fashionable ladies, exercising loudly, were up and out.

It was months since she had accepted that spirits could communicate with her. She never wanted to talk to the dead, but they seemed to find her. She had overcome thinking it was a load of hokum, now it was simply fact.

This morning, her timing was spot on. Not a soul. She left the road and took the inconspicuous path alongside the youth centre. The shell of a rusting burnt out car was rotting in the undergrowth. She had been here enough times that she was no longer concerned the culprits might be lurking nearby, and actually thought this was a good way to keep the woods private and casual walkers away.

The summer had gone, and it seemed that the earth had turned overnight, from sufficiently hard baked that it needed a pickaxe to break it, to a squelchy sea of mud. The sun was low in the sky, glinting on the water left by the overnight showers and showing off the yellows and oranges of the beach trees against the clear blue above. She hopped from side to side of the path, to avoid the worst of the puddles and muddy tracks left by the off-road bikes, finally, getting deep enough into the woods to have a carpet of leaves underfoot. Now she could breathe. There was a warm silence. The smell of the earth felt right, restorative. Her spirits lifted.

Maeve, wasn't sure if it was the effect of the colours or that earthy smell that did it, but as she picked up her pace she felt happy and at peace. Walking on her own was the time that she could let her thoughts flow, she noticed the vividness of the green in the moss, as she mentally set the world to rights.

'How much has changed in the last year? Who would have thought that a pandemic would sweep the world? Sure there were films like 'Contagion', but that's Hollywood not real life. Yet, here we are in 'Lockdown 2', where wearing face-masks has become the new normal, and you are more nervous of strangers getting too close because they might infect you, rather than rob you.'

The family dynamics had radically changed too. Maeve hadn't consciously processed this, and was still living day to day, which the pandemic was helping with. Her daughter Marianne, had gone to college, this was her first term. Of course, there had been that debate which most families in the same situation had probably had, 'what was the point in going to University if all the lectures *could* be online and at some point most likely *would* be online? Especially if the second wave was going to be as bad as they thought it might be!' In the end Marianne had been both logical and firm,

"I need to get used to being away from home and to settle in, and even if a reasonable amount of the course is online, I will still get the tutorials. I need to start managing my life on my own." That was that.

Maeve and her younger daughter Orla, had driven Marianne up to Cambridge.

They had made plans to go for a last celebratory lunch together, before leaving Marianne. They dropped all her belongings off and Marianne took bags and boxes up to her room straight away.

Then, as they should have expected, the students were told they had to 'bubble' in groups, and the family were told not to meet them again in person. Marianne, made signs through the door indicating she would FaceTime them. She did, and was able to show off the interior of her new home, telling Maeve that her rooms were clean and friendly, and that she would be fine.

All in all, it was a rushed and brutal parting, where Orla and Maeve suddenly found themselves standing by the car not knowing what to do. Neither wanted to celebrate without Marianne, both feeling a little lost. Instead they opted for a service station take-out on the way home.

'Thank God for FaceTime', thought Maeve, at least we will be able to talk to her and won't feel so far away. She hated the thought of Marianne being lonely. She didn't want to think of the gap Marianne would leave in her own life, that wasn't fair. She reflected 'your job, as a parent, is to prepare your children for flight'. Still she didn't like to think of all the students alone for the first time, and probably many now quarantined in their own rooms.

A squirrel jumping from tree to tree dropping acorns, brought her back to the here and now. Part of her loved the random noises in the woods but another part was still nervous of coming across something more sinister. Some years back, she had stumbled upon a homeless gang who had either been on drugs or alcohol, and who made her realise that in the middle of the woods she was pretty far from help. They hadn't seen her and she had turned smartly, back-tracking out of the woods, but it gave her a fright.

In the cold of the first lockdown, the Council had gathered up all the homeless and given them shelter.

Maeve, needing a change from nosy passers-by, had come back to give these woodlands another try. She found that the atmosphere was completely different. Now, you were more likely to meet a poodle in a Burberry coat, than a crazed stranger.

As she passed the hollow with the big oak tree dripping with curtains of ivy, she wondered how old it was, guessing definitely more than a hundred years. Inelegantly, she scrambled up the incline to where the woods opened out to reveal gorse and rabbits. 'Kissing is out of fashion when the gorse is out of bloom', she remembered from childhood. She stopped, to carefully sniff the flowers avoiding the thorns. As she breathed that slightly coconut smell in, she was immediately taken back to summer holidays in the north of Ireland, and the joys of a Wall's smiley face ice cream at the end of mountain treks.

Smiling to herself, she walked on, slipping on the muddy edges of the tracks, she descended back under the trees thinking of her mother Ada, who, if she was there, would be shouting 'hands out of pockets!' She guiltily took her hands out, just in time to stop herself falling over on another slide.

This brought her thoughts firmly to Ada. Lockdown had been hard on both of them. Maeve and Ada, had faced some pretty raw truths this last year and they were building a new relationship. Ada, had a heart condition and had turned seventy, so was in a high risk category, hence she had been self isolating or 'shielding', pretty much since March. They had managed weekly outings over the summer, still being careful, keeping the two metre distance and staying outside.

Beach walks in Sandgate, with a takeaway coffee perched on the concrete slipway, overlooking the sea and the honey coloured shingle. But it wasn't the same. No hugs, no dropping round and staying for dinner. The children, who were of course young adults but still her children, had been adamant, 'we want to have Ada around for years, we don't want to be the ones who killed her!' So they kept their distance.

By now, Maeve had done a big loop around the reed lake and was heading back, when she heard some rustling noises. She was idly thinking that there must be more squirrels this year, or maybe it was the blackbirds, rooting through the leaves for worms. She caught a smell of something. It was like a passing feeling of sadness drifting in the air.

Then, crack!

In this part of the woods, in the hollow under the tree canopy, there were no other sounds. The traffic from the city was far away, and the little plane that had been buzzing around had gone. That was definitely a crack, a stick breaking.

Abruptly pulled out of her reverie, Maeve stopped, turned around, and looked. Nothing. Silence. A bit too silent.

She had had the woods to herself this morning. When she moved she had disturbed the wildlife, the birds flew off and settled back after she passed. The field mice and the squirrels had rustled or jumped to a safe distance. But here, nothing else was moving. She looked as far as she could see. The trees had been shedding their leaves and the undergrowth had died back, so she could clearly make out the structure of the trees and the layout of the woods. Slowly, she did another three-sixty degree turn, and took it all in. A few stray leaves fluttered down to the ground, the wind was blowing gently through the trees, nothing else. 'Sometimes there are just cracks', she thought, 'a branch that finally can't take the weight anymore, it has to happen even when there is no one to see it.' Still, it put her on edge.

Then, in the stillness she was forcefully hit by a wave of incredible sadness. It passed. It was not her sadness. She felt a sense of direction, something was calling her to follow it.

As if she could smell it, Maeve instinctively knew, where to turn, knew, exactly which direction this sadness came from. Her experience was still limited but it felt like a spirit reaching out from the other side, this time no words, just emotion. As she moved closer the waves of feeling were so strong that she had to stop and stand still until it passed. It was draining and the tears were flowing down her cheeks, she knew this wasn't her sorrow, but she cried all the same. She came to an area with dried bracken under the trees. If it wasn't for the sharp intensity of feeling that stopped her moving, she might actually have stepped on the body.

CHAPTER 2

IT ALL STARTS AGAIN

L eaves had almost covered the corpse and his clothes blended in with the brown, yellow, gold of the natural debris. Lying in a foetal position, maybe he was squatting when he keeled over, or maybe he just lay down to die. Either way, she didn't need any official autopsy to know that he was long dead.

Maeve still had Steve's mobile number in her phone. It hadn't been used for some time now. Not since their disastrous last encounter. Steve, officially Detective Inspector Stephen Maguire, came into Maeve's life when she discovered that the dead or, 'those who had passed over', could talk to her, and it turned out that those who were murdered, wanted to talk.

Maeve and Steve almost had a thing going, but there had been too much pressure, too many things changing in her life, and a new relationship was the one that tipped over into being the one too many to handle. However, she thought that now wasn't the time to mull over her romantic life. Now, she needed to talk to someone who would do the right thing, someone who would believe her and not think she was crazy, and that was Steve.

His voice was warm and confident, he let her know that he was happy to hear from her. They were both old enough to slide over any potential embarrassment, and move on to the practicalities of Maeve's discovery. Maeve said there was no rush, this person had been dead for some time.

She was surprised that she was so calm. Putting her phone back in her pocket, she stood there looking down at the body. She felt a sense of closure, peacefulness, this person was not sorry to leave this world. But something was niggling at her. Something didn't quite add up. The sense of sadness that had brought her here, still lingered in the air. She wasn't sure if it was actually connected to the dead body at all.

Steve was there in minutes. He loved to jump on his motorbike whenever he could, and it was a short ride from the police station by the back roads towards the Council offices, and on up past the Courts. He called Maeve again, and got her to 'share location' so that he could pinpoint her, rather than describe tree types, he wasn't a walker and so he didn't know the layout of the area.

She was quite near what she thought must have been an old military communications tower, now a satellite mast, not far from the road. Steve found her easily.

Maeve hadn't moved, she had stayed looking at the body, waiting to see if the spirit wanted to talk to her. Nothing. She felt nothing coming from this person. But… she felt something else moving around.

Steve took photos, to confirm the situation precisely as it had been discovered, in case there were any questions later on, and before anything was disturbed. They both thought that any evidence was long gone, but best to follow procedure.

Steve, set the police machinery in motion. Maeve knew that this would take time. The forensic team would cordon off the area. The ambulance would be waiting to take the remains to the morgue. And Steve's team, plus the others, would fill the site with activity, so these few minutes were the best time to take in the whole picture, before the hubbub started. They stood side by side, but not too close together, in contemplation.

First impression, was that this was a man, perhaps in his fifties, not too young anyway. Hard to tell his age precisely, especially if he had been living rough, which was their surmise. It didn't look like suicide. If it was an accidental drug overdose, that would show up in the autopsy. Steve stepped to one side and squatted down for a closer look at the head, careful not to disturb the surrounding area. Nothing. Well, nothing obvious.

He stood up, stepped back, and whilst keeping the appropriate two metre distance turned to Maeve, as if in the middle of a conversation, and said,

"Maybe we are overthinking this. Sometimes people die. His hands and fingernails suggest someone who has had a hard life, so if he was a rough sleeper, it might be due to natural causes."

He was right, Maeve had been feeling the same.

"I feel a sense of calm, as if he wasn't holding on to life." She didn't mention the other emotion that she had picked up moving around her, not the right time, she thought.

Now that they were just standing there waiting, Steve and Maeve became conscious of each other's presence. 'Oh God,' thought Maeve, recognising that emotional attraction which was still there between them, 'even if I wanted to have a relationship, how does anyone do that, with social distancing in a pandemic?'

What she said was, "So, how are things with you?"

CHAPTER 3
ADA THE MENTOR

B y the time Maeve got home it was late morning and the residual dampness had penetrated her jacket, crept up her legs, and chilled her to the bone. She could have left earlier; she didn't have to wait for the police to finish their business; in fact that was still on-going. She had stayed, because felt she owed the dead man some respect, as if, by being there as a civilian witness, he had a mourner, someone concerned with his passing. To the police, he was either a corpse, or a victim, neither of which recognised him as a person.

Luckily, the house was still warm from the morning burst of central heating. The house had been put on strict limitations of energy use, since Orla had taken on her personal crusade to save the planet. Maeve felt a twinge of guilt as she put the kettle on watching the meter flip into the red, but the sun had been shining earlier so the solar panels should have compensated to some extent. Then she thought, 'what am I doing, boiling a kettle is fine! There is a global pandemic, people are dying, let's get this into perspective.' She wanted to do her bit for the environment and felt that her generation really had accelerated the mess the world was in, but it still needed a sense of balance. Right now her priority was to warm up and recover, before talking to Ada.

Edward, her resident house spirit, was fussing around behind her. She was used to him by now and generally didn't pay any attention. She was talking aloud to herself, when he reacted as if she had scalded him.....what had she said? Playing it back in her mind, Maeve had been describing the wood, the specific trees, the location and that very strange feeling of someone else's grief. She couldn't see the logic in his reaction, so asked him directly,

"Edward, what's going on? What's up with you?"

Edward always looked the same, like he was in a faded fancy dress costume, or doing a bit part in a period drama. He had been in Sir Edward Hales' service and only found peace when doing domestic chores, he thought this was his home. In practical terms, he couldn't make tea but he could move objects, he could also tidy things and surprisingly, he could make beds. Normally he was happy and Maeve found that she liked having him around. At the moment he was hopping from foot to foot wringing his hands.

"You shouldn't go there. You shouldn't go into the woods. People live there, you know, thieves, bandits, bad people. They have been living in the trees for some time now."

Maeve frowned as she considered this.

"Hmm" she said as a noncommittal holding noise, while she finished making the tea. Thinking this was another question for Ada.

Ever since Maeve had accepted that she had the gift of communicating with certain spirits, or more bluntly, that she could hear the dead, when they wanted to talk to her, she had been working out how to control this gift. Her mother Ada, was the official medium, but, following on from her heart attack, Ada had lost her ability to reach over to the other side. Ada, still said it was a temporary glitch, but now many months on, Maeve wasn't so sure.

In the meantime, Ada was still the frontman, handling the publicity fallout from the dramatic events of earlier in the year. The paranormal communications and police chase leading to saving the life of the young PhD student, Adam.

Ada, was the kind of medium people expected to see, with striking make-up and dramatic outfits. She fulfilled the role with aplomb. She didn't see herself as a charlatan, more like 'on a career break'.

She had also nominated herself, as Maeve's mentor. They had worked out a way of doing things that suited them both. Maeve would encounter a situation, they would talk about it, and then Maeve would decide how to act on it. There were no abstract theory lessons. Primarily this was because Ada was a terrible teacher and Maeve who wasn't in a rush, had decided that learning through practical examples might be slower, but it was something that brought them together, and that was her first priority.

Now, Maeve wanted Ada's considered opinion on two things, first, to know what she had met or felt in the wood, and secondly, how best to interrogate Edward, to elicit the most useful information. Clearly he knew something which might be important, but wasn't telling her directly.

She texted Ada, who at that precise moment was in the process of doing her Cyanotype prints. Always an artist, Ada had revived her creative skills since lockdown, and was rushing to catch the daylight. So they agreed to make this an afternoon tea session.

This was another system they had come up with. It was a way to make it feel as if they were in the same room. In advance, they would agree on a food type, today it was toasted crumpets, dripping with butter, there was no disagreement here, with honey or the last of the summer's homemade raspberry jam. Accompanied by their favourite drink depending on the time of day, Barry's tea in Ada's case and, the now wholly compostable, PG Tips tea bags, approved by

Orla, for Maeve. They would set up their respective iPad and laptop, positioned halfway along their own table so that when they Zoomed, or FaceTimed, it felt as if they were sitting opposite each other, on a weird composite table. It was strange, but it was a lot better than nothing.

Maeve was impatient, she wanted to tell Ada her news and work out what was up with Edward, who was still jumpy. She had painfully learnt that not all spirits were good, they could be wily, and manipulate you into doing their bidding. Equally, you could demand things of the spirits. She still wasn't sure if they were obliged to do what you demanded, but sounding authoritative had worked for her in the past. This was still an area she thought of as, 'work in progress'.

To get out of the house before her teatime rendezvous with Ada and avoid Edward's fidgeting, Maeve went shopping.

Over the last year Maeve had gone from being part of a family of three, plus a wonderfully renewed relationship with regular visits from Ada, to being just Maeve on her own most of the time. Orla, was out championing environmental causes, Marianne, was in college and Ada was self-isolating. The house felt particularly empty when Orla was out on one of her missions. Even though Orla had just turned seventeen she had followed her hero Greta Thunberg, and become an environmental activist. Maeve and her ex husband, Pascal, had agreed that she could take time out of academic study so long as she got reasonable grades in her GCSE's, to give her some qualifications for later on, if she needed them. She had done fine, so had held them to their promise. In the moment it felt like the right thing to do. Of course, hit with the reality of their child becoming an Eco Warrior, it was a different kettle of fish. They were all still taking this a day at a time and had agreed to review the situation at Christmas.

Orla had been away for some time, but she was coming home today, and would be back in time for supper tonight. At the moment, the activists' focus was trying to save ancient trees, growing in the path of the planned high speed railway to Birmingham, HS2. They had been camping up in the trees. Maeve couldn't imagine the sanitary conditions, and didn't really want to think about what they did when they needed an emergency trip to the toilet. They had just lost some hundreds-of-years-old oak trees, so she thought Orla would probably be feeling bruised.

Maeve wanted to cook something nice for both of them. So, she was off to Waitrose to get some edible Spanish chestnuts, planning to be back in time, to get rid of any single-use plastic wrapping before Orla arrived. Not that she didn't want to do her best for the planet too, but for some reason vegetables without plastic, were more expensive than those in wrapped packs. It didn't make any sense, but for now finances were tight, Maeve was one of the lucky ones, she had started a new contract in the summer, and with the second lockdown they had put her on furlough, rather than let her go. The chestnuts in Waitrose were still a luxury, but one that she could afford once in a while. They were for Orla's new favourite dish, which was butternut squash, chestnuts and rice with sage butter. In fact, it was the butter in the sage butter that had stopped Orla from going completely vegan, for the time being.

Maeve parked her bike. Her bicycle was another concession to Orla, which she now loved and was grateful for. As she wandered past the plant section outside Waitrose, she saw John, the Big Issue seller, and waved. Maeve liked to give something to someone she knew, in her view, if you were lucky enough to be okay, it was time to share good fortune. There was a lady in front of her handing over a five pound note with a whispered

"You keep the change, I think you will need it this time. Take care, and hopefully I will see you on the other side of this lockdown, fingers crossed it will be before Christmas."

As she watched, it gave Maeve the time to think about how to approach the delicate questions, she wanted to ask John. It had occurred to Maeve, that John might know more about the situations that led to the homeless people camping in the woods. She stood there and she wondered about the body. Not a body, a man, the man that she had come across. It dawned on her that it might be someone John actually knew. Maybe this wasn't the time to mention it, and maybe it should be Steve asking the questions.

CHAPTER 4

WHAT'S GOING ON?

"Jesus, you don't want to mess with those fellas!" Ada had a turn of phrase that was at the same time easy to think you understood, while really needing a lot more explanation.

"What 'fellas' are you talking about? And what do you mean by 'mess with'?"

Maeve had learnt to take a slow breath, and let go of the tension. She didn't want to be short with Ada, but from years of dismissing her mother as 'away with the fairies', she still found Ada frustrating at times.

"I mean the fellas in the woods!" As if it was completely obvious, and Maeve was trying to be difficult, Ada did not hold back. "The fellas, you have been telling me about for the last half an hour."

"What fellas? I didn't see anyone except for the man who was dead, and I didn't feel his spirit anywhere either." Maeve's exasperation was coming through, despite her best efforts.

"Okay, okay, let's not fly off on one, we can take this handy. You were walking in the woods, right? You felt a very strong emotion that wasn't your own? Am I right so far?" Ada was now the calmer of the two.

"Yes, yes, of course, that's what I have been telling you." Maeve was now almost in tears of frustration.

"Calm down." Ada didn't seem to notice that these were the very words that drove Maeve to distraction. "Okay, so." Ada stopped speaking as if she had just made everything clear.

"Okay, so, what?" Maeve no longer knew what to say, to get Ada to explain herself.

"Ach! You know what I mean! The emotion wasn't just 'a feeling', it was a thing. They don't have a name that I know of, but they are like poltergeists, to normal people. I mean you can feel them, the same way a normal person can see some-thing flying about in their house. They are just some sort of fella! Well, don't mess with them, they are trouble and if they can, they will lead you astray, or into real trouble. There may be some that are good ones, but the only ones I have met, are more like a 'Will o' the Wisp', leading strangers into bog holes to drown." Ada stopped talking.

Silence. Ada was thinking of past experiences and Maeve was taking it all in. They had set up their screens, a pot of tea on each side of the digital divide, along with the remains of their individual, freshly toasted crumpets. Pouring some tea from the pot into her cup to heat up her unfinished remains, Maeve said,

"I haven't met anything like this before, how do I manage it or them, so that they don't lead me into trouble?"

Ada was thoughtful for a few moments, and then declaimed with confidence,

"Practice! You need practice. I think we need to come up with something a little safer for you to get used to, before getting involved with those 'boyos'. I am thinking that you have only communicated with those you wanted to help, or thought that you could help. And you have shut off any others. I mean Canterbury is teeming with spirits, so it has been a good policy to shut most of them out, or you would never get any peace. Maybe it's time to change things."

She paused,

"I need to make a fresh pot of tea to think this out."

With that, Ada disappeared from the screen and left Maeve in contemplation as the sounds of the water heating in the kettle grew in the background.

They were now officially in lockdown and not supposed to go out except for exercise, or essential shopping. Maeve felt that she had to admit that she was going into Canterbury the next morning. She had arranged to get a takeaway coffee at Fond's, at the same time as Steve. Fond's, was her new favourite haunt, it was behind the High Street, in a quiet, discrete back lane, with a table and chair outside for the take-away customers, and the 'flower-bikes', decorously perched on the other side of the lane, to make you smile. She didn't want to share that she was meeting Steve, because she knew Ada would want to know all the details, and she wanted to work out what she felt about him, for herself first.

Ada sat down with her steaming mug and started where she had left off,

"This is it. You take your exercise through the centre of Canterbury tomorrow. Walk, don't take your bike, you would be too fast on a bike to feel a spirit, even at the dawdling speed you go at. Walk slowly, down one of the side lanes, ideally without any other people on it, sometimes other people can cause interference. Then open your mind." Ada paused with a frown, "Jesus, I bet you are going to ask me how to do that now, aren't you?"

Ada was not a good teacher, when she was in the right frame of mind Maeve could laugh at her. This time she was following Ada with rapt attention, and of course Ada was right, she was just about to ask, so she did laugh,

"Well, how else will I know what you are talking about?"

"Okay, okay. I'll do my best." Ada sighed.

"You know the way people talk about the 'flow' of something, or getting into the flow? Well it's like that. To start with, it's probably best to close your eyes, stop thinking, try to empty your mind of all the normal stuff like shopping lists, or where you are going, or what time it is."

Ada hesitated, trying to find the right way to describe something that was completely natural to her, but which she had never put into words before.

"If you focus on your breathing, that can help you to stop thinking. Feel the air coming in cold and going out warm, nothing else. Then do that for a while, and if there is something there, you will feel it."

After the call Maeve was enjoying processing this interesting task, or piece of homework, she was intrigued.

Then hearing an "Ehemm" behind her, she remembered Edward, and thought 'bother I forgot to bring that up with Ada. Never mind, it's a good subject for another session tomorrow.' And on the upside, she didn't have to admit to her coffee date with Steve. For the moment, she was happy that she had a new challenge which felt under her control and she had kept her private life to herself.

In reality, she had no idea what she had let herself in for.

CHAPTER 5

THE NEW CHALLENGE

Orla being back, really cheered Maeve up. She didn't have to think about her future; she could focus on Orla's present. They could bang the table about the unfairness of something, the ridiculousness of some politician, or policy, or the American election, and what Donald Trump might or might not do. It felt like they were doing something, even if they were just wholeheartedly agreeing with each other. It was active and positive.

One of the things she had recently read on Facebook rang true, someone posted 'I thought 2020 was the year that I would get what I wanted. Instead it was the year I appreciated what I had.' Maeve truly appreciated her family. And her garden. And living in Canterbury, where her neighbourhood had bonded through looking out for each other, it had become a real community. A lot of which was online of course, but in general, people seemed to care more for each other, and were doing things like the pimped up flower-bikes, to make people smile. Values had changed, hopefully that wouldn't all disappear when this was over.

Earlier, Maeve had opened a bottle of organic red wine as a celebration to go with the food. Once supper was on the table, they called Marianne, and again ate together in a virtual sense, as they shared all the domestic gossip.

Maeve didn't mention that she was going to see Steve in the morning, though he was on her mind, and she knew that both Marianne and Orla approved of him. That was probably why she didn't want to say anything. Last time there had been too many people in the know. It would be better to keep it to herself for now.

With an extra glass of wine the conversation got silly. They could still do that, tell jokes, laugh till they were giddy. It is much harder to do when you are not in the same space, both emotionally and physically, but they all needed the release.

Orla started hiccuping, which set the others off laughing again till they realised that she wasn't laughing, she was now crying, sobbing.

At least this time, Maeve was in the same room, and could envelop her in a hug. Marianne had started crying too, laughing and crying are often closer than people think, it's the level of emotion that can switch. For Marianne, it brought home the loneliness that she felt and underlined that she wasn't there to help Orla.

After a few moments had passed, Maeve said,

"I know this is tough on all of us. Let's talk it through and see what we can do." Part of her felt glad that it wasn't just she who missed her children. She felt needed, if traumatised,

"Orla, love, what is it? You're okay, you're safe, you're home now." Maeve held onto her as they rocked back and forth.

Orla took a few minutes to stop sobbing and blow her nose.

"It's not that. I'm exhausted and it's all shit. We only ever slept on and off for a few hours at most. And then after days and days, and actually weeks of all that, they cut down the trees anyway. Trees that were hundreds of years old. But they said, 'it's okay', because they planted a seedling somewhere nearby. It's not okay. We lost hundreds of years of life. It felt like murder!" And she started crying again.

Maeve could feel her fatigue, and thought that this wasn't the time to be logical, it was time to be the support refuge of 'home'.

"You are right Orla. And you are completely done-in. You need sleep. I am going to make you a hot water bottle. You go on up and get ready for bed. We can resume this conversation tomorrow, whenever you wake up, which I am guessing will be in the afternoon."

Redirecting herself to the screen, Maeve went on,

"Marianne, can you make a cup of hot chocolate for yourself? I'll make some tea, and in ten minutes or so I'll call you back?" Maeve knew that this wasn't the time to leave Marianne out of anything, they were reshaping the family bonds.

Orla gave in immediately, overcome with tiredness and was fast asleep, even before Maeve had called Marianne back.

Going through the domestic mechanics of boiling water, checking towels, and bringing the hot water bottle to Orla, had given Maeve a little time to catch her thoughts. When she reconnected with Marianne, she launched straight in,

"Marianne, how much of your course is online now? I mean, how much could you do from home? I know it's not the same but really, it might be better to make a fresh start in the new year. Vaccines are coming. By the summer we should be almost normal. It's not forever." In fact, Maeve was saying everything that Marianne had been thinking, and had already come to the same conclusion.

Marianne, now smiling, said,

"We are alike. That's pretty much what I thought too. So I have been self isolating just in case, and I could have a test tomorrow if that's negative, could you come and pick me up?"

Privately, Maeve was thrilled, but didn't want to seem too keen.

"Yes, yes of course. Let me know and I'll be there. It better be what you really want, because it will mean staying here for the rest of this lockdown at a minimum."

Ever practical Maeve went on,

"For the drive up to you, I won't stop on the way. When I get to you, I'll text, and you can meet me outside."

Maeve couldn't hide the fact that she was beaming, and even on screen she could see that Marianne's demeanour had shifted from feeling helpless, to planning mode. Orla's melt down had forced the three of them to face their emotions. It was a good way to end the day. She might have her family back in a few days.

The next morning, Maeve still had that lift in her step, and was more likely to laugh at Edward than let him worry her. She was walking quickly, so that she would have time to do her homework before her coffee with Steve. Since her experiences earlier in the year, unless she was in the right frame of mind to talk to the spirit in Beverly Meadow, she tended to skip the park and walk by St Stephen's. She had discovered a green pedestrian route, past the Kent Ballooning field, by the river Stour, at the back of Sainsbury's car park.

As she walked, she was trying to think of a good 'quiet' lane, to carry out Ada's practice session. Finally she fixed on Butchery Lane, it was a little out of her way but just off the High St. And the shops on it were shut for lockdown, so it was likely to be completely dead at this time of day.

She passed in front of the Cathedral main entrance, now covered in scaffolding and plastic for the current renovations; in a fleeting thought, she felt sorry for any tourists who had made the journey to see the Cathedral, and would miss out on the surprising archway entrance and Cathedral reveal beyond. Passing on down Burgate, she turned into Butchery

Lane. Town was already quiet, here, it was absolutely silent. No one at all. Perfect, she thought to herself.

She walked into the middle of the lane, opposite the half hidden entrance to the Roman Museum, now shut. Guessing this was probably the absolute quietest spot, she stopped. Feeling a little silly she closed her eyes, she could hear traffic in the distance, the occasional baby crying, a seagull who had come inland to shelter, or steal someone's chips. She tried to slow her thoughts down. She brought her attention closer, focusing on her breath. The sounds faded.

She could hear her breath, then just feel it. In cool, out warm. As she let go and allowed her breath to flow, she began to feel something or someone nearby. She could feel warmth, the atmosphere was close and she and they were in the dark. She felt in a tight space. Then, rushing at her she was over-whelmed with a blood red rage, a roar, warm flesh, hot breath, she could hear nostrils flaring. It was cramped, no room to move. She couldn't move. Then crunch, slash, crunch and she felt blood, warm, everywhere, pumping out of a living being, she had no way out, she was rigid, paral-ysed. 'Stop!' She was aware that she wasn't making a sound, but inside she was shouting, 'Stop!' It all stopped. Then, the close feelings began to fade, they receded, still there, but more, and more, distant.

At last, she could open her eyes. She hadn't moved, she was still in the middle of the lane, now, she could hear the passers by, smell the sausages from the street vendor cooking. She became aware that it was only a few steps away to the High St where everything was normal. She was the only one who had 'witnessed' the killing.

As if emerging from some kind of unconscious state, to find that she had been sleep-walking, Maeve had lost all sense of place and time. It had felt so real, she was completely shaken, her hands were trembling, she was weak. She lifted her head up slowly, looking around her, nothing, no clues. She looked at her hands to see the blood. Nothing. She was still partly in the trance, slowly, coming back into the real world.

Not sure what she was doing, but putting one foot in front of the other, she walked onto the High St, turned right heading for Jewry Lane, completely on auto-pilot. Was that an evil spirit, or had she just felt a murder?

CHAPTER 6

RECONNECTING

At some point, she registered that she was walking towards Steve, and felt some comfort. Here was the person who could make things better in the real world, who wouldn't need explanations. She needed a bear hug, and he was good at that.

Steve, was standing outside Fond's, the coffee shop, he knew something was wrong as soon as he saw her. Maeve was deathly pale and walking as if in a dream.

They'd had previous experiences, and seeing her like this made him forget that any time had passed at all. He walked towards her, wanting to wrap his arms around her and say it was all okay. But he was a policeman, and he knew that he had to set an example of how to behave in lockdown, so he couldn't. Instead, he gave her a reassuring broad smile to indicate how pleased he was to see her and said,

"Hot chocolate? Or something with a lot of sugar? You just sit down here, before your legs give out, and I'll get it." He guided her to one of the seats on the pavement. Leaving her for a minute, while he got the hot drinks.

They didn't say anything until she had warmed up, some

colour had returned to her cheeks, and she was breathing normally. Steve started.

"Okay, I can see that you have had a shock. There is no obvious sign of damage and you are not on your phone, so I guess you saw, or heard, something. Can you tell me what happened? Was it something real or, was it of a spiritual, or otherworldly, nature?" As he looked at her, he could see what looked like panic in her eyes.

She didn't speak, she couldn't. Maeve drank some more, the heat and the sweetness were working on her, at last she said,

"I don't know what it was. I hope I never experience it again."

After another pause, she started to describe what she had been through as best she could. It took a few goes before he could capture what she was trying to convey.

"Let's see if I have got this right. You were trying to 'feel' a spirit as an exercise, so you opened your mind?"

"Yes." Maeve had not fully recovered and was still having difficulty finding the right words.

"And you were on Butchery Lane, near the entrance to the Roman Museum, so you were also just outside where Timpson's the key cutting place was? Right?" Steve had that half policeman half friend tone, the confidence of which Maeve found very reassuring.

"Yes."

Steve went on, he had a hypothesis to share,

"I don't know if this is useful but years ago I remember a story that was in the paper. A girl called Emma, I don't know why her name stuck in my head. Anyway, this Emma who worked in Timpson's somewhere in the North of England, had won some sort of prize to spend the night in the most haunted Timpson's in the UK. It's coming back to me now, it was Halloween, that's it, and it was like a dare. She was to see if she could spend the whole night in the basement, and she got stuck on a train and nearly didn't make it. Something had happened in the basement. The staff who worked there wouldn't go down at night. Let me think about it a little longer, there was some story…."

Maeve had been happy to have Steve talking, his voice sounded safe and normal. She didn't want him to stop, so she said nothing and waited.

"Of course, the name, it's in the name of the Street. Butchery Lane. The basement under Timpson's was an abattoir, I mean a long time ago, maybe hundreds of years ago. There was a story that one night, some poor butcher went down to do his business, but something happened, maybe he was just careless, anyway he was gored to death by the bull he came to butcher. I think you would have been standing right above the spot where it happened."

Steve was pretty pleased that he had managed to drag it out of his memory. "I don't remember if the girl did stay the night. I remember thinking at the time, that I wouldn't do it for love nor money."

Silently Maeve agreed.

Steve couldn't officially give her a lift home on his motorbike, so when she had recovered to a more normal state, he suggested a taxi. Then Maeve looked at him a little dolefully and said,

"I know it might be a risk, but I would rather be with you, than in a car with a stranger. Depending on the autopsy, our man in the woods might be police business, plus there is someone I think you should talk to."

Sometimes, human need overcomes the official line. Steve was thinking, that everyday he had to go into an office and meet a wide variety of people, under much less careful conditions. She was right, it was official business, Steve already knew that he needed to have an 'on the record' conversation with her, but didn't think she was in the right state of mind today.

So they agreed, masks on, sanitised the bike, and then they were off. It was what Maeve needed, to be able to hold on to Steve, and feel that warmth and security. This was real, she thought, if she could just hold onto that thought, then she felt that she could deal with the trauma from the other side.

Steve left her at the door, with an arrangement to meet again. This time he suggested lunch, fish 'n' chips, on the pavement opposite Close & Hamblin fabrics, where, if it wasn't closed, you could go in and see the remains of the Roman baths.

As he left her, Steve remembered all the reasons that he liked Maeve, she might not look it, but she was strong. She would manage this, and by tomorrow would be ready to hear his news.

When she got inside, Maeve just sat for a moment. Not at all sure what to do next. Then she heard the noises of Orla getting up. Going in and out of the bathroom, water on, for her shower, cupboards opening and closing. Maeve realised that she was following the sounds, because they were so normal, so grounding. She picked herself up and began to think, I'm fine, I'm here, and it's time to get on with the day. So first things first, food, it might be mid morning but it was time for breakfast with Orla.

Yes, Orla, and her issues with the life she had chosen. It felt good to think about other people and not focus on herself. The routine business of sorting things out in the kitchen, of preparing boiled eggs, and toasting some homemade brown bread to build Orla up, all helped, and pretty soon, she felt like herself again. She made her own double strong Aeropress coffee with hot milk, and tea for Orla.

By the time Orla came downstairs, it was all ready and waiting.

"I love you, Mum. You know just how to make things better. I am starving and in need of a proper breakfast.

Mmmm, I might even ask you to make me a coffee too, it smells delicious."

This, was exactly what Maeve needed to hear. All good. Now they could tuck in and set the world to rights.

Orla had got the family to move from being everyday meat eaters, to a 'flexitarian' diet, where they had radically cut down on their meat and fish consumption. She had decided that she was a 'lacto-ovo-vegitarian', or in Maeve's language, no meat but she could eat cheese, milk, and eggs, though she usually had oat milk. Initially, Maeve had had trouble keeping up, but once she had got started she had found that it was relatively easy to cut down on meat. She had found some delicious and simple recipes. Now she was taking it as a voyage of discovery, but she was in need of some people to feed.

Following on from their breakfast-lunch, a brunch in the true sense, Maeve could see that Orla was recovering too, her cheeks were pink, and she had regained her ironic sense of humour. Overall, she clearly needed more sleep and decent regular food. Maeve gathered, Orla had spent most of the last month living on pot-noodles and cup-a-soup. Not ideal. Despite the set-back of losing the trees, Maeve thought that it would take Orla a few days, then she would reassess the situation and decide the best next step. Maeve was glad that Marianne would be home shortly, it was always best when they could talk things through together.

Now that Maeve felt stronger herself, she needed to talk to Ada. She was not expecting the response that she got.

CHAPTER 7

WHAT DO YOU WANT?

First, Ada burst out laughing. Then, seeing the shock on Maeve's face, and registering that she was still trauma-tised, Ada was contrite.

"Sorry, love, sorry. That was some experience." She couldn't help herself, tried to stifle another laugh, which made it worse, so she laughed out loud again. "I am sorry, I really am. But what you felt happened long ago. That poor man probably died a hundred years ago, or more. You must have great empathy."

Pause, as Ada tried to calm down,

"Oh my God, you must have listened really hard, or maybe I am a good teacher after all. You really zoned-in to yourself, you must have gone into a deep trance for it to affect you like that."

Another roar of laughter, Ada had given up trying to hold it in, and then went on,

"I didn't mean that to happen. I thought I had set you a simple task and you would come across someone doing some-thing mundane, like pulling the curtains, or lighting a candle. Those are the kind of small things that linger around us and I wanted you to learn how to hear them and then how to shut them out. I never thought you would pick up a brutal murder on your first outing! Oh my God! You are some case, you are. Who would have thought it? There you were, shutting it all out for most of your life."

Ada was recovering her composure.

"Okay, I'm back to normal, I have it all under control, I think." Ada went on as she wiped the remaining tears of laughter from her eyes. Like everyone else, she really needed to laugh and once she had started, it just got a bit out of control. In the family, it was known that she could shake with laughter, no noise coming out, and tears streaming down her face. She could laugh like this at her own jokes, and then be incapable of sharing the punch-line. They had had situations with all of them laughing and no idea why. Some time later, Ada would manage to tell them the funny story, which might, or might not, actually be funny.

"Okay, okay, okay. It's as if I asked you to buy a pound of butter and you came back with a cow ready to be milked, thinking you had done what I asked." Ada smiled again as she took a sip of water helping to return to normal.

Then the tone of her voice changed radically as she said,

"This is really serious."

Maeve thought this was singularly ironic, as Ada had been the only one laughing.

Ada carried on,

"This is crunch time. Decisions have to be made. I can't set you exercises, if you can go in that deep without any of the normal set up that we use. It's no good if you are going to come back in a state every time. You would be an emotional wreck in a week. So this is it, you need to ask yourself what you want out of all of this. And then do it for real. At least that way, if there are consequences they are ones that you have chosen to deal with. You have made the decisions. It wasn't someone else sending you to poke a wasps nest. With your talent, I have some idea of the kind of trouble you could unleash, so I really don't want you digging up spirits for no good reason."

Ada sat back and folded her arms, looking at the screen with her head tilted to one side having left the question with Maeve.

Maeve was righteously indignant,

"It was your brilliant idea in the first place!"

In a much more pensive tone, Ada answered,

"It was. But you have a gift. I mean, you, me and Orla can all communicate, but this is different. The other spirits came to you, to get you to solve their problems, and stop another murder. Pretty transactional. This time you voluntarily called a spirit, and then you entered into that experience with them both, both the victim and the killer. I am not sure if you were channelling the animal or the man, you may even have switched from one to the other. You did that, and then you controlled the situation, you made it stop. This is very advanced stuff."

As a way of trying to make up for her initial reaction Ada added,

"I don't, sorry, didn't, get into things like that. Mainly I dealt with spirits who wanted to say 'good-bye'. I mean sometimes they had unpleasant messages, and wanted me to tell the one left behind that they never really loved them, or even despised them, which of course I wouldn't pass on. Why create unnecessary pain?"

Digging up the past, Maeve remembered the sessions where as a child she had hidden under the table, mortified at Ada's indulgence in creating a dramatic atmosphere. Ada used every trick in the book, dim light, incense, anything and everything to make her clients satisfied that they were communing with spirits on the other side. Maeve had believed that it was all made up, until she 'met' her first spirit. Thinking back to Ada's clients she reflected, it was true she never gave them any bad news or said anything unpleasant, now she knew why.

Ada had started talking again,

"This is on a different level. What you have just done is really deep. You will need to be careful. As I said, the first and most important thing right now, is for you to decide what you want. I am not asking you for an answer this instant. I am asking you, to find a quiet space and ask yourself that question."

Leaving a pause, to let it all sink in, Ada finished with,

"Let's leave it there for now and we can talk again whenever you are ready."

Maeve had not really contributed to this conversation at all. On the one hand she had a sense of pride, that Ada thought she had done something impressive, on the other hand, she didn't entirely know what she wanted. She knew she had to help, she knew that she could no longer pass by when people or spirits were in trouble. The question that was uppermost in her mind was, could she really control her gift?

To help her think straight, Maeve needed to take a walk. It was still bright. She was waiting for confirmation from Marianne, to be able to sort out the logistics of picking her up. Orla needed to spend a while on her own, so now was a good time.

If she had taken a little longer to plan her route she probably wouldn't have gone back to the woods behind Military road. But her mind was thinking of somewhere quiet and her feet were on autopilot.

En route she passed John, the Big Issue seller, now because of lockdown, not able to sell the Big Issue till it was over. He always had a lovely smile and positive attitude, never pushy, always polite. She wanted to make sure that he was okay, and didn't want to just walk by. So after confirming that he was fine for the moment, without prying into his private life, and having had the obligatory exchanges of, 'It's getting

colder now, will they keep the lockdown till Christmas?'
Maeve decided she had to ask about people who might camp
in the woods, but maybe not to mention the body that she
had found in particular. Just in case.

Happy to oblige, John gave her the lowdown,

"Hard to tell. I've moved around over the years and I can
tell you, Canterbury has more homeless people than most
places. It's like London. There must be some kind of magnet
drawing people here."

He was happy to talk and didn't seem in a rush, so she
continued to ask questions,

"But there are those who seem to be in some kind of
gang. They have certain spots in town that they stick to and
seem to be pretty aggressive. The ones I am thinking of are
mostly young men."

"Oh yes, the scene has really changed over the years. You
can spot some of them who are in pretty organised groups,
because they have the same sign. I mean the actual same
physical cardboard sign, asking for money. They pass 'em
around. Some of them are Eastern European, some are
British. The drunks in town at the moment, are mostly
English. I keep myself to myself. There are a lot of them who
stay in groups, and stick to their own group. I don't think they
have been camping out. Since the first lockdown, most people
have got somewhere. Or are waiting for somewhere, unless
they are still 'on' something," indicating drugs or alcohol, "so
won't get anywhere..."

Maeve wanted to know more, so asked the direct question
she had avoided in the past,

"What brought you to the Streets?"

John warmed to his subject,

"Divorce. I left home thirty years ago and it was the best
decision I ever made. I wouldn't go back, I choose to be on
my own, I want the freedom. I love to wake up in the
morning and hear the birds, nothing else, no other sounds.

35

No one around." There was a wistfulness in his tone as he relived the moment, before coming back to the present,

"But things have changed. Years ago, it was different. I had friends and we used to meet up in different places around the country. Most of them are gone now. Homelessness is still a hard life, hard on the body."

He paused thinking back on his life,

"Of course, when the Big Issue started back in the '90s, it made it all possible. With that you can survive. You are your own boss. You earn your money. Keep your own hours. There are stories I could tell you about that too......and how that's changed. But really it all changed when serious drugs arrived. I'm talking crack cocaine. If they're on that I'm off. You see 'em, move on." He was emphatic. Silence.

He reflected on his experiences, then in a more positive note,

"Mostly though the homeless, they don't stay in one place that long."

Maeve was really absorbed so she went on,

"We hear about people with mental health issues and soldiers who are on the streets, are they?"

John was thoughtful,

"Yes, there are some, but not many, ex-service men around, only those who can't cope. There are a lot of charities too. Here in Canterbury, there are a lot of charities, Catching Lives, Porchlight, and Lily's Cafe, in the Baptist Church, I get a cup of tea there in the mornings. Or I used to before lockdown." A little pause of regret.

"But do you remember that guy, the young-ish blond guy who used to cover for me sometimes?"

Maeve nodded, so he went on,

"I never would have thought it, but one day he just come up and punched me in the face! I laid low for a bit; didn't come into town. After a while, I asked around to see if he was about. No one has seen him since. I don't know what happened to him. Maybe he had an episode. But I don't think he was ever in the army."

They had been standing on the street for nearly a quarter of an hour, and John was starting to hop from foot to foot, clearly on his way somewhere. Becoming aware of this, Maeve said,

"Take care and stay safe. I know people say that, but I really mean it. Be careful with this virus."

John laughed,

"I only know two people in all my customers who've had it. Yet our numbers in Canterbury are still high, where are these people?" and with a shrug and a wave, he was on his way.

Maeve felt she now had a picture of the homeless, that was much more nuanced than her natural bias. Confident that it was very unlikely that there were any in the woods, she headed straight there. So often, things are not what you expect.

CHAPTER 8

NOT WHAT SHE EXPECTED

As if to banish any remaining ghosts, Maeve went up towards the entrance to the disused barracks and, part way up the steep hill, by the telecoms mast, using the hidden stile, she dived into the woods.

As soon as she had taken a few steps, she breathed in the smell of fresh leaf mould, as the sounds of traffic died down, and the blackbird and robin took over.

This time she was nervous. She was worried about relaxing, in case by accident, she tuned-in to unpleasant spirits. The image that Ada had left her with, being that she might unwittingly poke a wasp's nest from the other side, was not one that gave her any comfort at all. So she concentrated more on the real world, on nature and her surroundings. She made her way through the blackthorn bushes that were laden with juicy sloes, and was passing the strange little apple tree, noting the remains of the small yellow apples on the ground, when she heard a sob.

A real world sob, and then someone speaking and blowing their nose. She dodged round the tree and walked a few steps through bracken, where she found the source. A middle aged, reasonably well dressed woman, who must have been talking to herself, was sitting on the trunk of a fallen tree. She had a much used cotton hanky clutched tightly in one hand, and was emphasising her point with the other. As Maeve got closer she thought she heard,

"Yes, yes, I know, it's all for the best. But why? I am good too. Am I not good enough?"

The woman became aware that Maeve was approaching and stopped abruptly. She seemed to give herself a shake, as if to pull herself together. Then she turned, and managed a smile.

With some trepidation, Maeve, who never liked to intrude on people's private business spoke,

"Are you alright? Can I help?"

Still smiling, the woman replied with a confident voice, as it to indicate that this was quite normal,

"Thank you for asking. I'm fine, just resting for a moment. When the wind catches my eyes they stream." She said, by way of explanation, as she waved the hanky in Maeve's direction.

"So long as you are okay? It's a lovely day for a walk." Maeve finished on what she hoped was a positive, everyday sort of comment. She back-tracked through the bracken.

'Well at least that was a living experience. And, not a drug fuelled psycho.' She thought to herself and immediately felt bad at calling anyone a 'psycho', even to herself. When she was uncomfortable with a situation, or she hadn't really thought it through, she found that it was all too easy to pick up and use old stereotypes. They gave her a feeling of distancing herself from whoever or whatever it was, she could imagine that it's 'not us' or 'well, that's not me anyway'.

Since finding the body and talking to John, she had decided that she didn't know enough about other people's situation. And the pandemic had made her want to help the living. She had already discovered that her 'gift' could save lives in the real world, as well as helping those on the other side find peace. Ada's question was weaving its way through all of these thoughts. What did she really, really want?

She would have picked up her pace but the woods hadn't dried out yet. However, the benefit of stopping herself from sliding in the mud, was that she had to 'be' in the present and this released any stress or tension, while letting her mind do its work. She found herself laughing, as she grabbed at a leaf to regain balance, as if that would have been of any use, but balance regained, she went on.

Keeping her thoughts on the present, she noticed that the woods had gone quiet again. 'Uh oh', she didn't like the idea of that. Again, there was no rustling of small animals. 'So what are my options', she thought, 'that woman is not very far away, but I'm not sure she would be much help.' She decided to press on as quickly as she could and make for the open ground, with the gorse bushes and rabbits.

Still slipping, and now cursing the off-road cyclists who had muddied the path, she was scrambling up the last bit of steep incline before the open ground, when she heard a voice in her ear. She nearly jumped out of her skin, but that's hard to do when scrambling upwards. So her feet lost their grip, she slid back down, and almost gracefully, fell flat on her face, well mostly on her stomach, but she had felt it on her chin and her nose too.

The voice was still talking, as she tried to get up, and kept repeating,

"Miss, miss, spare a few coins. I'm hungry, haven't had nuffin to eat in days, nothing."

The mud, and the cold, and the shock of falling over, dispelled Maeve's fear, now she was irritated,

"Well if you want some money, the least you could do is help me up."

"Oooh, I can't do that. Nooooo, can't do that, can't do that, no, no, no."

So Maeve gave up, stopped trying and half-turning

towards the voice, sat down in the mud. Her 'would be' assailant was right beside her, too close, he had indeed been whispering in her ear. As soon as she could see him, she knew that he was a spirit. Now she was really cross with herself.

"Bloody hell! If you want some help, why on earth did you give me such a fright?"

"You was walking so fast, you didn't hear me. You slowed down a bit here and I got closer. Didn't mean no harm, miss. No, no. No harm, miss."

There was something about him that felt familiar, he reminded her of someone, but she didn't have time for that now, she was still sitting in the mud. She did notice his clothes which were threadbare and caked with mud, old-fashioned, more like rags really. And his boots were leather, that had been repaired many times, but still had gaping holes in them.

She was about to ask him another question, but he had gone. She understood why, as soon as she reached round to push herself up, and looked straight into the face of a man, who was holding his hand out to help her out of the mud.

This man was real. She was so grateful for a warm hand, that she didn't hesitate, and in an instant she was back on her feet. With the momentum of the upward movement, she briefly moved that bit too close to him. She smelt his body, which surprisingly, didn't smell of soap, it was more earthy than that, not unpleasant, but of someone who spent their life in the outdoors.

He was handsome, short, salt and pepper hair, with a warm smile and direct gaze, that made you trust him straight away, probably athletic but looking a little gaunt at the moment, and he had that trendy slightly unshaven look. All in all, it was enough to make Maeve feel embarrassed that she was covered in mud.

As soon as they were both stable, and had enough distance between them, to look each other over, Maeve's rescuer also looked sheepish, as if he didn't know what to do or say. His vulnerability gave Maeve confidence, and she wanted to relieve his discomfort, so stretching out her hand she said,

"Thank you. I'm Maeve and I really appreciated the help." As she offered him her hand, she saw the muddy state of it, and added, "Actually you probably don't want to shake hands, I'm filthy!" They both smiled, he still wasn't forthcoming, and Maeve was getting cold.

"I think I'll make my way home to a hot bath. Hopefully I'll see you another time to thank you properly." He seemed hesitant and either couldn't or didn't want to talk.

Then in a bit of a rush he said,

"I'm Matthew. I'm often here." His voice was rich, and warm. Safe. With that he turned and walked off on one of the side paths, that lead through the undergrowth to the reed lake. Fishermen often spent days there, with small green tents for shelter. Maeve guessed that was why he was in the woods.

Once the image of the hot bath had entered her head, she could think of nothing else. She stopped thinking of the mud and the cold, walking as quickly as possible, focusing instead on the bath. If there was still enough hot water after Orla, then steaming hot would be best. The big question was, would she have a relaxing lavender bubble bath soak, or rejuvenate with a fizzing bath bomb? And then she thought after the bath, maybe hot chocolate with a shot of brandy, to stave off any potential long term effects, yes that would work.

She didn't notice that the woman she had seen, sitting on the fallen log, was still there.

CHAPTER 9

A HOT BATH

"I'm *NOT* COVID positive! For goodness sake child, pay attention. I am just not going out, and I need to talk to your mother, where on earth is she?"

Maeve heard Ada's voice as soon as she opened the door. She moved into the hallway, and took off her coat and shoes, looking down at her muddy legs.

Orla had rigged up the same screen based system on the table and had been chatting to Ada. But just as Maeve had thought, Orla still needed some rest and regular food, so clearly was having trouble staying focused on whatever Ada was saying. That being said, Maeve often had difficulty keeping up with Ada as she flipped from subject to subject, so maybe it was just Ada.

This was definitely not what Maeve had been looking forward to, but she knew if she didn't make an appearance then there would be a string of missed calls and messages. So, she stuck her head into the breakfast room, interrupting their conversation with,

"Don't! Don't laugh! If you laugh I won't speak to you. Or I'll cry. I'm only dropping in to say, I'll call you back in an hour, and you can see why. Okay?" Maeve did have a comic look with mud splashes on her face. And as she came a bit further into the room, they could see the extent of slip, she was caked in mud. However neither Ada, nor Orla, were laughing, they were both more concerned that she had had a fall.

"You okay Mum?" "What the hell did you do to yourself?" Orla and Ada's concern came out at the same time, in different flavours, but genuine on both counts.

"I'm fine, it's just a bit of mud, no damage done, other than to my ego. But I am going for a bath, the vision of which got me home double quick. Talk to you later. I have more questions for you Ada."

With that Maeve was gone and the digital conversation resumed.

"Right so." Ada had settled back into another cup of tea, "Tell me the rest of your adventures. How on God's earth did you manage to sleep in a tree! I ask you. I never thought a grandchild of mine would get up to such shenanigans, and you are telling me that all this is to save the planet?"

Orla was patient but firm, "Ada, if you really *do* want to know, then you will have to stop talking and let me explain."

Ada missed social interaction, and it had emphasised her habit of talking over people. Dialogues, had become monologues, replete with questions and answers already filled in by Ada. Maeve had noticed this before, and had warned Ada to be careful, and that she, Maeve, was not prepared to become Ada's version of Wilson, the football that Tom Hanks talks to, in the movie 'Castaway'. So Ada took Orla's comment in good part, and stopped talking, well almost.

Orla got on very well with her grandmother and loved her eccentricities. But she wasn't prepared to have this conversation yet, so she instead she changed the subject.

"Tell me what exactly are Cyanotype prints? And what are you doing with them?"

This was all that Ada needed, someone happy to listen,

"Where were you brought up? Not to know Cyanotype prints! Have you ever heard of a blueprint?"

Orla nodded, and smiled at how Ada put it, mixing mundane and obscure as if it was self-evident that everyone who had heard of a blueprint, knew what a cyanotype print was.

Ada resumed,

"Well blueprints are the original type of photography. And they are the most natural, safest way to print, children can do it. First you prepare the paper, then put an object on the paper, and expose it to sunlight. Then the magic happens. You put the paper in water and like a photograph the image emerges. Everywhere you blocked the sunlight will stay white and everywhere else turns deep blue. Like a negative." Now that she was in her stride Ada didn't stop.

"I used to sell prints, years ago. Well with all this isolation I had to do something, so I started again. This time gathering seaweed and objects from the beach. Making images. People told me they were beautiful and wouldn't I sell them? Right ho, I thought. So I asked for more advice, 'You can do it online', they said."

Orla was half listening, half enjoying Ada's burbling.

".... you know how terrible I am with a computer?....and neither you nor your sister were around to help me. So guess what?"

Orla was just about keeping track of all this, particularly as Ada had been holding up some of the prints as she spoke. They were lovely ghostly images coming out of a fabulous indigo blue. Meanwhile, Ada was clearly making decisions, laying the prints in two piles and then switching them from one to the other.

"What? You said 'guess what'? So '..What'?" Orla prompted.

This brought Ada back to the principle point of the call, she got excited as she went on,

"There's this brilliant new shop in Canterbury called….."

Frustrated that she couldn't remember the name, Ada was clicking her fingers for Orla to fill in the gaps.

What's that game you used to play…?"

"Monopoly? Scrabble? Risk?" Orla tried her best, but Ada was looking at her, as if she was mad.

"No, no. The one with your hands. What's it called? Paper, scissors, stone, lizard…."

Orla suddenly got it, "I know, you mean Rock, Paper, Scissors."

With that, Ada was happy to continue,

"That's the one, that's the name of the shop 'RockPaper-Scissors'. Anyway, the people who run it are lovely and they are going to take some of my prints. Now I need Maeve to come over and collect them. I have them ready and waiting, and I don't want to miss the Christmas rush."

Orla didn't want to throw cold water on Ada's new found excitement, so hesitantly she put it as a question,

"What about lockdown? I thought only shops that sold essential items could open?"

"Ach, keep up girl. That's where I started. Charlie has got it all sorted, they have a website and do the 'click 'n' collect' thing. Huston, we are good to go!"

Orla was piecing together parts of the earlier conversation, and it was beginning to make sense.

"So Charlie runs the shop? I was wondering who this Charlie was, now I see."

"How long have you been away? You have missed all the excitement. Yes Charlie and his cousin Liz. It's Liz's idea and he's making it work. Go in with your mother, and have a look in the shop windows, see for yourselves. Talking of which, I had better finish framing them in case Maeve gets a fit and decides to come over asap." Abruptly she was gone.

Orla was glad to be home. She had promised herself a few days of rest and recuperation, which of course would include some of Maeve's cooking. She knew she needed some good food and lots of sleep, but she was already feeling more positive after her marathon lie-in this morning. Both Maeve and Ada shared a positive 'can-do' approach to life. In their view, nothing was impossible, you just had to think it through, then work out the steps to take. Orla needed that kind of back-up, to give her the belief in herself to plan her next steps.

Maeve was still soaking in the bath, so Orla was the first to see the message. It was from Marianne, who was letting them know that she had already had her COVID-19 test, and was due the result shortly.

Marianne didn't like unknowns, so she wanted to make a plan on the basis that the result was negative, and then if it turned out otherwise, she could move to her plan B.

Plan B, if the result was positive, was to stay in college accommodation until she had two negative tests in a row. She wasn't keen on that, she wanted to stay optimistic, so was scheduling Maeve to come and pick her up in two days' time, pending confirmation of the test result.

Orla was delighted, she thought that would give her time to sleep and be fully recovered by the time Marianne arrived. Orla wasn't ready to say it yet, but she really wanted to talk her plans through with Marianne as well as Maeve, before coming to any decisions.

The two sisters were very different people, but as they got older they appreciated each other more.

At last, a fresh and fragrant Maeve emerged from the bathroom. Orla sorted the hot chocolate that Maeve had been planning on, while Maeve called Ada back.

Rather than get sidetracked with her recent mud bath, Maeve confirmed that she was fine and went straight in with,

"I'm still working on your question, Ada. But I have a few other things to talk to you about. First is Edward. He has been behaving oddly since I went to the woods for a walk. I don't think it was connected to the body. He knows something about the woods and he is not sharing the information, he keeps warning me that there are thieves and 'bad' people in those woods."

Maeve was focused so didn't let Ada interrupt until she had finished.

"Another thing. Today, just now, when I slipped and fell in the mud, I slipped, because there was a spirit whispering in my ear. He was asking for money to buy food. What's that all about? Spirits can't eat or use money, so why is he asking for it?"

Unusually, Ada was calm and waited patiently until Maeve had finished talking. Ada knew that she had a favour to ask, so she was on her best behaviour.

She was reflective, when she answered,

"Hmm, could they be connected? It's not like him, I mean so far Edward hasn't got into a tizz about any of the others. Anne was your neighbour, and he didn't really react, but if there was something connected to him personally, or to his time, it might cause a greater reaction. More of a fuss. Could your man be from the same part of history as Edward?"

Maeve frowned, concentrating on the brief encounter she had just had, and after a pause said,

"Maybe. His clothes were covered in mud, so it's hard to tell. But I remember a badly torn heavy, overcoat, with large pockets. Possibly it was brown, dark anyway. And I did notice his boots, they were old fashioned, repaired many times but still with holes and broken laces."

Ada was mulling it over as she replied,

"I think you might, you know, ask him straight out. Be direct. You've never really dug into Edward at all. We know next to nothing about him. He might be the blaggard, not your fella in the woods!"

This was going in an uncomfortable direction for Maeve,

who liked having Edward around. If she solved his issues he might leave, but... maybe it's his time.

After a moment Ada added

"This could be like an exercise, but it should be a whole lot safer than digging up spirits from a murderous slaughterhouse."

Now that Maeve's pressing issues were dealt with, Ada moved on to her needs. They agreed, that Maeve would be over first thing in the morning. Ada would prepare some hot coffee which they could share over the sea wall. She knew that she was COVID clear, so she wasn't going to pass it on to Maeve. That way, after Maeve picked up the prints, they could have a few moments talking over the wall and the coffee would keep them warm. Not like normal, but at least have a moment with each other in real life.

Maeve also wanted to spend time with Orla before Marianne arrived, so suggested an early start. They could watch the sun rise over the sea. Maeve had a new iPhone and wanted to test the camera on something beautiful in low light. Ada was up for it, delighted that her plan was working.

Maeve hadn't finished her calls. She had another one to make. Maeve knew that she had been saving her call to Steve till last. She wanted to be on her own for this one. There had been a time when he was the last person that she wanted to talk to, but the situation was different now. Now, she wanted to have that promised catch up, without any more traumas. She was savouring the moment.

She wrapped up warm, and took her phone out into the garden. She waved at Anne, her friend, ethereal spirit gardener, and next door neighbour. Then turned back facing the trees to make the call, where no one could see if she blushed a little.

As so often happens, if you save something up for the moment when you are ready, it can mean you miss out altogether. Steve was too busy to talk today, so they swapped text messages, and confirmed lunch tomorrow.

Steve had news for her but wanted to see her in person. Something to do with the body in the woods. Maeve was intrigued. Why wouldn't he tell her now?

CHAPTER 10
MAEVE'S QUESTIONS

The next morning, it was still pitch dark when Maeve made herself some porridge. Before she left for Ada's, Maeve wanted to have at least started the conversation with Edward. He seemed to be avoiding her, but she knew he couldn't resist making some comment on the state of the saucepan. She was right.

Edward hovering over her shoulder as she stirred the pot,

"Em, of course it's none of my business, but less heat would save the pot."

Taking the saucepan off the heat, trying not to make him feel cornered, Maeve went about her business as she addressed him, pouring out the porridge and putting the pan in water to soak,

"Edward, we haven't really talked about why you like to be here. I mean in this space, in this house, which was built long after your time."

Edward looked puzzled,

"Hmm. But I am here in Place Hall, built by Sir Roger Manwood, who was not a kind man, but a godly man." Edward had 'stamped' his foot to indicate exactly where they were standing.

"Sir Edward, my master, will build a grand new house, but we use the old Hall here, for the time being. And this is the kitchen." With that he disconcertingly waved his arms through the wall showing Maeve the outline of his kitchen.

She got the gist of it, Edward's kitchen was large, and they were standing in it. Maybe her pre-war home was built on some old foundations, even though she knew that Place Hall had been completely demolished so there would have been no other signs of the old building by then.

She tried again,

"So your Sir Edward was he Sir Edward Hales?" She was slowly drawing Edward in.

"Yes, yes, of course. Sir Edward Hales, son of Sir Edward Hales and great grandson of Sir Edward Hales."

Maeve thought they didn't have much imagination when it came to names. She tried a different tack, she knew that they were talking about the sixteen hundreds, or the seventeenth century, and took a gamble,

"So was he a Parliamentarian or a Royalist?"

Edward almost exploded,

"Shhhhh, don't say that, we don't talk about that. No, no, no we don't. NEVER!" And with that, trembling from head to foot, he was gone.

Maeve sighed to herself, thinking that it was a lot harder to get information from spirits who didn't want to share it. She didn't feel as though she had made any real progress and wondered if Ada had any other tips that might actually be useful.

The sky was beginning to lighten as she took the A2 towards Dover and then joined the A20 to the M20 motorway by Folkestone. She avoided the cross country roads this morning, she hadn't been back, to see if Kamal, the Iraqi spirit, was still there. She needed to have better control over her gift, before trying to sort that one out.

It was a clear run right through, and the light changed as

she drove, the stars disappearing as the sky brightened. Maeve wondered what would happen after the Brexit transition was over. Deal, or no deal with the European Union, there would be an impact on the roads around East Kent. Operation stack had not been fun for anyone living around here, with lorries parked on the motorway and traffic delays of up to five hours. That was with the normal cross channel traffic, before anyone had even heard of Brexit. The divisions that Brexit caused, upset Maeve, it made her sad, regardless of anyone's politics the practicalities of life for everyone she knew would be impacted. And now, with COVID-19 and Brexit, they were in for a double whammy. For Maeve, it underlined her belief that you have to enjoy each moment, of each day, as you live it. There is no knowing what might happen next.

She arrived and was parked in good time. The sunrise was beautiful, straight up over the sea, clear horizon with a slight misty haze, enough to provide fabulous colours. The coffee was delicious. Maeve's photos were perfect. Ada was in sparkling form. Maeve was very glad that she had come over. They were social distancing, and they were in the open air, and this was a business meeting. Regardless of the rules, Maeve would never want to unintentionally infect Ada, so they made sure to keep their distance. Maeve had brought her own cup, Ada filled it from a flask before stepping back. Maeve wondered what life would be like when all this was over, would everyone forget these gestures, and the impact on everyday life, or would we take bits of this as the new normal?

Picking up on their conversation about Edward, Ada said,

"Well, I don't know. You could fit my knowledge of English history on the back of an envelope. Get Orla, or if Marianne comes back, get her to look it up for you."

Ada drifted from subject to subject as they occurred to her.

"Aren't they two great girls? You are lucky to have them, and if they do a bit of work for you, and feel like part of the team, it helps them too. They are changing from teenagers to full blown adults,.... but it takes a lot longer than you think. One minute they are out changing the world, the next minute they need a hug from Mum. Sure, aren't we just coming to terms with each other?" Ada said with a smile, as she looked at Maeve. Raising her eyebrows as she said,

"My mother always said people don't mature till they are forty. I think, at least forty!"

Maeve said nothing as Ada chatted,

"You might get it easy with your girls, but it can all go pear shaped as they get to this stage." She shook her head as she went on,

"The trouble starts with boyfriends, men. Have you really thought about that? Sex in the same house as you, are you ready for that?" Eyebrows raised again,

"Either Marianne and Orla have been keeping secrets or they are late starters..."

Maeve nodded absently as she gazed at sea, indicating more, that she was considering the prospect than that she was already comfortable with the idea.

By now, Ada was almost talking to herself, expressions drifting across her face, occasionally glancing at Maeve,

"..or girlfriends." Ada was getting more animated with concern,

"That's a point though Maeve, as their mother, somehow you will have to let them know that whoever they bring home, or whatever they do, they will always be welcome. Don't make the mistakes I made, keep them in your life."

Maeve was hoping these were issues that she could put off for a bit, whilst at the same time recognising that Ada was spot on. Partners and sex, were things she didn't know how to deal with and would have to work it out. Maybe it was time to have a call with Pascal, their father? She thought it would be better to talk it over in person but, that's not an option, it would have to be another Zoom call. Preferably when neither of the girls were in the house.

Maeve certainly didn't want Ada getting involved,

"Yes, I know you're right, and I'm not ready, so let me think about it." That might have been sharper than Maeve intended. Not wanting to spoil the early morning coffee, Maeve changed the subject.

"In the meantime, how about I practice handling subtle relationships with Edward? I can try dealing with him as if he was a sex starved teenager."

They both laughed.

"That's a great idea. If you are up to it." Ada challenged Maeve. Then getting back to business,

"Whatever you are doing, it hasn't really worked so far, has it?"

Maeve rolled her eyes skywards with a 'tell me something I don't know' gesture.

Ada went on,

"Actually I haven't forgotten about your adventures in the woods."

Confident that she was on safe ground now,

"Why not take Orla there next time?"

Ada crossed her arms in satisfaction. Maeve looked puzzled not fully getting Ada's point, company is always nice but what difference would it make?

Exasperated Ada went on,

"She can sense things too."

Maeve was still frowning. Now exaggerating her gestures as if talking to a child, Ada explained,

"That way with two different heads on you, you can work out what you are dealing with."

Lowering her voice as if she was talking to herself Ada added,

"And if something goes wrong, you have some chance that Orla can bring you back from the other side."

The mention of Orla, made Maeve look at her watch,

"I have to dash. I was hoping to get back before Orla woke up. Actually, I had already been thinking of going for a walk with her. I thought of it as a time to bond, before Marianne gets back."

Maeve was nodding in agreement with her mother's idea, thinking of how to fit it all in,

"However, I'm not sure if I have time this morning, I have a lunch date in town." It had slipped out before she could stop it.

Ada pounced,

"A lunch date? When were you going to tell me about this? And with whom, I might ask? And how are you going to manage it in lockdown?"

Maeve wasn't awake enough to think of any evasive tactics, she knew that she had been rumbled,

"It's with Steve. It's business. There will be social distancing. I didn't want to say anything, because right now there is nothing to say."

That didn't stop Ada,

"Oh, he's such a lovely man. Now why wouldn't you settle for someone nice like Steve?"

This was exactly why Maeve had not wanted to share the information, that they had met again.

Ada was on a roll,

"Of course, I should have guessed you would come across him, when you found the body. Yes, yes I can see, of course it's business. Still, you could sharpen yourself up a bit girl. Refresh the make-up, and maybe get something with a lovely bit of colour from Clothesline. I'm sure they will manage Click and Collect!"

Ada was off on her own line of thought

"You know, I have a beautiful Charles Jordan scarf that I

56

got from Pam when I moved here, and I still get great compliments. You could do with a bit of juz-ing yourself up. Good for morale at least."

Maeve knew that Ada meant well, and maybe indulging in a nice scarf, was a good idea, however, non-essential shops were shut, and she didn't have time to buy online and pick up later. But Christmas was coming, so still not a bad idea.

"Alright, I will think about it. Which reminds me Christmas is coming…. we will have to talk about that too. But not now. I'm off. I have the prints and I will let you know as soon as they have been safely delivered." With that, Maeve walked round by the beach to the car park which was still empty, except for her car.

CHAPTER 11

MEN

O n the drive home, Maeve ran the logistics in her mind. She definitely wouldn't have time for a proper root around in the woods with Orla, if she had to be back in time for lunch with Steve. Plus, she might be a bit distracted. Maybe best leave it till tomorrow, and have the walk before driving up to Cambridge, for Marianne. If, fingers crossed, her test was negative.

Maeve got home in time to have a slice of toast and coffee with Orla. She explained the issues, her experience in Butchery Lane, and Ada's thinking about whatever was in the woods. It could get emotional.

Orla's view, was that she didn't want to face any trees today, but with a day to prepare herself, she should be fine. She didn't think that she would have another emotional breakdown. She liked the idea of going for a walk in a wood that wasn't currently under physical threat. And she hadn't faced anything from the spirit world in months.

Between mouthfuls of toast, Orla said a day in town was exactly what she wanted, just window shopping would be perfect. Just because she didn't want to buy anything new, didn't mean that she didn't like looking at it. Plus, to stop Ada raving about it, she had promised that she would look at Liz's window display, in RockPaperScissors.

So that was decided, as soon as Orla was ready, they would go into town together. Maeve told Orla about her lunch date with Steve, because being accidentally spotted was definitely not worth the risk. Maeve had made that mistake before, and had learned her lesson.

Orla, was a little more discreet than Ada, she understood that this was not something that Maeve was comfortable talking about. So, she tried hard not to react, seeing Maeve exhale with relief, Orla felt that she had been reasonably successful. Still, she hoped that it might work out for Maeve, they all liked Steve.

While waiting for Orla, Maeve turned her attention towards Edward. She tried again, this time not waiting for him to appear, just addressing the room,

"Edward, if Orla and I go walking in the woods should we be wary of anyone in particular?" Nothing. She waited a moment and then,

"Edward, if we went and got into trouble, and you knew something that you hadn't warned us about, then it would be your fault?"

With that Edward appeared behind her,

"Well, it's those vagabonds, they are the ones. I only tell you because you must be careful. There're many people who had to take to the woods after, you know, after the Christmas business. I'm not talking. I keep my peace. I'm just sayin' you need to go in company, not alone."

This gave Maeve something to go on. She could start checking things out online, she knew he was connected to Sir Edward Hales and she could cross reference that, with some event that happened around Christmas. Hopefully, that would be enough.

Orla appeared with a subtle, slim fit, down jacket which for some reason made Maeve notice that she was looking very smart. She had brushed her hair and put it up, and maybe there was a trace of eye make-up. Maeve was looking at her and seeing her daughter for the first time, no longer as an awkward teenager, but as a beautiful confident young woman.

Orla misinterpreted Maeve's moment of reflection, so as if in self defence, she said,

"What? Just because I want to save the planet doesn't mean I have to look like a sack of potatoes. Anyway, while you are on your date, I mean official business, I'm meeting a friend for coffee."

Deflecting any further comments from herself, Orla went on,

"I have heard, that they now do churros with melted chocolate in the Dane John garden, as 'takeaway' food."

Maeve smiled, she had a fair idea who this friend might be. It was likely to be Adam, the handsome young PhD student of archeology, who Orla had helped to rescue from a deeply unpleasant situation. But as advised by Ada, she didn't want to get this wrong, by being too interfering. And she wasn't sure how Orla's relationship with Adam would work out, so responded with what she hoped was a cheery sounding,

"Great, that sounds lovely. I didn't want you to feel as if you weren't welcome to join me, but that sounds like a much better idea."

The weather was in the process of turning cold, there was a misty feel, and the trees were losing their leaves with each gust of wind. Not ideal for eating outside, but not too cold yet either, and at least it wasn't raining. They both opted for a quick walk through Beverly Meadow.

From her previous encounters Maeve now knew that if she didn't 'call' the spirit, linked to the park, then she probably wouldn't appear. She liked the young woman, but didn't want to face her this morning, anyway, spirits who had issues seemed to prefer to talk to her when she was on her own.

The closer they got to Canterbury, the more anxious Maeve felt. She was only half listening to Orla. As she registered this, she glanced over to see if Orla had noticed. Maeve saw that, like her, the closer they got to town, the more animated Orla was getting, she now had a healthy touch of pink in her cheeks. Maeve smiled to herself, thinking that they hadn't got to the stage where they could share what they were feeling about romantic relationships. Neither of them was ready for that yet.

Trying to be sensitive, Maeve suggested that they split up, giving each of them some time on their own, to prepare themselves for their rendez-vous'. A relieved Orla, carried on walking along the High Street.

Maeve peeled off into Stour St, to drop off Ada's prints which she had carefully packed in her backpack. They weren't too heavy. She was happy that Ada wasn't doing large prints yet.

Maeve had listened to Ada's advice, and without going overboard had taken a look at herself in the mirror before she left home. She could do with a haircut, but that would have to wait till lockdown eased. Otherwise, she had gone for the 'enhanced natural' look, that being reducing the makeup rather than any femme fatale red lipstick. And had on her smarter navy Barbour jacket, as opposed to the much loved, full of holes, green with brown corduroy trims, Barbour jacket. It is doubtful that Steve would have noticed the difference, but Maeve felt that bit more confident. Anyway he had news for her so he probably wouldn't be looking.

Steve spotted her as soon as she turned into St Margarets Street. He had got there a little early, to make sure that he could reserve the bench resting against St Margaret's Church, in the alleyway beside the fish and chip shop. This was their idea for a makeshift outdoor restaurant. It wasn't romantic, but then this was supposed to be work, and Steve wanted to make sure that they wouldn't be overheard, so it would do.

Food bought, they sat at either end of the bench, as far away as possible. The practicalities of getting served, whilst distancing, had made them both laugh, so tension had been relieved.

Steve was chatting comfortably,

"...so the bikes around town with all the crazy colours and covered in flowers, you know the 'flower-power-bikes'. I found out, that they were inspired by a guy in Amsterdam who covered his wife's bike with flowers so that she could find it. That was nearly twenty years ago and he is still doing it."

Maeve couldn't wait any longer, did Steve just want to meet up with her or was something up, direct as ever she said,

"What did you want to tell me in person?"

Steve appreciated her straightforward approach to every-thing. Looking around to make sure there were no other customers lingering nearby, he leant a little closer before saying,

"After you left, the forensic team cleared away the rest of the debris. Then, as they moved the body, we could see the other side. The bit he was lying on. It was clear that he had been hit hard on the back of the head. Almost as if someone had swung a golf club and caught him just where the head meets the neck. That man's death was no accident."

Stunned Maeve simply looked at Steve as she took all of this in. As her colour returned to normal, she said,

"But, I didn't feel anything. I didn't pick up any sense that he was unhappy. In fact the opposite, it was calm, peaceful, and content."

Steve was trying to look her straight in the eyes as he said,

"Now you know, why I wanted to see you in person. Not only to tell you this, but to ask you to do something. Look at me. After your recent experience in Butchery Lane, I want to see your answer to this question."

She turned, with some trepidation.

They looked directly at each other, over the remains of the meal, the leftover chips now cold, gathered up in the paper they had been wrapped in.

Steve spoke slowly and clearly,

"Will you call the dead?"

CHAPTER 12

IT'S BEEN A TOUGH YEAR

After Maeve had left, Steve cleared up the debris, dumped it in the bin and walked down St Margaret St to pick up a takeaway coffee from the Micro Roastery on his way back to the office.

He always ran some background music in his head, now he was in the '80s with Sade and 'Smooth Operator', though he didn't feel that he had been very smooth. He was reflecting on this last year, it felt like years, not less than one year.

It was spring when he met Maeve. Steve liked her right from the start, she was his kind of woman. The warm, practical, 'takes no shit', kind of woman. But there was nothing normal about how they met or what happened after that.

Steve didn't believe in ghosts, or rather before meeting Maeve he didn't. Now he knew that Maeve had something, an extra sense, or a gift. He believed that she could communicate with the dead. That didn't mean that she would, or that he would get any useful leads from it if she did. Nevertheless he hoped that this time it would give him the excuse to spend some time with her. To try again, and see if there was anything there between them.

Due to Maeve, he had arrested a serial killer and they had

saved one, possibly two lives. Back at the station he was a hero. Tim, his 'colleague' or nemesis more likely, had been put in the shade, and Steve, with his team, got all of the glory. They'd had to manage the media, it was clear that the police put the case together that would keep the killer in jail even if the medium, 'Mystic Ada', had helped. In fact Ada was great and the more she played down her part the more the media loved her as an eccentric and didn't believe a word she said. The press headline ran 'Local Mystic Finds Serial Killer in Canterbury Cathedral'. Regardless, the police line is always the same, 'we do not work with psychics, or any paranormal practitioners.' This time they had to add that ' a neighbour Ada McPhilips had been helping the police with their enquiries.' When the media frenzy had died down and things got back to normal, it hadn't actually changed anything in the station. Steve didn't get the promotion, neither did Tim. COVID happened. Everything else was sidelined.

In that all too brief gap between lockdowns during the summer, when everyone had been encouraged to 'eat out to help out'. He had tried to have a date with Maeve.

It was a beautiful evening and Steve had booked one of the tables outside the Miller's Arms. The sun was still warm but not too hot; laughter, clinking glasses, the sounds of summer were all around, the smell of fresh cut grass wafted past. It's a quiet part of Canterbury, so even though the tables opened onto the street you could still hear the water racing through the old mill run in the adjacent park. Perfect.

Maeve looked wonderful, soft, a touch of make-up to make her sparkle but not overloaded. Steve hated seeing lovely faces layered up with foundation cream, particularly with young women determined on masking perfection, on plastifying nature.

That evening they were seated facing each other, it should have been idyllic. But you know when the little things start to go wrong, it's not going to end well. The table was too small, dishes were on top of each other, finally the garlic bread fell onto the ground and the plate smashed. Or maybe Steve was too big, he had felt nervous, he hadn't been on a date in years and years, maybe he knocked the plate, either way it was a bad omen.

Maeve said it was fine, it didn't matter. But they both knew it wasn't good. They ordered another bottle of wine, as if to start again. That was another sign, both of them had drunk the first one too quickly. Nerves.

Anyway, one way or another they ended up in an argument. It was a stupid argument. Steve shouldn't have said anything, but he was used to being in charge and having people listen to him, so he mouthed off. He didn't even mean it, it was just something to say.

Maeve had said something about the government scheme giving away this 'ten pounds a head' towards their dinner when there were people that needed the help to survive who had been ignored, like all the freelancers. He said they were all hand-outs and he didn't believe in handouts. She got really mad, the extra wine probably played its part, she got louder, and pretty soon was almost shouting 'it's not their fault, all their work has gone'.

Then the killer blow, it was like lighting touch paper, Steve had said 'Shhhh, we don't want to make a scene.' Well that was that. Maeve started with 'Don't you dare tell me what I can and can't do.' Then her voice dropped to an icy cold, icily polite, 'thank you for offering to take me for dinner. I think it's over now.' And with that she put her share of the bill, in cash, on the table, and left.

As he re-lived it now, he could see that he had been crass, recognising that she was one of the freelancers who had lost work. And that evening she got very emotional very quickly. She probably hadn't had enough time to deal with the full emotional roller coaster that she had been on since she discovered her gift.

Thinking back he counted the issues Maeve had dealt with, one, she was reconstructing her relationship with her mother Ada when Ada had a heart attack, Steve had been the shoulder Maeve had cried on. And it made him feel good. He liked that closeness, he liked having someone need him. At the time he hadn't been sure that he was ready to give up his single life, now he was thinking, what was it that he was so afraid of giving up? Lockdown made him crave company. Two, she thought that she had lost her daughter; three, there had been the adventure that had led to his utter humiliation, and finally going on to that mad chase to save Maeve's other daughter's life. Now, with reflection, he knew that he should have cut her some slack. At the time, he was just hurt.

That summer evening, he had been thinking of what he wanted, not what she needed. It was time to try again. So this was a nice, hopefully safe, little project that they could work on together. The body had been dead for some time and had not been reported as missing so as much as it was good to solve any crime, this was not an urgent case. Steve could use this to repair bridges, and calmly see if there was still anything there between them.

There was still an elephant in the room, he knew he had one other problem that he would have to face. Steve had spent ten years lighting a candle for his first love, who had been killed in a car crash. He needed to know that she was okay about this. That he wasn't betraying their relationship, and that she was okay for him to move. How could he be sure?

There was only one person he could ask to communicate with the other side, and that was Maeve. He could never do that.

CHAPTER 13

COURAGE

M aeve worried about it all the way home, so without any of the normal preamble, she opened her call to Ada with,

"How do you call a spirit, who isn't looking to talk to you?"

Ada had a feeling that this call would be coming at some point,

"You are not going to like it!"

Knowing that Maeve still had an inbuilt resistance to the 'dressings' or staging of most mediums' performances.

Ada waited till Maeve seemed calm, if still impatient. She sniffed, "Well. If it was me, I would have a seance, and probably use a ouija board. With the board, if they don't speak, at least that way they can communicate. It's a bit slow, but it does work" Ada dealt with the behind the scenes mechanics, as if she was describing how to use a new remote control, or a clever App.

Maeve cut her off mid flow,

"Well, that's not going to work this time. It's in the middle of the woods. And I am *not* going to have a seance at home, goodness knows who might appear. I do *not* want to have an 'open door' policy to any old spirits, I would never be able to get back to having a normal life."

Ada could feel, and to some extent, understand Maeve's upset.

"I am trying to control who I speak to. This is for a very specific question." Maeve's anxiety was clear. She did not want to open a floodgate to the other side by accident. She was not at all confident that she could manage this.

Ada wanted to help, but it was tricky,

"I'm guessing it's to do with the body you found, and not the strange woodland spirit?"

Maeve nodded but didn't say anything.

"I'd do it myself but I can't." Ada was referring to the 'temporary' loss of her gift.

They looked at each other for a moment, one frowning puzzled, the other at a loss.

Ada took a deep breath, and then said,

"Okay, here's what I think. Go to the woods with Orla."

Maeve settled back to listen, she really wanted someone to tell her what to do.

Ada went on,

"Take a wander around first. Look around, take the temperature of the place. Make sure it feels safe, and you are okay."

Maeve was getting impatient.

"When it's all good. Come back to the place where you found the body."

Ada took a sip of her now cold tea, as she gathered her thoughts.

"When you are ready, concentrate on the man, and do your slow breathing, like you did the other day in town. Stop thinking about all the everyday things, keep the man in your mind. Hold on to the thought of him. And if he is prepared to talk to you, he should appear. Or at least you should feel him nearby, and you can ask your question. With Orla there you should be fine."

Maeve was breathing quite heavily, but she was calmer, the plan was practical. She still wasn't too happy about it,

"One other thing Ada, before, when I spoke to other spirits they didn't actually remember how they died, except for Anne and she was a special case. I mean they could remember events leading up to it, but then blank. Maybe he won't know anything about who killed him?"

Ada shrugged,

"I said it before, you are in a different league to my experiences. I don't know. But it would make sense, so yes, he might not remember anything useful. Still, it's worth a try. Isn't it?"

Maeve wasn't so sure. This could open a door, she wanted to keep closed.

That evening she had a yoga session. Of course it was another Zoom session, but during the lockdown Maeve had become addicted to yoga. Tonight she really needed it. A good way to prepare for her ordeal in the morning. Saskia, the yoga teacher, had a way of calming everything down until you were truly 'in the moment'. The flow of movement between the poses didn't allow time for Maeve's thoughts to wander. Today's focus was on heart opening. Maeve hadn't realised how tight she was across the chest. Stress had rounded her shoulders. As the session slowed down and flowed into the last moves, Maeve was leaning back on her elbows with her heart rising up, shoulders and head gently stretching back, when the tears began to flow. Saskia had warned them all that at some point during yoga practice, this might happen. Emotion is held in the hips and in the heart, everyone is different, but whenever it is right for you, and you let go, it can come out. For once, Maeve was glad that it was a Zoom session.

She heard the key in the lock, Orla arrived back in time to see her mother still with tears streaming down her cheeks.

"Oh my God! What's the matter? What's happened? If you weren't still sitting on your yoga mat, I would think it was Steve, maybe it is anyway, is it? Or Ada, or Marianne?"

Maeve was smiling, as she wiped away the tears trying to answer Orla, in the end she said,

"Everyone is okay, and I'm fine. Nothing that I can explain has happened. But I think I am ready for this next step."

The next morning, plans rehearsed, Maeve and Orla set out as soon as it was fully bright. It was one of those overcast, almost foggy days, when you never see the blue sky. It had rained overnight so everything was still dripping. On the drive over, Maeve told Orla the full story of her strange experiences in the woods and her overwhelming moment in Butchery Lane. Orla was taking it all in, and checking her facts for this mornings project,

"So, wait, Ada thinks that I can be your minder? I don't know how to do that. She didn't say anything to me. That's some responsibility she had dumped on me. What if I can't do it?"

Maeve found that talking over the plan helped to clear her mind,

"Ada thinks that you may pick up on any younger spirits. That way we can begin to sort out what is happening. Then, we walk back by the other path and end up at the spot where the man died. If we are lucky and it all goes well up to that point, I will try to call him. Having you there, just being there, should act as a sort of anchor for me. But, if I end up going in too deep, then you will be there in a practical, common sense manner, to 'wake me up', or 'bring me back' as she says. Ada, is not saying that you have to commune with the other side to bring me back, she means physically make sure I get home."

They looked at each other, and Maeve said,

"Yes, it doesn't sound brilliant, does it? But at least it's a sort of a plan, we can see how it goes. That's it really, isn't it? We just do our best and see what happens. And at worst there are two of us."

Orla wasn't fully reassured, but they had arrived.

Maeve led the way, heading straight for the reed lake this time, so that they could go around it and then up to the open ground, finally back to where she had found the body. They had hardly absorbed the quiet of the first thicket, when Orla said,

"Wow, I see what you mean. I feel a tremendous sense of sadness. Oh, I can see her now."

Orla stood still for a while nodding, and after a few minutes said,

"I'm sure you are. You are."

Wide eyed she turned to Maeve and said,

"So what do you make of that?"

Orla was a little pale, Maeve guided them over to a fallen willow tree and they both leaned against the trunk for support.

When they were stable, Maeve said,

"I didn't see anything. What was that?"

"It was a girl. She was young, maybe four or five years old. And she just kept saying 'I want to be a good girl. I am a good girl.' She repeated it over and over. But when I said that she was, she looked at me frightened and ran away. She left that awful sadness."

"Ah, well, I felt that." Said Maeve.

"Both this time and the last time, so now we know where that feeling is coming from. And it didn't seem to come from the body that I saw, so that makes sense. Did she ask you to do anything?"

"No, no. She just looked terrified as she ran off. She went

in that direction." Orla pointed towards the spot where Maeve had first picked up the feeling.

Maeve nodded. They were silent. Both lost in thought.

Maeve thought she heard a branch crack, she looked around for an animal, a dog or a fox, but couldn't see anything. She turned towards Orla, and saw that Orla was looking up, she must have heard the noise too. Maeve followed her gaze. Up above, them in the tree canopy of the large oak, someone was lying against one of the boughs. They were almost invisible, but there was a slight shadow as the bough was too narrow to fully mask the body. It didn't feel like a spirit.

CHAPTER 14
MORE THAN ONE

"Oy, you up there, what are you doing?" For some reason, the fact that it wasn't a spirit made Maeve fearless. She was sure that she could handle this, so sounded authoritative, like someone you should answer.

"Ah, um, nothing really, just keeping a lookout." The voice came back. It sounded familiar,

"Is that you Matthew?" As Maeve peered up into the branches, she was glad she had remembered his name, it was the plummy accent that made her think it might be the same man. And there is nothing like the power of using someone's name, to get them to do what you want. Turning to Orla, she explained,

"It was Matthew who pulled me out of the mud."

Orla was leaning back, admiring his tree climbing skill, strength, and agility, as he came down to their level. Her voice was warm as she said,

"I didn't know there were any tree huggers in Kent. Glad to meet a fellow eco-warrior." She held out her hand.

"Um, well, I suppose so. Thank you." Matthew shook her hand, smiling ruefully.

"You are here to protect the trees, aren't you?" Orla went

on, "I didn't know that any of these were under threat? Actually they don't look that old, what are they, two hundred years?"

She had been looking up in the boughs of the tree, where he had come from,

"Oh, now I can see, you have been sleeping up there too. Well, I know what that's like, bloody uncomfortable." Unwittingly Orla had hit the nail on the head, only Matthew wasn't part of any movement.

Matthew, was slightly uncomfortable as he said with a self deprecating laugh,

"Well, I am more of a lone wolf, really. I keep an eye out to make sure that everyone is safe."

Maeve picked up on it in a flash,

"Safe? From what, or from whom?" This might add a different, and maybe dangerous, perspective to the situation. After an uncomfortable pause, as Matthew didn't answer, Maeve went on,

"Is there something we should know about?"

Matthew spoke.

"You know."

He affirmed with a nod, as if this was enough to communicate his thoughts. The blank look on their faces, indicated that they were waiting for more.

After another pause he shrugged and went on,

"You know, the woman in the river." No reaction on their faces.

"Didn't you hear about the woman in the Stour? It was just over there," he waved in the direction of the river, beyond the woods past a small housing estate. They got the sense that he didn't often talk to people, as more words came out, his voice got stronger and with growing confidence,

"It's only about a ten minute walk from here. She drowned. People said it was suicide. I don't think it was, I think it was made to look like suicide. So I make sure that nothing bad happens, to the civvies in the woods on my watch."

As he was talking Maeve had stepped back, and was taking a good look at him. When he rescued her from the mud, she had noticed that he had an athletic body, and was attractive enough to distract her. He hadn't seemed to be in a rush, so, not a walker she thought, maybe he had been fishing in the lake. She often saw men who seemed to spend the day there, or even camp, by the reed pond. Now, on closer examination, she saw that he was wearing army fatigues rather than fishing, or forestry, gear. When he referred to people as 'civvies', it rang a bell as 'army speak'.

Maeve took a risk,

"Were you, are you, in the service? In the army? Ever based here?"

Matthew hesitated,

"Look, I'm okay, I'm fine, I don't need any help."

Running his fingers through his hair, as he took some time to think,

"It's like she said," gesturing towards Orla. "I look after the trees, and I keep watch. It keeps me sharp."

His shoulders sagged a little, and his voice lowered,

"Not ready for civvy street yet. I need the space. Soon. One day. When things are better." He seemed to think that this was sufficient explanation, then as an afterthought looking directly at Maeve said,

"But you are okay, I won't frighten you again. Must go."

He had clearly had enough conversation because with that, he turned and did a sprint up the steep incline that led to the flatter open spaces and gorse bushes before the old barracks. He was out of sight before they moved.

"What was that all about?" Orla asked.

"No idea," Maeve said, "but I wouldn't be surprised if we found out that he spent some time in this barracks, and maybe it was a good time for him, or he felt safe, or he had friends here, but there is something acting as a draw to this place."

They started to move off, and resume their walk, as Maeve went on,

"I really know nothing about people who leave the army, but from things you see on the news, the military doesn't seem to do a lot for them. Once they are out, they are out. I know there are a number who have PTSD, so he might not be that stable, he might have unresolved issues."

Still thinking aloud, Maeve changed her tone and was more upbeat when she added, "Anyway, at the moment he seems harmless, and frankly I am glad to know that if I hear any more strange noises, or twigs cracking, it's probably Matthew and not someone going to mug me. Plus he is a good looking man, and I love that accent, he's like a cross between George Clooney and Hugh Grant, playing someone who's gone a bit wild."

Orla was thoughtful,

"There is something about him that makes you trust him immediately. Shame he's not an eco-warrior, it would be great to have someone like that. I bet he wouldn't take any shit from the digger drivers and the developers. And with a voice like that the money men would listen to him."

Good humour returned, they were both enjoying stomping through the woods and had almost forgotten why they were there. Orla was showing off her new found knowledge and green credentials. Oak, willow, poplar, hawthorn, blackthorn, rowan, she was listing them off as they walked past, and Maeve was enjoying it. Orla might not be in school, but she definitely hadn't stopped learning, if anything it was giving her a new appetite for knowledge. Orla was about to launch into her most recent preoccupation, which was how to effect change in government policy, when Maeve stopped suddenly.

"Ehm, Miss? Please Miss, did you bring us something to eat? Anything'll do."

Maeve jumped, it was that voice in her ear, she almost felt his hot breath down her neck. Far too close. She really didn't need this, she had business to do today and this wasn't it.

"Stop!" She held up her hand to keep him at a distance, and said the first thing that came to mind,

"Tell me about Christmas? What did you do?"

The man had almost the same reaction as Edward, when she asked if he was a Parliamentarian, or a Royalist. Agitated and clearly nervous, looking around to see who might be listening, he now backed away, voluntarily

"What did you see? I did nothing. They were chasing all of us. We just had to get away and hide. For God's sake, it was Christmas, we don't trade on the birthday of our Lord. We are right. It's always been like that, for ever. They can't just declare Christmas Day a work day!"

Maeve felt she was clearly onto something, but didn't know exactly what, so taking another risk,

"Do you know Sir Edward Hales?"

The man spat,

"Bastard! He'll have us all hanged if he has his way." He took a breath,

"But you know what," he moved closer leaning into Maeve. This time she noticed his clothes and they might be from the same time period as Edward's. But she wanted more than anything to get away from him, she felt that he hadn't washed in a long time, maybe not ever. She thought she could see lice, it made her skin crawl.

"But you know what?' He said as he got closer still, "It's not going to go all his way. I hear tell of a thousand Men of Kent joining a force, from Nonnington and Canterbury and all round. That number of men will be something to be reckoned with. I'll join them for food, if they'll have me."

Maeve could feel it slipping away from her, she was losing

the thread of who was who, so she made one last push to get some information that she could work on,

"What's your name? I think you have a friend in Edward Hale's household, over by St Stephens."

He laughed, a chesty laugh, which didn't sound too good and wasn't a pretty sight either, as most of his teeth were missing or rotten.

"Oh, Edward Hale, you mean the grandson, they say he's on our side. It's the grandfather as what wants us strung up. A friend in his house, you say? Yes, I know a man works there. He's no friend, he's a coward, and that's being kind, some might say 'he's a traitor! You speak to him, you tell him Thomas Apps knows where he is. I may need food in my belly, but I never sold no one out!"

Then Thomas turned to face Maeve full on, and with a sly, menacing attitude said,

"'Here, you give me an idea. Maybe I'll go and find him meself." He tapped the side of his nose, grinning to himself,

"I knows where you come from."

With a menacing leer, the spirit Thomas, turned, and now facing the direction of Maeve's home, disappeared.

CHAPTER 15

WALKING IN THE WOODS

The more he thought about it the more anxious Steve became. Since he wasn't a true believer in the spirit world, at times he could be flippant about it. When he had been thinking about finding some extra investigating that he could do with Maeve, selfishly the idea had been for him, and he hadn't thought about her, and what she might be going through.

Steve knew that Maeve had resisted, or in fact completely suppressed, her ability to communicate with the other side for many, many years. When he met her, it was because she had responded to one person and then to a few more people, or spirits, who wanted to talk to her. She certainly hadn't opened herself up to the whole spirit world. Yet, he had asked her to do just that, for a case that he thought was a cold case, which even with her help they weren't likely to solve.

Steve was piecing this together, and guessed that this 'next step' of calling, or tapping into spirits at will, was something Maeve was working through. But her experience in Butchery Lane had not been good.

Now, he was kicking himself, because he had just asked

her to go into the woods, probably alone, and face something that might be terrifying. He should have gone with her.

Looking for reasons to excuse himself, he thought that in his world, things had not eased up since the summer. The second wave of COVID seemed to catch everyone on the hop. There was no clear strategy from number ten Downing St, or central Government. Laws had been passed, but there were no extra police on the ground to make sure that people abided by them. Plus, the rules changed with no warning. And of course the infamous Dominic Cummings from number ten's trip to Barnard Castle to 'test his eyes', had undermined any moral authority the police might have had. He couldn't count the number of times people had said to him, 'we're just off for our eye test - ...in Scotland!' So how could they prepare?

Amongst all of this, in Canterbury, they had had an unusually high, non-COVID related, death rate. People said it was suicide. His team had discussed this through their partnership with the charity 'Mid Kent Mind', who manned their helpline. The counsellors confirmed the team's suspicion that it was probably the effect of isolation in lockdown, on vulnerable peoples' mental health. Steve thought that was fair enough, in most cases, but there had been a few that didn't seem to fit. He had been looking at the map and noticed that the recent body pulled from the Stour, was actually pretty close to the woods where Maeve found the body.

He should have gone with Maeve, he shouldn't have asked her to do it alone. He would call her.

❧

"That was very disconcerting." Maeve said to Orla as she recovered from the encounter.

Orla hadn't seen Thomas at all, so Maeve had to recount the conversation verbatim, or as close as she could get.

"Well the gist of it is, that he knows, or knew, our Edward, there is some issue between them. He said Edward was a coward and he was heading over to our house to sort it out. Probably not in a pleasant way either."

Orla exclaimed,

"Shit! Can they really do that? I mean, can spirits move around and 'sort people out'?"

Maeve was drained, it had been an unpleasant experience,

"I don't know. But if they can, do we have time to warn Edward?"

They looked at each other for a solution. Orla could see that it had taken a lot out of Maeve, and today her role was as support, so she spoke first,

"Regardless, I think we should head home. We have had enough adventures for one morning. That way, if it is possible, you can warn Edward, then we can get some food and head out to pick up Marianne."

Maeve looked relieved, she appreciated Orla's clear thinking, and she felt it gave her permission to avoid Steve's mission. She was glad she did not have to try to call up a spirit that wasn't forthcoming, well not today anyway.

She nodded agreement, and reached for her phone to call Steve to let him know, so that he wasn't waiting, or thinking that she was avoiding him. She didn't want to admit it, but really Maeve wanted to hear his voice; she wanted the reassurance. She was still walking as she pulled out her phone and wasn't concentrating on what she was doing.

It was one of those moments that you play back in your head later, thinking, if only I had......

Maeve hadn't put the protective cover on her new phone yet, so it was thin and really slippery. She didn't know how it happened, but as she pulled the phone out of her pocket, it flew out of her hand, through the air, actually skimmed across reed lake, and disappeared under the surface in the middle. They both dashed over, but all they could see were the ripples widening on the surface. The lake, more of a glorified pond, was deceptive, there were some reeds around the edges which gave it its name, but then the sides dropped and it was deep. Not the place to try and wade in to get your phone out from.

"Shit, shit, and double shit!" Maeve didn't know what else to say, this was her new phone and she definitely couldn't afford to replace it.

"Will it be covered by the house insurance?" Orla's first thought was helpful and gave Maeve something less negative to focus on.

She sighed,

"I'm not sure, we can have a look when we get back to the house. I have an old BlackBerry that I can dig out for the moment. I think I can get a 'pay as you go' SIM until I figure this out. One thing for sure, if we are dealing with an insurance company, then it's not likely to be quick."

Heading back in the direction of home, their good humour of earlier had evaporated. They were trudging along. Orla had been getting cold from hanging around. Maeve, just wanted to be home, when she spoke it was almost monosyllabic,

"Orla, your phone? I need to let Steve know."

Orla handed her phone over, and didn't mention that she was surprised that Maeve knew Steve's mobile number off by heart. She noticed it, and kept it to herself. Maeve texted Steve, explaining that this was Orla's phone, implying that this number was not to be used unless for 'official' messages. She got a quick 'understood - but we need to talk' back from Steve.

By this time, they were not far from the telecoms mast and that was only a few minutes walk from the spot Maeve had parked the car. As Maeve handed Orla back her phone, she looked up and noticed the woman that she had seen before. She was sitting on the same tree stump. This time she was definitely talking to herself, gesticulating, and not aware of them approaching. She was large, overweight, heavily made up, had brittle blonde hair, now with grey roots showing. Maeve tried not to catch her eye, she really didn't want any more issues to deal with, and so looking down was surprised to notice that the woman had on platform boots, not at all suitable for a walk in the woods. No wonder she was sitting down, maybe this was as far as she ever got.

As they got closer, Maeve and Orla, did the practiced nod of country walkers, to indicate that they had seen the woman but had no intention of striking up a conversation. She had stopped talking as she saw them, she nodded back, saying nothing but watching them move on.

As they moved, definitely not wanting to stop here, Maeve tried discreetly to point out where she had found the body. She needn't have bothered, it was pretty obvious, because they could clearly see the remains of the plastic police hazard tape flapping around some of the trees. Like joining the dots, the tape marked the spot. Maeve didn't slow down. So she almost walked straight into Orla, who had stopped abruptly.

Orla was rigid and had turned a deathly pale.

This time it was Maeve's turn to be the support act. She didn't think that either of them could handle much more today, so taking charge, she gently but firmly put her hands on Orla's shoulders, saying, as if to the spirit that she couldn't see,

"It's all right, we will be back. Soon. But we must go now."

Then she turned Orla to face the right direction, and again gently but firmly propelled her forwards. Orla moved as if she was sleepwalking, saying nothing.

CHAPTER 16

REUNION

M arianne got her negative test result, which cheered
her up, she was cleared to go home. She texted
Maeve with relief, even though this was her anticipated
outcome, the relief of knowing for sure that she could go
home, lifted her spirits.

Marianne had a very strong sense of fair play, and always
abided by the rules, so she was never going to go against official guidelines. She resented the fact that students had taken
the principal blame for this second wave of the virus. Being
an undergraduate and in accommodation on campus she had
been part of the testing pool. She already knew that their
pool had tested clear a week ago, and she had kept herself to
herself since then, in the hope that she could go home.

Although she didn't have the sense of drama that her
sister frequently displayed, she did want to make the world a
better place. Hence her choice of course, PPS 'politics,
psychology and sociology', which she felt would allow her to
choose a career that suited her, even if she wasn't quite sure
what that would be yet. Marianne imagined she would have
worked it out by now, but she hadn't.

She thought she was heading for politics, but was exasperated with the current set of politicians. If she got an internship in Westminster she didn't think she could keep her opinions to herself. Also, by now she had discovered the depths of the Oxford-Cambridge rivalry, and if she wanted to get into politics, she should have gone to Oxford.

This first term had not been a success. The campus was beautiful, it definitely wasn't the location that was the problem. Although everyone had been perfectly nice, she hadn't appreciated the amount of online lectures and self supervised reading involved. She hadn't had any of the real Cambridge experience. She knew her way around the town from her many walks, and knew Ellie, the girl who had a room next door on her landing. But effectively she had not had a social life at all.

Part of the reason Marianne had come here, was because she really wanted to challenge herself. Academically she was fine, the course was stretching her, but not beyond her limits. For her, the question was much more personal, she didn't find relationships easy. So far she had put her energy into study, rather than romantic or sexual relationships. And if she was going to find someone, she wanted it to be without any family around. No matter how loving they might be, her family members were smothering. The last thing she wanted was other people involved, before she knew what she wanted herself. In any event, social distancing had ensured that experimenting with relationships was not an option. At least, not within the rules.

Marianne had decided that if she had a break, with any luck the vaccine would be approved and available, so that she could do a reset and start again. Now, she just wanted home, wanted to put on cosy clothes, and be where she was loved, unconditionally.

As a result, she was ready with her cases packed, long before she got the test results. She had a lot of bags because she was taking everything that she might need, in case the

COVID lockdown situation changed, and she ended up staying at home for the rest of this academic year. She would be happy to do that now, independence had proved to be lonely.

But Maeve hadn't replied to her text, where were they? She tried again, this time she phoned Maeve, but no answer, it went straight to voicemail. 'Bloody hell! I thought they would be waiting to hear from me, she could feel her irritation rising as she thought this. There was nothing she could do but wait.

∽

Maeve got Orla into the car, messaged Marianne, and drove, giving Orla a moment to come back from whatever had happened. They were home before Orla even began to look normal.

Maeve was in the kitchen getting some hot sweet tea for both of them, when remembering Edward, she shouted out to the empty room, "Edward!"

He wasn't her priority at the moment, but still, she wanted to give him a head start if she could, "Edward, there might be a guy called Thomas Apps, on his way over here to 'sort you out'. He didn't seem like someone you'd want to meet. If you're hiding, then stay that way. We can talk later."

No reply. She had done her bit. Now she could concentrate on Orla. Walking back into the sitting room with two mugs in one hand, as she opened the door she asked,

"Are you ready to talk about what happened?"

Orla nodded, "It was the same young girl. She was shouting over and over, 'I want to be a good girl' and then 'I am a good girl'. But separately, I could feel fear, a trembling fear, of something I couldn't see." Orla stopped, her colour had drained again, her hands were shaking, she sipped her tea to give herself some time before going on,

"I could feel something else too. I think there might have been someone else there but I couldn't see them." Re-living the experience was clearly traumatic for Orla,

"I have never felt anything like this before. It was like an all consuming wave of emotion. I don't know what would have happened if you hadn't been there."

Maeve was now sitting beside her on the sofa, she wrapped her arms around Orla, and they rocked in silence for a few minutes, both of them with tears running down their cheeks.

'Christ', thought Maeve, 'I am going to have to learn how to deal with this, if not for my own sake, then for Orla.'

The trip to Cambridge and back, gave them some time when they only had to deal with logistics, and the lighter than normal traffic on the road. Being in a warm car on the motorway looking at the hedgerows, now changing yellow, red and brown, was comfortable, and safe; it gave a sense of ordinariness, a sense of 'everything is always going to be okay'. It was settling. Maeve had packed a bag of snacks with the totally unhealthy, crisps, chocolate biscuits and flask of good coffee. Orla had worked her way through a good half of them, before they even got to Marianne.

When they arrived, Marianne's bad temper evaporated into hugs and childish jumping up and down, not caring who was watching, just glad that they were all together again.

It was long dark, by the time they got home, but making plans for Christmas, deciding on favourite foods, what decorations were allowed and what had to be done beforehand, dispelled the gloom. They were laughing as they unpacked the car. Maeve was hearing Ada's words in her head as she watched her daughters maturing in front of her. She didn't need to say anything for Orla to offer to help Marianne, 'that wouldn't have happened a year ago', she thought.

Lights on, heating going, both girls in Marianne's room chatting. Maeve was in the kitchen sorting out the easiest supper she could think of. Too tired to prepare anything fresh, she opted for pizza from the freezer, with a bowl of cherry tomatoes as a token gesture to healthy food. She had closed the oven door before she thought of Edward.

"Edward! Edward?" She shouted to the empty room. No reply. She couldn't feel his presence either. 'I hope he's alright', she thought, and then wondered, in the spirit world what does that even mean? Time to call Ada.

CHAPTER 17

WHAT TO DO

The pizza, now with screen at the far end of the table, and Ada chatting as they ate, was a success.

"I don't care what you say, you've lost weight. Still, you are looking good."

Ada sighed, "I wish I was there with ye. Though pizza's not my favourite. I'm not keen on this eat with your fingers business. I have mine with a knife and fork because I am well brought up, not like you lot." She poured herself another glass of red wine on her side of the screen divide, and settled back,

"So where were we? There is a bunch of stuff to be sorted."

Although Maeve, Orla and Marianne, were all eating, they really wanted to hear Ada's answers, all eyes were on Ada.

"The fella in the woods connected to your Edward. I think he needs some researching. Marianne, could you do that? Check out the Hales family and see what you can find. Sometimes facts help, not always, but let's see what we are dealing with."

Marianne nodded, smiling. Maybe she was happy at the prospect of her task, or maybe just happy to be home.

Ada got out a pencil and some paper, on the basis that things were getting too complicated for her to rely on her memory. Alternating between sips of wine and tapping her lips with the pencil, Ada was thinking.

"Okay so." Pause.

"Here are my brilliant thoughts. Maeve you talk to Steve, and find out about any old cases." Ada tried to wink at Marianne and Orla without Maeve seeing her. Failing miserably.- Maeve interrupted,

"Everyone knows I've been talking to Steve, so no need for sly winks from the sidelines. Let's stick to the plot. What else have you got, Ada?"

Duly reprimanded, Ada went on,

"Well, we need to know more. I don't think that this is just one thing. You keep tripping over things so let's go at them, one at a time."

Another sip of wine,

"If you are going to help Steve, we need to know what goes on there, in the woods. Let's start with your man, the real one. Is this chap Matthew, really homeless, or camping out like Orla? How do we know if he's an ex-service man?"

Maeve could see that Ada had only written down a few words. Maeve thought the whole pencil and paper act was just to have something to do, so that they wouldn't notice if she drank the whole bottle in front of them.

"So someone has to find out what happens if you're homeless in Canterbury. To be honest, I'm thinkin I haven't a clue. I give money at mass if they are collecting, and then if someone is begging in the street I'd give them a bob or two. But beyond that, I have no idea."

She looked at them over her glasses with eyebrows raised, waiting for a reaction. Ada never used her glasses in front of strangers, it spoiled her image, even though her arms weren't long enough to hold print far enough away to read. Still no reaction from the Canterbury side of the screen, so she went on,

"Drugs? Would you know if he was on drugs?" Again looking over her glasses, to see if there was any response from Maeve, or Orla. This time taking off the glasses and tapping the piece of paper,

"See what I mean. Your Steve would know about these kinds of things."

Maeve wasn't expecting this. Real world problems were something they could handle between themselves. She was getting annoyed, maybe Ada didn't have any of the answers they needed,

"Ada! We want to know about the spirit world. Can a spirit move? And what would 'sort him out' even mean?"

Ada went back to her pencil, and another sip of wine. Maeve thought that by now, they wouldn't get any more sense out of her. Irritated, but at the same time guessing that Ada was never going to say she didn't have an answer, when it came to the spirit world, Maeve suggested that they leave it at that for the night. Apart from Ada, who was happy with her wine, the rest of them were exhausted and needed the sleep.

First thing in the morning Maeve went into town to get a SIM card for her Blackberry.

Steve, was the first number she put into it, and then he was the first person she called. A coffee break at Fonds would give them a little private time, without breaking any rules.

It had been raining, but they got one of those wonderful gaps when the sun comes out and lights up the world, as if it was always going to be like that. They dried off the seats and sat down. Maeve was well wrapped up and not bothered by the cold. She wanted to make this all sound normal, as if seeing Steve wasn't anything special, so she started as if they were in the middle of a conversation,

"Kieran and Colin, got the grant."

Steve looked a little puzzled, so she filled in,

"I'm sure they told you. Inside. In Fonds." She nodded backwards, indicating the coffee shop behind them, "They want to train young unemployed people to become Baristas, and they got a grant to help the trainees. Isn't that cool?"

Steve smiled, he recognised this as a diversionary tactic, as a way to fill out their conversation, their time together, without getting into anything too personal. Nice, but not necessary.

"That's great." He wasn't in the mood for chitchat this morning, he went straight into what he had come to say.

"I'm sorry. I shouldn't have asked you to do that. I am going to come clean."

Maeve was scrunching up a paper tissue in her hand, colouring slightly, clearly nervous that he was about to make a declaration that she wasn't ready to hear.

He noticed, and decided to change tack,

"It's okay," he took a moment to rephrase what he was going to say "I mean, the guy in the woods. We probably won't be able to solve it. I wanted to give it a try. But it is a cold case and realistically we don't have the bandwidth at the station right now." He didn't say that he wanted to spend time with Maeve. He didn't think she had noticed his change of direction.

She breathed a sigh of relief. Although she wanted to be with Steve, she still wasn't comfortable with it. Like with everything else in her life, when she didn't want to face the reality of the situation, she put off dealing with it directly. A little more time, she thought, I do like him, I'm just not ready right now. She reflected on how many opportunities she had missed this way. Regardless, she was still happy to delay.

Tension relieved, Steve went on,

"There have been more deaths than normal in Canterbury." He sighed,

"Yes COVID-19, does account for many," glancing at Maeve whose eyes were widening in anticipation.

"I think you can guess that some of them, sadly, are suicides. People who find all of this too difficult to cope with. But,.."

Steve paused for a moment, hesitating. He thought, better she knows than that she lands herself in more trouble by accident.

"...I have my own theory." He knows this is a personal opinion that has not been backed up, so takes his time.

"I believe that some of them are not what they first appear to be. Your body in the woods, might be one. The woman who drowned in the Stour, might be one."

He didn't want to worry Maeve unnecessarily so was examining his fingernails as he thought how to put it.

"It's very hard to drown yourself," he said looking at Maeve as if everyone knew that.

"I didn't know that. I never thought about it. I suppose I am lucky enough to never having contemplated suicide." Somehow, Maeve felt guilty for not knowing, maybe she could have helped someone.

"What do you want me to do?"

~

All three of them got home around the same time. As Maeve closed the door, she heard Marianne and Orla swapping updates. Just in time, she thought.

Twenty minutes later, the table looked like a military campaign was being planned. Remains of tea, crumbs from sandwiches and butter smeared where it shouldn't be, like an island of debris in the middle of maps, printouts, and sheets of scrawled notes.

Maeve was impressed, both girls had been working hard, and had come back with lots of information.

Marianne was the first to launch in with the Hales family, she was confident that she had pinpointed the issue,

"It was called the Christmas riot of 1647, or the Plum Pudding Riots. The puritans had outlawed Christmas, they said it should be a normal working day. This Christmas, fell on a market day, so the Mayor ordered the market to go ahead. The people thought this was against God's will, they wanted the shops shut, and Churches open. In the fracas, some heads were bashed, but the local people won the day. But this is no Hollywood story, so it wasn't long lived."

Marianne had it all down in her notes, with references. But she was telling the story 'in precis', with relish, just glancing for confirmation of dates or names.

"So…. the really interesting bit is that we have a family feud in the middle of all this. The Christmas riot, triggered an uprising in support of Charles the first. Now at this point, old Sir Edward Hales sat in the House of Commons and was a 'hang-em, shoot-em, flog-em type' of Parliamentarian, but his grandson, Edward Hales aged twenty-four, was persuaded to lead the Royalists against Parliament! So they were on opposite sides. No wonder Edward doesn't want you mentioning Royalists or Parliamentarians."

Maeve and Orla were taking it all in, this was a lot more drama than any of them had been expecting, and was beginning to sound like a prequel to 'The Crown'.

Maeve had questions,

"But, do we know which side Edward was on? Or which side the guy in the woods, Thomas Apps, was on?"

"Good question. I have located the gravestone of a Thomas Apps in St Dunstan's dated 1755 so there definitely was a family Apps still here. And…" Marianne was getting excited.

"…I found more Apps, sometimes written as Epps, and

95

they were carpenters or wheelwrights." She finished with a flourish, as if that explained something. Looking at the anticipation on Orla's and Maeve's faces, Marianne saw she needed to go on.

"Don't you see? A carpenter. Outside craftsman. Our Edward was a house servant, probably young Edward Hales's servant, because he mentioned the new house. So he probably employed Thomas Apps on behalf of his boss, and if anyone was on a different side then our Edward could be caught in the middle, regardless of what side he was on." She ran out of steam here, "Okay, I may be jumping to conclusions, and I thought that made more sense that it really did. I'll do some more digging."

Marianne looked down at her notes, "There is definitely more on the ground research to do."

Throughout all of this, Orla was hopping from foot to foot. She had information to share but she also had a big favour to ask. She was going to bust if she couldn't get it out.

CHAPTER 18

DISCOVERY

Maeve was still the only one who could see Edward. Ada, had 'temporarily' lost her gift, Orla, seemed to communicate with younger spirits, so for the moment it was only Maeve. Maeve had already gone into the kitchen for tea and snacks and she called him.

Now she was whispering his name, in case he was hiding. Nothing. He wasn't there. Or he wasn't showing himself.

Before Marianne could finish with her projected next steps, Orla blurted out,

"Can Adam bubble with us?"

It took Maeve by surprise. Less than a year ago if someone had said they were 'bubbling with someone', she wouldn't even know what they were talking about. Now she knew all too well.

At the same time, this wasn't a school ground play date. Ada had warned her that the girls were growing up. She hadn't found the time to talk to Pascal about it. But that didn't really matter; she already knew what he would say, he was very relaxed about physical relationships, and would be delighted at the prospect of a potential romance for Orla. Maeve knew that she was the problem, she had been putting off making her own mind up. Is Orla old enough? Am I being over protective? No way out now.

In those few seconds, which felt like hours, she regretted not facing up to her feelings for Steve. If Adam stayed in the house with them, then she wouldn't be able to add Steve to their bubble. She smiled to herself thinking, well at least I know what I feel about Steve now.

Orla misinterpreted Maeve's smile as a 'yes'. So launched in with,

"I love you Mum. You are the best. He can't go home, and if he doesn't come here, he will be all on his own for Christmas."

Well, that's that decision made, thought Maeve, who didn't have the heart to crush Orla's excitement.

"But for Christmas?" Marianne was not happy.

For her, Christmas was a sacrosanct family time, just the three of them, with of course, Ada coming over on Christmas Day for present opening and Christmas dinner. This year in particular she had been counting on Christmas as a special time of childhood rituals. Like a puppy that's outgrown its basket, she was trying to convince herself that it didn't matter what happened, she could always snuggle up at home, and that would never change. Her reaction was extreme, unleashing pent up emotions, more related to her upset at her college experience, than anything else.

"How could you! You don't think of anyone but yourself!" Marianne shouted at Orla, as she burst into tears and ran upstairs to her bedroom. Of course there was also an element of 'how could Orla bring a man into the house before she did'. It just wasn't fair.

Maeve was taken by surprise for a second time, she hadn't seen this coming at all. Looking at Orla's stunned face,

"Orla, that's fine, we will work it out. But there are practical things to be considered. Where will he sleep?"

Orla flushed. Practical solutions were Maeve's forte; she

would probably muddle through that way, without ever talking directly to Orla about rules and relationships in their shared home.

"I can move into your office, on the camp bed." Orla offered, as they didn't have a spare room.

So, thought Maeve, either Orla is too embarrassed or the relationship hasn't gotten to that stage yet.

Maeve had resigned herself to the new addition to the household, by the time she went upstairs to see Marianne, having first suggested, that Orla tidy the table and get the Christmas Panettone out. Time for the first seasonal treat, it might tempt Marianne out of a sulk.

Neither Marianne nor Orla ever doubted how much Maeve cared for each of them. But sometimes Maeve found herself in the middle, seeing both sides and having to mend fences.

She knocked on Marianne's door. Hearing some muffled sobs, she didn't wait for an answer. Maeve opened the door quietly, slipped in, and sat beside Marianne, who was lying face down in her pillow, on the bed. Maeve rubbed her back.

"It's okay. I know you want things to be like they have always been, but they aren't, so maybe this is a good year to try new things and make some new traditions." No response, but the sobs were easing. "I know it must have been hard this year. Your first year in college, mostly in isolation. Not at all what you were expecting." Her voice was soft and it was having a soothing effect on Marianne, who eventually moved round, swinging her legs off the side of the bed, she sat up.

"I was so looking forward to it. Just us. Normal. Everything as it should be." A few more tears escaped. Maeve handed her a tissue. Marianne blew her nose and the tears stopped. That was that.

Maeve smiled at her, as she gave a good hug,

"Well, that was never going to happen. We couldn't have done our 'Christmas Eve' Bluewater trip with lunch at Eddie

Rocket's and a big movie, Harry Potter, or Lord of the Rings, or whatever it should have been. The cinemas are closed, and even if they were open there are no big releases this year."

There was something in the reality of the facts, and Maeve's grounded attitude, that made Marianne laugh,

"I suppose." She blew her nose again.

Maeve took advantage of the change in mood, "So this year should be a year of new traditions. First one being that we can start the Panettone today, now. Hot chocolate and cake is an excellent new tradition."

Within minutes they were round the table again, Marianne having apologised to Orla. Maeve got her notebook out.

"Ada was right, it is getting complicated. We need a re-cap, and then let's start a 'to-do' list."

Marianne said, "Oh, first, I found a place where you might look for Edward. I didn't go and have a look because I couldn't see him even if he was there. Apparently, it's the only remnant of the Hales mansion, which the young Edward built, it's an old dovecote. But now it's a chapel." She shrugged, "I know, sometimes the reasons for things get lost in history."

Refocusing,

"And, there are some strange stories surrounding it, including tunnels and more importantly, ghosts."

She had their full attention.

"It's not far. It's about a ten minute walk away. But I don't think any of us have ever been there."

Lists forgotten, the idea of a short walk, something physical, sounded great. So, wrapped up, they were out the door in minutes. They stomped down the hill trying to remember the silly walks Maeve had done with them as children, to make the journey home from school shorter. Giggling at the silliness, good humour was recovered. There were times, Maeve thought, when she could still see the two little girls, but those moments were fast disappearing.

Marianne was the guide and had the map out on her phone,

"Okay so we turn left here, along The Terrace. Of course, it all makes sense now, it's called The Terrace because it was the terrace in front of the large Hales' mansion."

As they walked, she filled in more of the detail. The leaves had completely fallen from the trees by now, allowing them to see the layout of the valley through the bare branches stretching round to St Stephen's Church in front of them.

"So this flat bit of grass, would have been their lawn, looking down over Canterbury to our right. Directly across there, is the wood where you have been walking. And behind us on the hill, where the post World War Two houses are, that's where the big house was. It was huge."

This was very familiar to all of them, they just hadn't thought about it before. Within a few minutes, they were walking into new territory beyond their everyday world, into a housing estate that they never needed, so had never noticed. Round the bend, up a steep incline, and there it was. Bizarre that none of them had noticed it before.

Here, was a strange tiny circular chapel set back from the road in its own green. The building was made of flint with red brick columns, striped with bands of knuckle bones; a porch had been clearly added. The roof was domed with a glass cupola to let some light in, and the whole thing was surrounded by a circle of large lime trees, between the trees were gravestones. The gravestones fanned out radially from a central point, probably the chapel. The gate in the outer railings, was locked.

Orla, was immediately walking round the full circle, and shouted across from the far side,

"Hey, you can get in here, something has driven into the railings, it's easy to climb in."

CHAPTER 19

THINGS CHANGE

Marianne dashed off, following Orla, Maeve hung back.

Something's not quite right, she thought. Tuning into her feelings, something was pushing her away from the dovecote. Using her senses like a divining rod, she closed her eyes, and turned round, with the chapel now at her back she began to move forwards. Once she felt sure of where to go she opened her eyes. Luckily, she was just in time, to stop herself from walking under a bus.

Recovering her breath, she crossed the road, and walked back towards the Terrace. Under some large trees was a short section of a red brick wall, probably the remains of the old walled garden. There, cowering by the wall was Edward. He was sitting on his haunches, holding his head in his hands, mumbling, "Oh no, not my time, no, no, no. It's not."

As soon as he saw Maeve, he put his fingers to his lips,

"Shhh. Whisper, don't let him hear you." As he registered certain thoughts, expressions drifted across Edward's face. Looking at Maeve he grew anxious, eyes open wide, as he stood up and looked around them. "He didn't follow you did he? He's sneaky, he could be following you." With that Edward disappeared.

Maeve took a good look around, then as she was about to try this concept of 'tuning in' to herself, she stopped. "Edward, if I 'call' him then he might feel me and know where you are. So far, he is not here nor at the house." She felt pleased with herself, this was progress. She was controlling her ability, albeit in a limited sense.

Edward did not reappear.

Maeve waited for a few minutes, and then said, "Okay, you stay hidden for the moment, that way I can't show him where you are by accident. I will try to get to the bottom of this."

He still didn't appear, but she could hear him clearly as he said,

"Let him know that I left food out for them every night by the dovecote. But he never came. My master was looking for men, good men. Thomas, wasn't a good man, but I couldn't let them starve, could I?"

As soon as she couldn't feel him anymore, Maeve crossed back over to the dovecote. Orla and Marianne had done the recce, by the time she arrived.

As it was Orla who got over the railings first, she was taking charge of the find,

"We can't get inside. But there is something wrong with this. From talking to Adam," slight pause of embarrassment,

"I know that Christians are normally buried facing East. So all the graves run in an East-West direction. Look at these ones. They are like spokes of a wheel coming out from the chapel. What is that about? And what's the story with the trees? One for each grave."

Marianne added, "There are thirteen graves in a ring, then there is a second ring so twenty six graves in all. Does that signify anything? Apart from the obvious. I mean, two times thirteen is twenty six dead people."

Orla said what they were all thinking, "Thirteen. I'm pretty sure that's not a good number."

They looked at each other for a moment. Maeve said, "It doesn't feel good to me and I don't want to draw any spirit's attention, to the fact that I am here. So I'm not going to try and see if I can find anyone. This is not a good place. I am heading home, right now."

The girls got back over the bent railings and ran to catch up with Maeve. On the walk back Maeve shared her conversation with Edward.

"Back to our list. We have different things that need to be sorted out. One, we need some more historical background. Marianne, so far this has been really useful, at least to have some idea of the world that Edward's coming from."

Going with the random flow of her thoughts, shifting from historical puzzles, to potential affairs of the heart, Maeve changed the subject.

"Maybe we should work out when we are going to start this bubble with Adam, and get him over to pick his brain too?" Maeve was thinking that it might reduce any awkwardness if he had a role, something to do, but she had moved her mouth, before she had engaged her brain.

It set Marianne and Orla off, talking over each other with various platforms of indignation. This historical research was Marianne's area, and she didn't want Adam taking over. Orla was excited that her 'friend', could be a part of this too. And Orla used her trump card, Adam owed Maeve, since between them, Orla and Maeve had saved his life. This was an area where he could genuinely make a contribution.

Bickering, reminded Maeve that they still knew how to irritate each other, and were childish enough to do it. She thought that the sign that they were really growing up would be, if they were also mature enough to make it up later. Time would tell.

She didn't have time for that now, so Maeve just up-ed the volume and talked over them,

"We need as much help as we can get. Also, we do need to get some more background info on Matthew, and whoever else might be in the woods. That's your department Orla. Plus, I can call Steve." By now Maeve wasn't paying any attention to the bad atmosphere between Marianne and Orla, she was lost in her own thoughts.

She went on, almost talking to herself,

"But this idea of shutting out everything else and concentrating on 'feeling' works. It's as if emotions are what connect, or guide us on the other side." She looked at the girls as the revelation dawned on her, but clearly wasn't expecting an answer.

"The big question is, when I 'zone in' does it act like a beacon? Do I suddenly appear in their world with a flashing neon light over my head, saying 'can I help you?'"

~

Hours later, back around the table, Ada had asked to listen-in to all the news, so she was on screen as Maeve exploded.

"But that's ridiculous. Canterbury Cathedral is the centre of the Church of England, and you are telling me that they don't do anything for the homeless? That's not possible." Maeve was outraged and kept interrupting, as Orla was recounting her discoveries.

"No, they do do something, just not directly. Or at least I couldn't find anything." Orla flicked through her notes. "They do have a soup kitchen but that's to raise money for the homeless charities. So they give money to Porchlight and Catching Lives, but they don't do it themselves."

"Don't like getting their hands dirty." Maeve muttered to herself.

She had forgotten that Ada was 'there', until her voice emerged from the table.

"I'm sure that they do good things that we don't see too."

Marianne chipped in, "Well, one of my friend's mothers had a shop. And you know, the Cathedral is the landlord for a lot of the shops in town. Anyway, they are not a kind, or compassionate, landlord. She'd been there for years, a perfect tenant, but they wouldn't give her any kind of break when times were tough, and in the end, they put her out of business."

Orla jumped in, "since lockdown, I've heard that the Church is still charging the shops full rent, even though the shops can't open!"

"Ah now. You can't know that for sure." Ada wasn't keen on the direction of the conversation.

"I heard that there was a lovely deacon, or someone from the Cathedral anyway, who at the worst part of the first lock-down, made sure that my friend had a lovely funeral. So the family said. Small, but proper and personal. This man made a big effort when it mattered. So, they are not all bad."

Maeve brought them back to the matter in hand.

"It does mean that there's no point in going to them to find out about the homeless, or any ex-service people who might be in difficulty."

Orla, jumped up.

"I forgot about that. I do have some information. I spoke to a lovely woman, who knew everything about ex-service people, and how to get help for them."

She was now reading directly from her notes.

"Her name is Jan. She said 'sometimes you see people begging, and they have a sign saying they were in the service, well, ask them for their service number. If anyone has ever been in the service they will never forget their number.' " Looking up Orla added, "Jan left the WREN's in 1962 and she rattled off hers."

"That's good to know. Did she say where they could go for help? Is it to the army?" Maeve wanted to help Matthew if she could.

"Well, she laughed when I asked that exact question. She said, 'when they're out, they're out.' So back to Catching Lives. But Jan will help, if she can. She has been doing it for years. They are lucky to have her." Orla sat down as she finished.

Ada had been looking for the right moment to jump into the conversation.

"We mustn't lose sight of the big picture. You have something for Matthew which might help, which is all well, and good."

She wanted to shift the discussion to her area of interest,

"But the stuff with Edward is a brilliant way for you to practice, Maeve. His pal, what's his name, in the woods? You can try controlling your access to him, and getting stuff out of him. You did it before. And, if you are in the woods, you won't be letting on where Edward is."

Ada was rubbing her hands, pleased with the way things were going, so far. Then her expression changed,

"However there is something else, deeper, going on. The stuff you picked up there before, Maeve. And that Orla had an even stronger reaction to. Something else definitely happened there."

Ada paused for dramatic effect.

"You have to talk to Steve. If it's that strong, it might be recent."

CHAPTER 20
THE RIVER

That night, Maeve waited till she was on her own, before calling Steve. The proximity of his voice in her ear was intimate but at a safe distance. Maeve found it easy to flirt with Steve on the phone. She was giggling at silly things like a teenager, and he wasn't much better, he seemed to find everything interesting. 'What are we like', she thought to herself, enjoying the moment.

"But seriously, Ada says something bad must have happened in the woods. From Orla, we know it has something to do with a child. She said it could be recent. I was thinking it might be the opposite. Could you see if you could find anything in the last say fifteen or twenty years? That's still recent, compared to Cromwell!"

"Nothing's too much trouble for you..." Steve was only half joking, he couldn't remember anything off hand, but he didn't think it would take long to check it out.

Steve was enjoying the intimacy of the late night call too. He was comfortable. Which is probably why he started talking about things closer to home.

"You asked about PTSD, or the effects of trauma. Of

course, I imagine anyone that has been in a war zone is a prime target, but there are others too."

Steve was moving the conversation between official and personal, as though trying out boundaries.

"I mean, in the police, we get called out to domestics. Some of them are bad, really bad. And I know that many of the kids suffer long term from watching their Mums being done over. And they see worse than that. The cuts and bruises are what we deal with, but the effect on the kids...."

Then his tone shifted, lowering his voice it became more personal,

"You know, we get that in the force too. In fact you never know the people who are suffering..." He left the sentence hanging.

Maeve allowed a warm moment, before almost whispering,

"And you?"

"We don't talk about it. Not macho. The flashbacks, the triggers." Pausing to decide how much he was prepared to share,

"Lads don't talk about feelings. Any sign of weakness and you're a wimp, 'not a real man'."

He sighed, his voice was almost a whisper,

"You push it down inside, tell yourself it's okay and try to forget about it."

Steve had never spoken about his own experiences. The phone made it feel safe, and Maeve was listening, not passing judgement. Checking in on himself, he felt okay, so went on,

"For me, I had a bad day early on, when I was a first responder."

He stopped talking for a while, and Maeve just waited.

"I was called in after a jumper had thrown himself right in front of a train at the station. He made it across both rails of the tracks before the train hit."

Pause, Maeve could hear Steve shifting position on the other end of the phone.

"The train never had a chance to stop. It cut his head clean off, and the rest of his body in two."

Maeve could hear him breathing, this was hard.

"The ambulance guys dealt with the body. I had to go further up the track and find his head. Then bring it back." Pause,

"That frozen expression of surprise, still haunts me."

Maeve was no councillor, but she felt that in telling the story, Steve was allowing some of the emotion out. Thinking that must be a good thing, she imagined the tears, and wished that she was there for him in person.

After a few minutes, he cleared his throat, and in a stronger voice, went on,

"It was worse for the driver. On the day itself, he was in total shock, deathly white, trembling. But he never recovered; couldn't put it behind him. He left the job after that; said he couldn't get it out of his head. Just kept seeing it over and over, every time he came to a station."

"For me it was a smell. I don't know what exactly, oil, blood, metal, the wet of the day, but sometimes I get a whiff that reminds me of that mix, and I am right back there. Right in front of that face and that look of surprise."

Maeve stayed silent, feeling that Steve was talking as much to himself as to her.

"I know you're not supposed to, but I keep thinking, if I'd been there twenty minutes earlier, I could have stopped him. Stupid really, he was a stranger, there were other people there, no-one saw it coming."

"But still, I think if only….." a few more moments of silence.

"Anyway, that's a long time ago."

Maeve wasn't sure now what was the right thing to say, but something needed to be said,

"Accepting is good. I mean just acknowledging something, not saying good or bad, just that it happened. I think that's good."

Steve exhaled, as if he hadn't noticed that he had been holding his breath.

"It feels good to let it out." Then with a recognition of the importance of this moment "You are the first person I have ever told."

Maeve steered the conversation round to the normal, the mundane, until she felt that Steve was okay.

By the time they hung-up, they had agreed that Maeve would go for a walk along the river Stour, with Steve, as soon as possible. Ostensibly to see if she could communicate with the woman who had drowned recently. However, Maeve was pretty sure, that if she was with Steve, no one from the spirit world would contact her.

Thinking back on the call, Maeve guessed that this was just the beginning, Steve needed to open up to someone. She also thought she wanted to be there for him, to let him talk some of this stuff out. And if she was really honest with herself, she wanted to know who he really was, before…..Before what? Was she ready for there to be a 'something' between them?

On the other hand, if the sun came out, the idea of spending time walking along the river bank together, sounded good. Maeve needed adult company, she felt she needed him too.

❧

The following morning, the hubbub of the station was the usual, and full of the normal frustrations. They were stretched. Some people simply wouldn't take the pandemic seriously. It was the house parties that they just couldn't ignore. Everyone knew it was hard on young people, but these parties! With up to fifty or even a hundred drunk kids, you had to do something, and they used up a lot of resources.

Other crimes hadn't stopped. And now they were being pulled into Brexit preparations. Just what they needed. Miles of container trucks or pantechnicons, parked up on the M2 and the M20, and in Manston Airport, which was a pig to get to in a truck. Steve's early experience, in the Roads Policing Unit, meant that he was the one they were most likely to call on

Being pulled in all directions, Steve decided the best thing to do was to walk out the door, and leave it all behind, and come back in an hour or two when priorities were established. Coming back with a clear head, sounded like a good idea to him.

The rain had stopped, the sun was shining, it was a glorious morning. He signed out, and he called Maeve as he walked,

"You up for that riverwalk now? I'll pick you up. Wear a mask, I have a helmet, and you'll be fine on the back of the bike." Steve felt lighter. He didn't think that they would find anything either, but sometimes just talking out loud to someone else helped.

Ten minutes later, like a teenager bending the rules, Maeve hopped on the back of Steve's bike. Full of hope for some quality 'me' time, Maeve enjoyed holding on to Steve. The journey was too short for both of them, so Steve decided to go a bit further out of Canterbury. Get them in the right frame of mind, he thought. He followed the river on to Fordwich, the smallest town in Britain, more importantly, home to the George and Dragon pub, still open for takeaways. In reality, they were about twenty minutes walk from the spot they had planned to visit, just, on the country, rather than the town side of the river.

Hot coffee and a bacon roll in hand and still giddy, they

crossed the road away from the pub, facing towards the river bank. Glad that the car park was pretty empty and no one was watching them.

As they finished up their takeaways, Steve took the debris back to the bin. Looking back at the pub Maeve sighed, shame it was closed.

The sun had the remnants of warmth, the grass was still a brilliant green, the pub garden stretched towards the river, it was idyllic, with the perfect traditional pub, red tiled roof and window boxes full of flowers.

She waited for Steve, before walking through the gap in the car park edging towards the river itself. She turned to her right, facing the red brick bridge, noting the weeping willow touching the water, as she looked down into the flow.

The morning had lulled Steve. He didn't feel on duty, so he wasn't prepared for what was about to happen, and at first he didn't react at all.

Maeve was walking towards the water. Steve was still talking as he followed behind her. But she didn't stop at the water's edge. She kept on going. Straight into the river.

CHAPTER 21
NEW BEGINNINGS

S teve was mesmerised watching her, as she kept on walking into the water, then he switched into official mode.

"Stop! Stop! What are you doing?"

He was shouting as he moved into action. He ran to the river bank and followed her into the water.

Maeve carried on wading into the river, the water was up to her waist. She reached her arms down into the flow, then pushed off with her feet, almost diving into the river. She was right at the bottom, touching the river bed, before Steve got to her. He put his arms around her middle and pulled her out of the water, dragging her over to the river bank.

Coughing and spluttering, he held onto her until they were lying on the bank, safely on dry land.

"What the hell are you doing?"

Coming out of the water, woke Maeve from her trance, she was holding tightly onto Steve, like a security blanket.

"Oh my God! Did you not see her?"

Even though Steve was relieved that they were both okay, it had given him a fright, which came out as exasperation,

"What the hell are you talking about?"

Maeve was too shaken to react badly, she was coming out of a dream state,

"That woman, lying there, at the bottom of the river. I needed to get to her. She needed me. She wanted me down there, at the bottom of the river with her."

Now Maeve was sobbing with relief.

"If you hadn't been there….."

Steve had recovered enough by now to be comforting Maeve,

"It's okay, it's okay. There's no one there now. There wasn't any one in the river. Well, not anyone that I could see. You were reaching for some of that river weed. But you're fine now. And I am here." He held her tightly.

She opened her hands, and she was indeed clutching some trails of long flowing weed.

"I thought that was her. I was trying to get hold of her clothes, to save her. But I couldn't get a proper grip. And someone, or something, was pulling me down."

She stopped talking, looking at her hands in disbelief.

"It was so real."

Steve let her talk. They were lying on the ground recovering. As their levels of adrenaline dropped, they both became aware of the cold, and of their wet clothes.

Trying to lift the mood, Steve laughed,

"If anyone saw us they would think we were mad. Let's get you home and into something dry."

Maeve was white and still trembling, she nodded without saying anything. She was processing what had happened.

Propping her up, Steve guided them round to where he had parked the bike. Once on the road, he was fast. They were back outside Maeve's house in a few minutes.

Steve sorted the bike. While struggling to get the keys out of her wet clothes, Maeve saw the note pinned to the door.

'Gone shopping for provisions. Marianne & Orla XXX'.

She managed to open the door, thinking, good I can get myself warm and dry before they get back.

Once Steve was happy that she was safe, and on the way to a hot bath, he left to go and do the same thing, shouting over his shoulder on his way out.

"I'll be back in half an hour for that tea you promised. By the way, we may not officially be in a household bubble, but after this morning's adventure, I am telling you that we are in a 'care bubble'!"

Maeve smiled as she closed the door. As soon as she was alone, Maeve began peeling off her wet clothes, managing to smear herself with more mud in the process. She was too cold to care. Moving into the bathroom, running the bath and then back to her bedroom to get clean clothes. Heading again for the bathroom, now fully naked, holding the dry clothes out at arm's length, she saw a young man standing in front of her. She stopped, extremely annoyed that Edward had chosen today to make someone else appear.

Edward often appeared at inappropriate moments, Maeve had tried to ban him from her bedroom, without complete success. Irritated, she stood there, not wanting to actually walk through him.

"For Christ's sake, out of my way!"

She moved towards him, as he backed away turning puce with embarrassment. Not registering his discomfort, Maeve carried on,

"Where's Edward? And who are you? I can't deal with any new people today. I've had all I can take. So, whoever you are, get out of my way!"

"I'm Adam." The young man managed to get out, as Maeve slammed the door to the bathroom behind her.

A pause.

Still in shock, Adam stood there not knowing what exactly he had seen. Possibly a naked woman streaked with mud and bits of pond weed in her hair, who might actually be his hostess, and his previous saviour? Who was inexplicably angry and shouting at him?

He was wondering if had made the right decision to take Orla up on the offer of a place to stay. Christmas might be more 'interesting' than he had bargained for.

A moment later. Gingerly, the bathroom door opened. Maeve stuck her head out, keeping the rest of her body covered by the door.

"Oh my God. You are Adam."

"Em, yes?" Adam didn't know where to look, or what to expect.

"You are really here? In the house? In person?"

"Er, yes" by now his voice had dropped to a whisper, thinking that, even if this was her house, she was at best eccentric, at worst totally deranged. He wondered if he could get his stuff and creep out of the house without being accosted.

"Oh God! I am so sorry. I thought you were a ghost." Having recognised the extreme awkwardness of the situation, Maeve was still desperate to get into the bath.

"Well as you can see, I have to have a bath. Then we can have tea, and I'll explain."

She couldn't think of anything else to say, so closed the door. Shit, shit, shit, thought Maeve, who had by now remembered that it was her idea to get Adam over. Well, she reflected, it's too late to do anything about it, what's done is done, depending on how he reacts we'll know what kind of a person he is....

Stepping into the bath, luxuriating in the warm water, she forgot everything else for the moment.

Adam was standing on the landing, turning to the room, where he had been in the process of unpacking, and turning back to make sure the bathroom door was shut. Could he repack his bags and get out the door, before Maeve came out of the bathroom?

He was still hesitating when he heard keys in the front-door, this time, it was what he had been expecting before. Orla and Marianne, were back from the shops, with bags full of groceries. This he could manage, so he dashed down the stairs to help with the bags.

Seeing Maeve's clothes abandoned exactly where she pulled them off. Orla looked up at Adam as she said,

"I see you have met Mum", the girls looked at each other and back at Adam with raised eyebrows, wondering what exactly had been going on?

Looking deeply uncomfortable Adam said,

"She thought I was a ghost!"

The girls turned to each other and burst out laughing, Orla managed to get out

"Well you are as white as a sheet." Before collapsing into another fit of giggles.

Marianne recovered first,

"I have no idea what happened, but these clothes are wet, and Maeve wasn't expecting you to be here, so I guess it was a bit of a shock for both of you."

Their laughter signaled normalcy to Adam, maybe he could see the funny side of things,

"Oh yes, of course I know that Mrs McPhillips can communicate with the other side. I never thought she would see me as a spirit."

By now, he was smiling too, and as he told them exactly what had happened, their infectious laughter had Adam joining in. Things might work out fine after all.

Adam was a PhD student at the University of Kent, studying medieval archaeology, that was pretty much all that the family (except for Orla) knew about him. He was tall and slim, well, maybe skinny, and had a strange way of bobbing up and down when he was excited, which was quite often. Everyone thought he was English, but he had grown up on the Greek island Folegandros, his mother was Greek.

Canterbury was an escape on two counts, it was far away from Greece, and his choice of medieval history was far from the ancient world too. He needed the space. Folegandros is a small island, where everyone knows your business. He didn't know many people in the UK, he wasn't yet comfortable with any number of English customs, and equally he had some very strange misconceptions. He had only recently learnt from Orla, that Ireland was a separate country.

Over tea, and freshly made blueberry cake, Adam was reconciled to Maeve's strange behaviour, they had both decided not to mention, that she was actually naked when they met. Maeve had filled them in on her river spirit. At which point Adam said, "Ah yes, Ophelia."

The three faces turned to him as one, expectantly,

"Em, well you must know about the famous judge James Hales? Of course it's not really my period. But he was one that committed suicide in that river, the Stour in Canterbury. They say his death inspired the gravediggers' speech in Hamlet."

Well, maybe Adam could be more useful than they thought.

~

Steve didn't make it back for his promised cup of tea, he had been called into the station for a crisis, linked to Maeve. He was coming to the house all right, but this time it was one hundred percent on official business.

CHAPTER 22

CROWDED

M aeve had gone from no one in the house, to full house plus a guest, so private space was now at a premium. She had lost her box room office. Orla had offered to sleep there, and give Adam her room. Adam, chivalrously had said he wouldn't hear of it. The winning argument was Marianne's, who pointed out that all of Orla's stuff was in her room, so if Adam wanted any peace he'd be better off with Maeve's files, than Orla's clothes. She didn't add, that if Edward re-appeared he habitually tidied Orla's room, which might freak Adam out altogether. They had realised that he was a sensitive type.

Maeve was now lying on top of her bed, Skyping Ada on a precariously balanced iPad with the bedroom door shut.

"One minute I was feeling sorry, for myself, all alone, now I'm scheduling meals and fighting for a minute, to myself."

Ada sniffed,

"It's well for some! Don't complain, I've started picking up a pebble on my beach walk, to have someone to talk to. People are keeping themselves to themselves, there's not much 'cheery banter' in this lockdown."

Maeve smiled to herself at the idea of Ada talking to a stone, she must be desperate.

They'd caught up on Maeve's river adventure.

"So, any thoughts?" Maeve needed to hear about Ada's experiences, but they both feared that most of this was beyond her.

"I may have nothing to do, but I haven't been doing nothing."

Ada really wanted to help.

"I tried talking to my friends on the other side. Nothing. Spirit world is still out of bounds."

Maeve sighed, disappointed.

"Anyway, it started me off on a track. My other friends in the 'medium' world, told me to check out the International Psychics Association and the Spiritualist Association of GB. They were cryptic, just saying 'it's not like it used to be.'"

Ada took a deep breath launching into,

"And...Holy Mother! The world's gone mad. They do it all on Zoom now with huge live streams, PayPal, and hundreds of people, and I am seeing dollar signs!"

"I don't know how they do it." Ada was in awe.

"I can't imagine how you get the drama though? The dark room, the smell of the incense, the single candle casting mystical shadows."

Ada had always loved the trappings.

"I know it's not your kind of thing. But it helps me with channelling. I've always found smell important. Don't know how you could do it through a screen?"

Maeve was following the path of Ada's thoughts so wasn't surprised when she changed direction with renewed passion.

"There's an awful lot of scammers out there too! Those buggers are clever."

Ada wasn't feeling sorry for herself now, she was preparing for the charge.

"We've got to do something about it. We always had

trouble before, but with this social media and the internet it's exploded. Charlatans everywhere."

Maeve didn't want to crush Ada, appreciating the effort that she was putting into this, but online mediums was an area she wanted to stay well away from.

"Look Ada, this is your hobby horse, not mine. I'm trying to handle the things I can control. I'm not ready to save the world."

Ada was deflated.

"I suppose. I can see that. You're still learning. Talking of which, they did have some interesting things to say about 'natural spirits'."

Maeve was a little irritated that the main purpose of her conversation, had become a footnote,

"Aren't all spirits natural? How could you have a synthetic one? Made of plastic? That's ridiculous."

"Hold your horses! I mean, a spirit from the natural world, like the woods or the river." Ada wasn't bitter that Maeve had discovered her gift, but at times found it galling that Maeve didn't want it.

"Those of us who are ordinary mediums, not like your ladyship, we don't normally deal with them."

"This time it looks like you may have to."

Ada was back in control, with information to impart.

"Remember I went off on one about 'Will-o-the-wisps'? And you thought I was mad. Well I wasn't. They exist."

Infuriatingly, Ada was now taking her time, she was settling back, she knew she had a good story to tell.

"First, if you are Googling it, watch out, because 'nature, wood and spirit' comes up, with some kind of DIY treatment with white spirit and plywood."

Maeve raised an eyebrow, but said nothing, completely aware that silence was the best way to encourage Ada to get to the point.

"Okay, okay, so this is what I found. I think you may have

made contact with the Green Man, or as I now know, possibly the Green Woman. These fellas seem to be all over the place."

Ada was waving her arms to indicate the whole world.

"They are spirits connected with nature and rebirth, and of course rebirth comes after death, you have to have death first of course."

Ada looked thoughtful.

Maeve wanted to head off another deviation, so prompted "And?"

"Well you can imagine…." Ada nodding to herself, as she went on,

"You've seen them around, on Churches, outside people's homes. I've seen some in Canterbury…."

Maeve could only manage her impatience for so long,

"Seen what?"

"Carvings or paintings of the Green Man!" Ada was looking up at the ceiling, counting off the number of images she could remember.

"Thinking of it, I've never seen a Green Woman, have you?"

A glance at Maeve's face and Ada got back to business

"Obviously, they are connected with spring, plants, trees etc. And definitely busy at this time of year."

Maeve's expression showed that it wasn't obvious to her.

"You know. The way we bring lots of greenery into the house around Christmas time? It's just a tradition, well that's likely for them. To call the Green Spirits back so that spring will come again next year."

Ada checked to see if Maeve was following.

This time Maeve was frowning with concentration,

"I'm not sure what it would have to do with me?"

Ada was known for strange logic, and frequently lost herself in convoluted explanations.

"Well, I was thinking, Canterbury's been a sacred site for

a very long time, people have been living there since six thousand five hundred BC." Pause.

"It is a special place, a spiritual place. It may be why you wanted to live there."

Maeve understood that Ada was still thinking and just throwing ideas out there.

Ada was a little hesitant, but she went on,

"So far, you have been connecting with people who needed help. Maybe this time it could be a different kind of connection, maybe it's the wood or the river calling. The place, or something in it, might want you."

Almost dismissing the thought herself, Ada said,

"Talk to Orla, she's the eco warrior.

Maeve was considering this with a certain level of scepticism, it was beginning to sound far-fetched.

"Hmm, I'll think about it."

～

It was late afternoon before Steve made it round to the house. Maeve thought he might have timed it for some afternoon tea. The blueberry squares were still fresh enough.

Maeve had moved everyone out of the room, it wasn't really a dining room, but it was the room with the table that everyone sat around. It had french windows which opened onto the garden, now with draft excluders running along the floor. It meant that there was a table between her and Steve, making it more official, even if they had agreed that this was a 'care bubble'. Mostly, it was private.

Marianne, Orla and Adam were sitting next door, hypothesising, internet surfing, and listening to music. They were enjoying getting to know each other. Adam had had a pretty rough time since he came to the UK and was revelling in the company. The girls were competing for his attention.

Clearing the plates to one side, Maeve said,

"Thank God you were there. I've been going over it again and again. I still don't know what exactly happened, but I do know that I wanted to stay down there. Which is frightening."

Steve was smiling. Maeve was a little embarrassed by the level of gratitude she felt, so altered the conversation.

"We could chat for ages, but let's get the police stuff sorted first. What's the issue?"

Steve had been enjoying the easy feeling in the house. This was the kind of home where you weren't worried about where you sat, or if you had mud on your shoes. It was warm, in all senses. He thought that Maeve had the right priorities. He took his time, if he'd smoked a pipe he would have lit it now.

"The body you found in the woods had a mark on the back of his head, as if he had been hit by a golf club, remember?"

"Of course!"

"And indeed, the body wasn't that far from the golf course." He took an imaginary suck on the fictional pipe, he was in no rush.

"Your 'friend' who lives in the trees, he said he thought that there was something going on." Another pause.

"And I said I was worried about the woman who apparently committed suicide. Suicides, that don't really stack up." Steve was laying it out as much for himself, as for Maeve.

"Also, you asked me to check out any older incidents that took place in the woods."

He paused, to make sure that Maeve was concentrating on what he was saying before going on,

"That's the position and that's quite a few areas of concern. I doubt if there actually is any connection. But I want to check each one out." A beat.

Maeve wanted to know what he had discovered, but didn't want to seem impatient, so waited, though you could see the tension in her clenched jaws.

"So, I was called back to the station yesterday, because I had asked for more information on the 'suicide' in the river. When they found the body, it had been there for a while, there was some decomposition."

Steve wasn't keen on going into a graphic description. These images are hard to get out of your head, no need to put them there unnecessarily.

"Getting to the point, on first inspection, the police on the scene didn't look too hard, because it was so clearly a suicide. So things were missed. The forensic report came in later, but no one was asking questions, so it was filed. Case closed."

He paused again, before looking directly at Maeve,

"She didn't drown. There was no water in her lungs. She was already dead before she hit the water."

CHAPTER 23

BACK TO THE WOODS

Over breakfast, Maeve went through her plan,
"The problem with this lockdown, is that we are
all fed up with lockdowns, and now that winter is here it's far
too easy to cozy up inside, eat too much, drink too much and
forget about any exercise." As she was talking Maeve was
rubbing her hands together.

The other three were looking at her, waiting, they knew
that something was coming.

"So we need an exercise routine." As she wafted her
hands around, emanating a sweet smell.

Groans from Orla and Marianne, who knew that when
Maeve had an idea in her head, she wasn't going to let it go.
They liked exercise and the outdoors, it was the idea of a
routine that was the problem. Sleeping in till you felt like
getting up, was one of the joys of being at home, they sensed
that this was where she was going.

"Starting today, I'm suggesting 'group walks' first thing in
the morning, which should set us up for the day. Evening
yoga, is optional." Maeve liked to be on her own for Saskia's
online classes, but she was prepared to share.

"What exactly are 'group walks'? And what is that smell?" Marianne liked clarity.

"Well, since all of us will be in the same house twenty-four hours a day, we might get on each other's nerves. So I thought we should go in pairs for the morning walk, changing partners each day. Variety, but still routine." Maeve smiled, at least she thought this was a good plan.

"And this is 'Wild Rose' massage oil, because I won a goodie bag of Weleda stuff, and I know that a symptom of COVID is loss of smell. I am checking. And clearly you are okay. What about you two?" Maeve checked for affirmative nods from Orla and Adam.

"This morning, I am suggesting that Orla and I go on the 'woods towards Fordwich' walk. I want to see if I can sort out the issue for Edward."

By now, Adam had come to terms with the fact that spirits were part of this family, normal, in the way that goats were part of life for him in Folegandros. Wanting to participate he offered,

"Maybe I could show Marianne the medieval water conduit that's just by those woods?"

Marianne liked the idea of a long walk with Adam,

"We could start there all together, and then Adam and I could walk home via St Mildred's Church. I want to see if I can find the grave of James Hales's wife, Margaret. Apparently she's buried there. As neither Adam nor I are likely to be in touch with any spirits, it's nice to feel that we can see something personal, that's physically here, but from their time."

Adam nodded.

Maeve noted the use of 'we', as if they were forming a bond, she wondered how this was going down with Orla.

What Maeve hadn't shared with the others, was the rest of the information that Steve had discovered.

Steve had done some more digging. Not only was his 'suicide' a potential murder, but he had found that twenty-five years ago, a grim crime was committed in the woods. Someone had attacked a family of three, they had killed the mother and one of the daughters, the other child had run away, and survived.

It was also why she was keen on taking Orla into the woods with her, but she didn't want to prepare Orla, she wanted to see if Orla would connect with the child again, before knowing any of the background details. Generally Orla was pretty open to spirits, but the last time had given her a shock. Maeve thought that if they were together, and she focused on trying to 'pick-up' whatever spirit was there, maybe they could talk to the child together.

But first Maeve needed to see if she could get rid of Thomas Apps, so that if she was 'tuned-in' to the other side, she wouldn't be calling him by mistake.

They set out as a group. There had been a lot of rain overnight and the morning was grey, not promising. Not ideal for a walk off the beaten track. On the other hand, they were less likely to meet anyone else.

Adam took them to King's Place and showed them the collecting point for water that was used to supply the St Augustine's Abbey complex.

"It's really clever," he bobbed with excitement as he warmed to the subject.

"We believe that in the mid twelfth century, Prior Wilbert of Christ Church, which is the old name for the Cathedral, studied the Roman systems for managing water, and created this amazing system."

He had brought them to the side of a large stone circular pit full of water, luckily there was a diagram showing how the water flowed in from three nearby springs.

"It just looks like a pond, I don't see anything special." Orla was unimpressed, or maybe unimpressed with the rapt attention that Marianne was paying Adam.

"How does it work?" Marianne was enjoying Adam's passion.

"Well, there is a small lead pipe lower down that ….."

Maeve was holding on to Orla's arm, tightly. Orla turned to look at her and saw that Maeve had gone white.

"We're off." She interrupted Adam, and steered Maeve off in the direction of their walk. Leaving the other two absorbed in each other.

They walked on a narrow path overhung with trees, that was a right of way between some modern houses. Hitting the scent of the earth, of the fresh leaf mould, still wet, helped Maeve to ground herself. A few minutes later she registered the blackbirds and the robins, singing their hearts out, defending their territories, she was back to herself.

"I don't know what happened there, but I didn't want to find myself in that well."

"You were holding on pretty tight, I might even have some bruises on my arm." Orla was partly trying to make light of it, partly annoyed that they had left the others together, the pair who were too interested in each other to notice anything at all had happened.

Maeve had driven over, and had packed some coffee in a flask along with a packet of biscuits, in case they needed reviving.

Orla said,

"Let's just have some sustenance before we head in for any more ordeals. Limit the coffee though, there are no loos in the woods."

Opening the hatchback, they sat side by side on the back ledge of the car, each lost in their own thoughts.

Maeve turned towards Orla,

"I wasn't going to tell you this but I think I have to."

"Sounds ominous" said Orla with a mouth still full of biscuit.

"I've been sitting here thinking back to some of the things

that Ada did that caused the trouble between us. And I don't want to be like her."

"Mum, you're not like Ada."

They both smiled.

Not knowing quite how to put it, but wanting Orla to know that she was there for her, Maeve put her arm around Orla's shoulders.

"Your gift is different to mine….." Pause.

"I want to know if you can talk to that child again. Then I think if I empty my mind, I will be able to feel her too. Together we would be stronger."

Orla breathed out heavily.

"When you suggested this walk, I thought you had something like that in mind."

Orla spoke slowly, she was still thinking, in fact she was deciding,

"I don't want this 'gift' to define my life any more than you do. Like you, I need to understand what we can do. This may be tough for both of us. But you are right, we are in it together. Let's do it."

"Thank you love, I needed to hear that." Maeve gave Orla a hug, before putting everything away and locking the car.

CHAPTER 24

WALKS

T hey were focused on getting to the spot where Maeve had encountered Thomas, without slipping in the mud or getting waylaid by any other spirits. As they walked, both were looking down, watching at their feet, avoiding puddles and muddy drifts, Maeve told Orla, Ada's theories on 'natural spirits'.

"So she thinks I might have chosen Canterbury because I can feel them and that maybe you have become passionate about the environment for the same reason." Sidestepping the off-road bike tracks, now filled with water.

"You do seem to have an affinity for trees."

Orla was reflecting,

"Well it seems like a neat explanation. Maybe too neat. Just because a round peg can fit into a round hole, doesn't mean it belongs there."

"Quite right too." Said a deep voice from behind them.

Maeve and Orla jumped, Maeve landed awkwardly, lost her balance, ending up sitting in the wet path, with both hands stuck in the muddy edges. Matthew reached down and pulled her up. It surprised Maeve, because he felt warm, and he had that magnetic charisma; against her better judgment she found him very attractive.

He breathed in, "I smell scent, emm... rose water? Smells like…em…Mum!"

Then pulling himself back to the present,

"I'm so sorry…. It's nice to see friends…."

Maeve had noticed before, that he had that look somewhere between Hugh Grant and George Clooney. As she was still that fraction too close to him, without thinking and with a flirtatious look she said,

"We must stop meeting like this."

In the moment that followed, she looked directly into his eyes. They were red rimmed, troubled. Had he been crying, she wondered.

He spoke like he was picking up from the middle of a conversation with them.

"Sometimes I don't know who to talk to, who to turn to. It's all so bloody hopeless….." Running his fingers through his hair.

Meanwhile, Orla had taken wipes from her pocket and was cleaning Maeve up, working around her, as Maeve was clearly captivated by Matthew.

Matthew was strangely both distant and addressing Maeve directly,

"…I don't get the point of it all. It's not like I haven't tried. I took the office job, wore the suit and tie…pitched up everyday…on time….worked hard, more than most.."

Orla, deciding that this might go on for a while, started heading off, catching Maeve's arm, and pulling Maeve with her. She was right, and just as she thought, Matthew followed them while still talking. He had a large stick in one hand, which he waved about from time to time, to emphasise a point.

They walked on, to the far side of the lake where, for a

short distance, the path was more tame with a hard surface, and shin high railings designed to indicate the boundaries rather than protect them.

"..but who gives a shit about the size of your desk? How does anyone work with these people? They have no idea what's really important. In the office, there are no lives at stake for Chrissake!"

Thwack!

He hit the short length of cosmetic railing, on the side of the path, a powerful thump, breaking the stick clean in two. Maeve and Orla glanced sideways at each other, signalling that it was time to put some distance between them and Matthew.

"Oh well," Maeve was trying a cheery voice to bring him back to normal. "I have been looking for people who might be able to help you. It sounds like you have some things to work through."

Matthew was distant, he wasn't paying them any real attention.

Maeve tried again.

"We'll come back another day and have a proper chat. Right now we have to meet someone over there in the woodland, who is very shy." Pointing to a different section of the woods off the main drag.

"So we have to leave you here. Bye for now."

Maeve took Orla by the arm this time, facing Matthew, they waved a firm farewell, encouraging him to carry on the path and not follow them.

"Er, oh, yes, of course." He was still preoccupied with his own thoughts but did start to move in the direction they had indicated.

"Phew, that was a little more than I was expecting."

Maeve was analysing her emotions,

"I do find him attractive but,.. Did you get the smell of

spirits from his breath? It is early, but he has been drinking or maybe hasn't stopped since last night?"

Maeve kept her arm linked through Orla's as they moved, and in a more conspiratorial voice went on,

"It confirms what I thought." She tapped the side of her nose.

"I have begun to look into it, since talking to Steve, and I'm no expert, but that behaviour sounds very much like PTSD."

Orla nodded, no need to say anything about Matthew. Matthew was a real world problem. She was preparing herself for whatever ordeal was waiting for them in the spirit world.

By now they were moving through some of the minor tracks in the wood, bringing them back to the incline where Thomas first spoke to Maeve.

Maeve continued working through the recent conversation,

"I doubt Matthew will even remember that he has spoken to us.

I wonder if that smell was a trigger? Maybe when the smell was combined with the alcohol it took him to another time, or person? Either way, he is not in a good place. He needs specialist help."

Orla was listening but not responding, so Maeve went on.

"I have read that in this frame of mind he could flip, become dangerous, and not even know it."

Getting close to where Maeve had last seen Thomas, they were facing the muddy incline. Orla brought them back to the problem at hand.

"So. What are you going to say to this guy?"

"Say to who?" A rasping voice startled Maeve.

For a second time that morning, a voice from behind, made Maeve jump. But it was Orla who missed her footing, and it was Orla who elegantly slid, while falling forwards onto the steep bank in front of them. She got away with minimal damage, just dirty hands. She righted herself, and turned to Maeve.

Maeve now had her back to Orla, and with one hand out in front of her, like a policeman stopping traffic, was using her most authoritative voice as she almost shouted,

"Stop! Stop right there. I have some news. And I have some questions for you."

Her firm tone and action, had the desired effect. Thomas stepped back, took a battered hat off his head as a sign of respect, revealing more grime and greasy locks of hair.

Maeve pressed her advantage, she had memorised Marianne and Adam's notes on the aftermath of the Plum Pudding Riots.

"You wouldn't be hiding out here if you were not one of the troublemakers. Were you the one who started all of this and tore the Mayor's cloak?"

Thomas bowed his head further. Maeve took this as a sign that she was on the right track. Using words and events that Thomas might understand she pursued him with,

"And after that 'melee', did you smash any of the Puritans' windows?"

Having known nothing about this before, Maeve was now fully aware that the Christmas riots in Canterbury in sixteen forty seven, were one of the key events in starting a second round of the civil war the following summer.

"We were just showing them, enough is enough. I didn't do no-one a permanent damage. Not like them." By not disagreeing, Thomas had accepted the charges Maeve had laid against him, but he wasn't going to take it lying down.

"It would've quieted down, if not for that bloody barber, White. They made him Captain White. He shot my brother dead, just for calling him a 'Roundhead', and that's the truth of it." Thomas looked around, in case anyone was listening.

"That's when the real trouble started. They were trying to catch all of us; they took some who weren't even there! Later we opened the jail 'n let 'em all out. Then I knew I was a wanted man. They put the other two lads in jail. I ran. Been here ever since."

"So you let others take the blame while you hid out?"

Thomas shifted from foot to foot, uncomfortable.

"Well Edward, wasn't your enemy. He didn't want any of you to starve, he left food out for you." Maeve was watching the reaction. It seemed to calm him.

"Maybe he wasn't so bad then. But he was in with old Hales, who wants us dead?" He was processing the information.

Maeve shook her head.

"No, he wasn't."

The fight had gone out of him, Thomas looked a little lost.

"I didn't think anyone gave a damn."

"It's all over then?" He seemed less present.

"Yes, it's all over. People celebrate Christmas now." Maeve didn't know what would make sense to him, but this seemed to be enough. She didn't feel him close to her anymore. The threat diminished. He was gone. Or so Maeve thought.

Orla had been watching throughout the conversation. Once there was silence she spoke.

"Fill me in that didn't make much sense."

"I had guessed that he was hiding out for a reason and Edward might hint at things but didn't want to get him officially into trouble."

It was too cold to stand around for long, so they started walking as Maeve finished the story.

"From the research that Marianne and Adam did, I took a chance that the locals who started the trouble were forgotten. And that's how Thomas might have ended up here, starving to death."

"Good detective work." Orla was impressed. "I heard them talking, but would never have figured that out."

Maeve didn't have long to enjoy that sense of satisfaction.

That distressed feeling of sadness hit them both at exactly the same time. The child was calling.

CHAPTER 25

FEELINGS

Adam was taking Marianne, the long way round. The sun, coming through after such a lot of rain was very welcome. The blue sky lifted their spirits. They walked through a small gate, to the back of the youth centre off Military Road.

"Are you sure we're allowed in here?" Marianne was not one for trespassing, even in the name of historical research.

Adam bobbed his head vigorously.

"Yes, yes, yes. This is a public monument. Sometimes it makes me sad to see things like this overgrown, broken down. But then, maybe that's what keeps it safe."

Backing onto the same woods that Maeve and Orla were walking through, they had arrived. They were entering what seemed to be a private garden, behind the parked vans belonging to the youth club. Moving nearer the trees, there was a small building fenced off. It was overgrown with ivy and brambles, but once they got close, Marianne could see that there was an ancient style, stone arch over a doorway, in a flint wall, which had bits of redbrick topping it, and a barrel shaped tin roof. In terms of dating the building, her limited knowledge of architecture stopped at 'old'.

"You see, what people don't understand, is that water is essential to life. This is ingenious." Adam was clearly in his element. "When Prior Wilbert came up with this system, which I am sure was inspired by Roman engineering......"

Marianne wanted to be interested, but really she was just enjoying spending time with Adam. Adam probably wouldn't have been her first choice, but she decided he was handsome in a 'boy next door' way, so not intimidating.

'Friend or love interest?' she wondered so she wasn't paying attention, as he explained the rivalries between the different monastic settlements, where access to water was crucial. She nodded, as that seemed to be expected, concluding that there were a lot of deeply unpleasant people connected to the church, with only a few good ones. Switching the conversation to something more inline with her own thoughts.

"And Orla. You two kept in touch since that awful night in the Cathedral?" Marianne was feeling guilty that she had made such a fuss, when Orla suggested Adam stay with them. Was there something going on between them, that she should know about? Orla hadn't said anything directly, but clearly liked Adam, again the question, 'friend or lover' was in Marianne's thoughts.

"Yes, yes. In different ways I owe Orla, and also your mother, my life. I don't know how to repay them. I thought, maybe if I came to stay I would be able to see what I could do." Adam hung his head. He wore his heart very much on his sleeve.

Marianne decided that so far, the Orla-Adam relationship was platonic.

"Well, let's enjoy the good weather and see if we can come up with something." The information added an extra spring to her step.

As Adam was still going on about water, and how it

shaped Canterbury, they took the path by the Stour through the town. Staying on green paths most of the way.

The river had broken its banks by Sainsbury's car park, and had flooded into two large puddles, one, with two little girls in boots splashing as the parents watched on, the other, with a little boy on a bicycle freewheeling precariously through the deeper water, with a father watching holding his head in his hands, as he shouted the useless "Be careful!".

It gave Marianne and Adam a sense of normal life. Lockdown, made it feel like a Sunday, everyday.

They passed the Miller's arms, going into the adjacent park and crossing the mill race.

"History has so many answers." Adam was still talking. "You see the mill, which used to stand over this part of the river, burned down because of shoes."

"Are you trying to make me ask the question, why? I don't like quizzes. So just give me the answer." Marianne had raised an eyebrow, indicating that this could wear thin.

"Ha, ha." Adam couldn't understand anyone who wasn't interested, so assumed she must be joking, "They say that one of the miller's staff had his shoes or possibly clogs repaired with nails in the soles. When he was walking on the stone floor he made some sparks. And poof" He clicked his fingers. "A little spark on dry corn made a big fire."

They left the park, staying by the river and passing the Marlowe theatre. Marianne tried moving off the history tour.

"So you grew up in Greece? But you are English."

"My father was English, and my mother thought it a good idea to have a British passport. I have two passports, so personally, Brexit is not a problem." Adam was less interested in present day matters so left it there.

Silence.

"Tell me about Greece." Marianne tried again, and quickly added, "not the history, tell me about your home. I've read Captain Corelli's Mandolin, and that's all I know."

"I love my home. But without history there is not much to tell. I can stand on the road by my house, and see the sea on one side of the island, then turn and see the sea on the other side. I can hear the bells tied round the goats in the fields." He was pulling up the familiar picture in his mind's eye. "In the distance in front of me I can see a row of three old windmills, that have been converted into holiday homes, and behind me there is an old church."

"That sounds pretty much like the descriptions I have read. Idyllic. Beaches?"

"Yes of course. You can take a car or a moped for two minutes to the beach. There are two restaurants right by the sea. Blue water. Rocky coves. For English tourists it is perfect."

His answers were short, and there was something about the idea of being an 'English tourist', which didn't sit well with Marianne. This time, Adam made the effort,

"Why Cambridge?"

"Actually, I may have made a mistake. I want to do something meaningful with my life and make a difference. I thought important decisions are made by the government, so politics would be the right way into government. And then I thought Cambridge was the best University, so Cambridge. Because my family are from Ireland and France, we never had that background knowledge or connections with Oxbridge."

Marianne needed to talk this through since she got home, but hadn't found the opportunity yet. This was helping her to think. "But I should have done PPE, sorry Politics, Philosophy and Economics, at Oxford, because in the real world, ten out of the last thirteen Prime Ministers went to Oxford. Cambridge, is for scientists and comedians, they have over seventy Nobel laureates to Oxford's fifty-five." She sighed, "Now, I'm not sure what to do."

She hadn't meant to pour her heart out, but he was the

first person to ask, and she felt he would understand. He was a good listener.

"Hmm, maybe you are looking at this the wrong way. For sure, one way to make a difference is to make laws, that way politics would be the path." Adam paused to see how Marianne was taking his comments, he didn't want to offend her.

"The other way to make a difference is how you apply the laws, defend the innocent people, or prosecute the guilty."

Sometimes, when he wasn't trying too hard, Adam could be very perceptive.

"I think you are better with brains than being an actor. Politicians have to be actors, to influence people with speeches. You seem more private."

He tilted his head to one side as he checked in again, to see if he had lost her, before adding.

"Law yes, I think that would suit you. You are good at research. But choose the area of your passion, then be careful not to be misdirected by money."

Marianne was impressed, now she was wrapped in her own thoughts, running scenarios through her head. They had been moving all the time, crossed the high street, and they were halfway down Stour street, when Marianne suddenly perked up,

"Oh yes, I'd almost forgotten. Fond's coffee. Let's get our coffees now."

Masks on, they ordered two piccolos, takeaway, and a slice of chocolate tiffin to share, chatting to Kieran and Colin, as they waited.

"We're all right, Pret and Nero's haven't opened this time. But we have our regulars, which is the most important thing."

They picked up their coffees as the door opened.

In walked Steve.

Kieran gestured that he had seen Steve, and automatically started brewing his flat white.

Not confident in the latest mask wearing and distancing protocols but glad to see Steve, Marianne said,

"Why don't we pull up a chair for you outside? If you have the time."

Steve had kept minimal contact with Adam, after the events earlier in the year, but he was glad to see that Adam was okay and hadn't suffered any long term damage.

By the time he joined them, the conversation had turned to Maeve.

"I look around, and I can not see what gift would be right?" Adam paused, "I mean this is not the occasion for a 'box of chocolates' or a 'bottle of wine'."

Then Adam looked at Steve as he sat down. Steve's presence caused a number of thoughts to drift across Adam's expressive face, as an idea dawned.

"Maybe it would be good if I give you a holiday in Greece, on Folegandros? What do you think?" Adam was beaming at his brilliant idea.

Steve looked uncertain, "Isn't this about Maeve?"

Adam was grinning,

"We have three holiday houses, so room for all of you. You get the flights, I do the rest."

"What about your mother?" Marianne was considering the possible obstacles rather than get her hopes up.

"She will be fine, she wants to know what I have done to thank you all, this way she will be part of it too. All good." Adam was absently humming to himself, foot tapping.

Steve and Marianne, looked at each other. Marianne didn't want to answer for the others, but it sounded fabulous.

Steve was wondering how the accommodation would be arranged, which could be exactly what he wanted and amazing, or a complete disaster. Steve came to the conclusion, that it was time Maeve came over to his place.

Turning back to Adam, in unison they said, "that sounds fantastic, but ask Maeve first."

CHAPTER 26

WHAT HAVE YOU DONE?

Steve had been thinking since Adam suggested Greece as a holiday. He needed to know what kind of relationship he had with Maeve. The more he thought about it, a forced date over at his place probably wouldn't do it for either of them.

He was sitting at his desk in the station, adding to the tower of used takeaway coffee cups, paperwork piled on either side, with a section in the middle for his laptop. He glanced at his less urgent pile, the case sitting on the top was the old case about the family in the woods. Looking at his watch and thinking, that's where Maeve was walking with Orla now, he picked it up.

By the time Maeve and Orla got back to the house, Marianne was in the breakfast room sitting at the table, talking to an onscreen Ada. There was something in Ada's tone that put Maeve on alert.

".....Where have you been hiding, that you haven't heard of TikTok? And I'm the ancient one here!"

Ada was chuffed that she was more 'with-it', as she would say, than her granddaughter.

Hearing the door shut, tilting her head to one side, Ada quizzed,

"Is that them I hear coming through the door?"

Even though they were both drained, Maeve knew she couldn't slip past without saying something. Nudging Orla in front of her they came in, still covered with mud, which had mostly dried, and was flaking off. Marianne took one look at them and disappeared to put the kettle on, coming back with all the biscuits, cakes, and any other snacks that she could find.

"So, what happened to you two? More rolling around in the mud anyway." Ada was not known for diplomacy but was dying to hear the story.

"Far more than I expected." Maeve smiled weakly, looking at the pile of food growing on the table. "I can see you won't give us the time to recover, but at least I can get changed, why don't you make some fresh tea for yourself?"

Orla was pale, and stayed sitting at the table as Maeve got up and left to wash her hands.

"It was awful, Ada," said the subdued Orla, as tears started to run down her face.

Maeve went upstairs, noting that Adam was now in the box room, almost bent double over his make-do desk, studying. Probably giving Marianne time on her own with Ada. He hadn't noticed her. This time, she made sure that her bedroom door was firmly shut, before taking off her muddy clothes.

Mud washed off, clean clothes on, feeling more human, Maeve took a moment on her own, before joining the call with Ada. It had been gruelling. Maeve had tuned-in, maybe it was thanks to Orla, or maybe it was the right time to see the child herself, but either way she had seen the little girl.

Maeve knew that Steve's case was about twenty-five years old, so she had been looking for clues to see if that tied in. The girl had red leather, buckled shoes, with white ankle socks, she had lost one shoe and her knees were muddy. She had a red dress, with a white 'Peter Pan' collar, the front of the dress was covered in tiny blue flowers over smocking, all of which were grubby from rolling around on the ground. The style suggested a different time, no Lycra leggings, or light-up trainers, but still not definitive, some people do dress their children in old fashioned clothes.

The child was trying to communicate something to them, but didn't have the words or perhaps couldn't articulate them. It seemed to be some kind of warning, but all that Orla or Maeve could make out was,

"I want to be a good girl!" Or sometimes "I am a good girl." Then the child pointed to her missing shoe. It could hardly be that, could it? Upset over a missing shoe?

Orla and Maeve had followed the direction that she was pointing, just like the first time with Maeve, she led them to where Maeve had found the body.

As they got closer to the spot, the child's distress intensified.

Orla tried first, "But you are a good girl, a very good girl." The child paused, looked at her, and with great insistence repeated, "I want to be a good girl!" Almost angry, as if Orla was wilfully misunderstanding her.

Maeve tried a different approach, "You are a lovely girl. Can we help you?"

The little girl stared at Maeve, as if considering the proposition. Looked down at feet, pointed to her missing shoe, stamped her other foot and wailed, "I am a good girl!"

With that she was gone.

This was the first time that Orla had met an unhappy spirit, it affected her badly, she was shaken. Maeve's being there, had kept Orla sufficiently present so she hadn't fainted, but it was close.

Back in her own bedroom, feeling stronger, Maeve was now ready to talk to Ada. As she came down the stairs she heard Orla sharing her side of the story. Marianne was being the caring big sister, rubbing her back and offering more biscuits.

As Maeve arrived Ada was doing the talking.

"Go on, have something to eat. I told you before this stuff takes a lot out of you, you will need the sugar. And I don't want to hear any nonsense about 'no carbs, I'm watching my weight'. Emotional experiences like this will burn through the calories."

Ada was walking a fine line between 'pull yourself together' and sympathetic grandmother. Ada knew that too much introspection was not good, you have to stay present in this world, plus, she thought this was a great adventure and was only sorry she wasn't the central character in it.

"This is a real spirit, with a real issue. Not some woodland or water spirit or evil 'will-o-the-wisp'. We can do something here. This is a good story."

It was the phrase 'a good story', that Maeve honed in on.

"What do you mean, 'a good story'? What have you been doing? What are you up to, Ada?"

Ada changed her position, she didn't quite squirm, but Maeve had definitely put her finger on something.

"Well remember I told you that everyone, all the Mediums, were going online and had thousands of followers?"

Maeve's heart sank, this was not what she wanted to hear.

"Ye-es…"

"I did a bit more looking into it. And I discovered, Tik Tok. Would you believe that my own granddaughter, didn't know what Tik Tok was?"

"Ada, stick to the point and explain what exactly you have done."

Maeve knew Ada's ability to distract people with shiny paper rather than tell them the crucial information.

"Okay so. I signed up. And I got followers. I looked at what Judi Dench was doing, and I thought, `I can do that'."

She stopped, clearly there was more that she was not so keen to share.

Maeve wasn't going to let her off the hook now.

"Back up a bit. What did Judi Dench do? And what did you do?"

Ada sighed, there was no getting around this.

"Dame Judi did what she does, she is brilliant. On Tik Tok, she does jokes with her grandson, and one where she even dresses up as a rabbit. It's really funny."

"And you?"

"I did what I do." Ada was dragging it out, "I put on my old gear, and did a good make-up session. I had candles for lighting, creating a great atmosphere. I used my iPhone to record it."

The mechanics of this part clearly pleased Ada, she was happy with her work.

"And I promoted what I do. Talk to spirits. In sixty second clips."

Ada folded her hands in her lap, looking as if butter wouldn't melt in her mouth.

"But you haven't been talking to spirits for a while….There has to be more to it than that. Go on"

Maeve knew her mother.

"Well, I have a few followers now." Ada stopped again.

"Really mother, you have to tell us, what's going on?" Maeve was too tired to play games, her irritation was clear, she never called Ada 'mother'.

"All right, all right, keep your hair on." Ada was going to have to spill the beans. She clearly didn't want to.

"So, I have millions of followers, millions of them from all around the world."

This didn't sound too bad,

"I am famous to a new generation and as a result all of my prints have sold. Liz and Charlie at RockPaperScissors are amazing, and they have already paid me."

Silence.

She had paused, but this time everyone was waiting. Ada knew there was no getting out of this and couldn't find a good way of putting it, so burst out with,

"The tricky bit, is that I promised I could still talk to spirits. And I used your story as the example."

"What?" Maeve exploded, "You have told millions of people about the child in the woods? Is that right?"

Ada was struggling between hanging her head in shame and wanting to defend herself,

"I didn't know it would go viral, did I?" She was defensive and contrite at the same time. It made her vulnerable, but right now Maeve was simply furious.

"Oh Christ mother, what have you done!"

CHAPTER 27
WHAT TO DO?

S teve had found something interesting in the file, something that might help him create an opportunity, for some time with Maeve. He didn't want to share it just yet, not until he had sorted the logistics. He could feel himself tapping to the beat of Dave Brubeck's Square Dance, he liked it when a plan started to come together.

Maeve, had had enough. She needed a change and something as normal as possible, so she arranged to meet her friend Kim for a coffee that afternoon. You could still exercise with one other person, from another household, so technically they wouldn't be breaking any rules. Maeve knew that Kim was shielding, and would keep her distance so they would probably be fine.

Everyone was missing seeing friends and family. There was the hope that Christmas would be the time for families, the government plan was for up to three households, to get together for up to five days. Ada had been planning to come over and stay with Maeve. Maeve wasn't so sure, particularly right now. Just this minute, Ada was the last person she wanted to see.

Kim, who referred to herself as 'the crazy cat lady', had

known Maeve since that first film festival, where they had both been volunteers. They shared a love of film, and good coffee, and had stayed friends ever since. She was the very person that Maeve needed to talk to right now. Grounded and supportive, Kim was also digital tech savvy, so a good person to work out what Maeve might do, re Ada and Tik Tok.

The sun was still shining, but already low in the sky, the atmosphere was heavy from the rain last night, giving the sky that strange luminescence, particular to this time of year. Coffees bought, they took a back route past the shop, Rock-PaperScissors.

Peering through the windows, it did look like Ada's prints had all gone.

"That's annoying. I was hoping that she had been exaggerating." Maeve sighed.

They walked on towards Greyfriars Gardens. Past the Canterbury Punting Company's cafe, and access point to the river Stour. The pleasant walkway linked Stour St with the gardens, by crossing two branches of the river. They stopped on the second bridge to look at the tiny Greyfriars Chapel, that was built to straddle the river.

Sipping their coffee, leaning on the railings, they were enjoying the company, Maeve was laughing and it felt good.

"Did you know that Saint Francis of Assis himself sent the monks over who built that building? Doesn't it feel as if you can touch the past sometimes?"

She didn't register the irony of the fact that she frequently talked directly to the past. Buildings are solid, and somehow that made it completely different, no one doubted a building.

Kim, who was more of a keen gardener said,

"And those are the Franciscan gardens. I wonder if they brought the plants with them too?"

Shifting to more contemporary thoughts adding,

"I think that they do weddings in the gardens in summer

now. What a romantic place for a wedding, if the sun was shining."

Somehow that sounded funny, the idea of relying on the sun in an English summer, they both started laughing again.

Maeve was watching the water flow, thinking that it might be fun to play Pooh Sticks, when she felt that pull again. The desire to get into the water. This time she reacted instantly, and clutched Kim's arm,

"We have to move now. Urgently."

Understanding the tone of her voice, Kim didn't hesitate, she walked Maeve over to the seat in the park.

Keeping her back firmly to the river, Maeve told the story of her experience in the river at Fordwich.

"Well it is the same river." Kim's logic seemed to have a meaning, if just outside their grasp. Kim went on, giving Maeve some time to recover,

"I've never had an experience like that. But whenever I have had a problem, something I can't control, I have found that I have to face it directly."

They had the kind of easy relationship which meant that Kim wasn't preaching, she was sharing, and Maeve appreciated it.

"The more I put things off, the worse they get. When I turn and deal with issues head on, it may not go perfectly, but at least I am in control. That makes a big difference."

Maeve was feeling herself again. They put their paper coffee cups into the bin and walked on.

"Hmm, I like the sound of that, not sure how...." Maeve was thoughtful as they passed through the narrow passageway between the houses, heading towards Westgate gardens.

"I think my real issue is that I don't know what *it* is."

Kim laughed, "Sorry, but abstractly that sounds funny. Clearly *it* is a river."

Laughter is infectious, she was making Maeve smile too,

"Laughing about it is helpful, it seems to make it less important."

Maeve was thoughtful and then began to look excited, "Actually I wonder if that is a way to do it. When I was laughing, I didn't have that connection with the water."

She was now very pleased with herself.

"It may not be the answer, but at least it gives me something to try."

The sun was setting as they came to Westgate, reflecting off the main branch of the Stour, the sky now full of startling oranges and deep pinks, merging into the deepening blue. The water level was high, it was so close to bursting the river bank here, that the access steps were almost fully submerged.

Crossing the river Maeve said,

"Jokes, I need jokes, as a safety precaution."

Kim offered, "What's a cat's favourite dessert?" Pause, "Chocolate mouse!"

Feeling comfortable enough to be a bit silly, Maeve was enjoying herself, which in itself seemed to have the desired effect.

"See, nothing, I felt nothing. That is such a relief."

They were about to go their separate ways when Maeve remembered that she was really looking for help with Ada and her online fame.

Kim didn't hesitate,

"With Ada you are on your own. She is a special case. This has nothing to do with technology, it has everything to do with personality."

Ada could turn the charm on, but over the years Kim had seen through the charm, and knew that Ada was good company, when you were doing what Ada wanted. Ada was not interested in cats, gardens or films; and mainly drank tea. Not much common ground. And Kim had always felt that Maeve was by far the more responsible of the two, Ada had a

154

habit of getting herself into situations, that needed some kind of rescuing.

~

That evening Steve called Maeve. He had enjoyed their last late night call. Warmth and intimacy without interruptions. Plus he had news. He had by now heard the Ada drama, which he thought was quite funny, till he realised that she might do something with all these fans to kick off another media storm. Getting out of town for a few days, could be a good idea.

"I went back over the details of that poor family's experience. And it was a dog walker who came across the terrible results. The witness was so traumatised by the experience that they moved away from the area, as far as they could get."

Steve was happy he had made some progress, and had an interesting proposition, but how to put it, so that Maeve would be as keen as he was.

Maeve jumped in, and retold their experience in the woods that morning.

"Was there anything in the file about the child's shoe? I can't figure out if she is using it to communicate something else, or if she is actually upset about the shoe itself."

This was just the entree Steve needed.

"Interesting that you should ask that. There is someone who might have some answers."

"Well don't leave it there, what do you mean?"

"The dog walker now lives in Scotland, in Cromarty on the Black Isle. Which I gather is a lovely place. Anyway I got in touch and he was a little cagey at first but was willing to talk to us, but only on the condition that we went up in person to see him."

"What! All the way to Scotland? And we don't even know if it will help."

"Well, I've got permission at this end for us to go on official business. And, I have found a lovely bed and breakfast in Cromarty. Given what Ada's been up to, it might be a good idea to get out of Dodge for a few days." He waited to hear her reaction. Softly he added,

"It would give us some time on our own."

CHAPTER 28

TAKING BACK CONTROL

Waking up the next morning, keeping Kim's advice in mind, Maeve decided it was time to think differently. Ada had lost her ability to communicate with spirits, so it was time to talk to someone with more recent experience.

Maeve thought of Anne. It was less than a year ago that Maeve's next door neighbour Anne, who had been suffering from early stages of dementia, was murdered. Her spirit had come back and often spoke to Maeve, when Maeve was in the garden. As a spirit, Anne didn't suffer any memory loss or confusion, so she might have the insight Maeve needed.

Autumn was moving to winter, the trees had lost their leaves, and the recent rain had put paid to much outdoor activity. Maeve put her garden to bed around Halloween, so hadn't been out there much since then. She hadn't forgotten about Anne, just didn't have the occasion to pop out for a chat.

Leaving Marianne, Orla and Adam, to tidy up after breakfast and make a second pot of coffee, Maeve went outside. Even though it was winter and things were closing down, she could see the cherry tree was already gathering strength and preparing to make buds for next spring. The robin was shouting out his territory and the blackbirds were picking something juicy from the ground. Maeve had a bird feeder, which they could see from the dining-come-work table, through the French windows. Since Anne died Maeve had taken to keeping an eye on the bird feeder next door too. Ray, Anne's husband, wasn't much of a gardener, it had never really been his thing, and he was inclined to let the feed run out. Maeve had a look to check the levels of grain and fat balls, popping an extra one in, just in case.

Turning back, there was Anne, leaning on the fence expectantly, gardening gloves on and a trowel in her hand.

"It's always so nice to see you dear. I know you have some questions for me, but first can I ask you to do something?"

Well, Maeve could hardly refuse, could she. She had a fair idea that it would be a message for Ray.

"You are always so helpful, Maeve dear. Yes, you are right. I've been watching Ray. And by the way, the birds appreciate your keeping an eye out for them." She smiled. "Could you tell Ray, that when he sits out in the garden on that bench," She pointed to the seat under the permanent sunroof that Ray had built years ago.

"Tell him, that I sit beside him. I think he feels it, but I just want him to know it."

Anne relaxed a little, she had been using the trowel to punctuate the conversation and point to the bench in question, now she was swinging it by the long loop for hanging it in the potting shed.

"Maybe tell him again, that I am happy here, and I'll stay around for him." She did look happy, with her soft but generous smile

"You know. I am ready to go, whenever he is ready to let go. No rush, but he shouldn't cling on to the past. He still has time and grandchildren to see as soon as he can. He shouldn't waste his time, living in the past."

Maeve reassured Anne that she would talk to him, at the

same time she had no idea how to explain the pandemic and lockdown, to someone on the other side. She knew that Ray couldn't go visiting anyone at the moment.

"No need to try," said Anne, "the spirits are bringing their stories with them, so much sadness." She shook her head at the thought of what she had seen. "I mean when he can, he should go right away."

She turned to face Maeve. "Now, you have questions for me. It's important that you think carefully about how you want to ask your question. Go on."

Anne put her on the spot, lots of thoughts were running through Maeve's head. She needed a moment to straighten them out.

"No rush." Said Anne, "I'm not going anywhere" as she twirled the trowel looking over both gardens.

When Maeve was ready, she said, "You probably know that I have two areas to ask you about." Looking at Anne, who was nodding affirmation.

"Let's start with the child in the woods. She doesn't seem to be able to tell us what her problem is. Why?"

Anne was pensive for a moment, she spoke slowly,

"You remember how for me, once I passed over, the fog lifted and I could remember things clearly?"

It was Maeve's turn to nod, how could she forget it.

"Well, I think this child has had the opposite experience. The shock of what happened, has made her speechless. Or at least just left her with a few phrases, nothing more." Anne had let the trowel hang from her wrist, crossed her arms and was rubbing her chin thoughtfully.

"She knows something. There is some urgency." She was looking for the right words to express what she was feeling, "Back when I called you, I knew I needed to stop that dreadful man, my guess is that she needs you to help someone in your world."

Maeve folded her arms and leaned back as she took this

in. Once processed, she was formulating her next question when she realised that she was on her own again. Bother, she didn't get the chance to ask about the river person.

Back inside, the house was warm, and the smell of the freshly made coffee was deliciously pervasive. The three sitting round the table stopped talking, as if Maeve had interrupted some secret planning. Or perhaps they were just anxious to hear what Maeve had found out.

"It seems like it's one question at a time. But our child in the woods may be more urgent than we thought. I can't see the connection to the body I found, but there must be one." Pause.

Are you going to tell me what I interrupted?" Maeve looked at each in turn. They had a sheepish air.

"Adam, now's the right time." Marianne was gently encouraging him to speak.

Adam had already called home and his mother was excited at the idea that they would come out to Greece to their island home, on Folegandros. She had immediately gone through the list of wonderful things she would prepare. Fresh bread from the bakery delivered by 7.30am. Greek yogurt and local honey, stocked in their kitchens, a daily refresh of ripe peaches. Wine, olives all on tap. He had to stop her. It was making him hungry.

Adam was so profoundly grateful to Maeve and her family that he had difficulty getting the words out. He mumbled his way through the offer to Maeve. Worried, it might not be something she would like, without giving her time to reply, or taking a breath, he was describing all the wonderful things that he hoped she would enjoy.

Orla tugged at his sleeve.

"Enough. Give her a moment."

They waited with bated breath.

Of course Maeve loved the idea, the images of sun

drenched beaches and delicious food, had won her over immediately, she only had one niggle,

"What a lovely idea!" She was smiling with pleasure, "When you said, 'you all', who exactly, were you referring to?"

Adam was beaming, this was a mere detail,

"All of you, this family" gesturing to the group around the table, "and Ada, and Steve."

"Ah." That made things clearer, "have you mentioned this to the others already?"

Adam was almost hopping off his seat with pleasure, at his good idea. Clearly Maeve was happy with the plans.

"Well we" indicating himself and Marianne "were talking to Steve, when I got the idea. But Steve said to ask you first."

So that's why Steve wanted them to go on a trip on their own. Actually, given the conversation with Anne, Maeve thought it might be a really good idea; and they should probably go sooner, rather than later.

Remembering herself she said,

"Adam, that is a fantastic idea. Thank you. Let me talk to Steve and separately to Ada before we finalise any details."

Marianne and Orla had picked up from Maeve's tone that this wasn't a done deal yet. Or maybe it was *who* exactly would be going, wasn't a done deal.

CHAPTER 29

TIME TO CALL ADA

Maeve shooed the others out of the room. Adam went back upstairs to work at his, Heath-Robinson attempt, at a workstation in the box room.

Marianne and Orla, had said that they wanted to join in the conversation with Ada, as soon as it was okay for them to be there. Maeve agreed to give them a shout, she wanted to sort out the TikTok business first.

Ada was sniffy. "Of course you know what I think, I think you overreacted. What's wrong with a bit of publicity?"

Maeve had already apologised even though she thought that Ada was in the wrong. However, if she was waiting for Ada to come around to that idea, then she would be waiting a long time and Maeve had more important things to do, things that were now urgent. Struggling not to allow herself get sucked into an unnecessary argument, she changed the subject.

"Hmm. Well, that's as may be. We can debate that another time, right now we need to move on, and quickly."

Air cleared, the girls miraculously appeared, before Maeve had remembered to give the signal. The dividing doors were obviously not soundproof.

Anne, having raised the stakes when she guessed someone was currently in trouble, set Maeve on a mission. She needed this Ada business resolved, so that she could plan the trip to Scotland, where they might get a critical lead.

"Let's pretend that I am interested, why would I go on Tik Tok?"

This was the best way to get information out of Ada, get her enthusiastic, and she would tell you everything.

"Well, you will be, when I tell you what's going on. There are plenty of people making a lot of money on it. Sure, Charli D'Amelio makes over fifty thousand dollars a post. That means fifty thousand dollars for a sixty second video. God Almighty, isn't that massive."

Ada had got their attention. Silence, as each of them started looking at Tik Tik on their phones, then a cacophony of exclamations, as they all talked over each other.

"This is a monkey opening a parcel and playing with zips!" Marianne.

"Oh my God! It's our friend Andrew, falling out of a hammock in the garden. With five hundred thousand views! Wow! And Nathalie made the video, she must be a star like you..." Maeve.

"I get it Ada, I've landed onto the paranormal activity, big numbers here too. Well into the millions." Orla.

Ada was sitting back, somewhat smug,

"You see. Interesting isn't it."

Maeve had put her phone down, watching the others carrying on finding more stuff, with more exclamations of incredulity. In a measured tone,

"But you see Ada, this is where we are different."

Ada sat up waiting for what was coming next, as Maeve continued,

"I never wanted to have anything to do with your 'events', seances, sessions, whatever you want to call them. I always hated the dressing up, the melodrama, the candles."

This was an old argument, Ada had her arms crossed defensively,

"Look-at, I was only trying to help people too. All the atmosphere does is help get them in the mood."

Maeve sighed,

"I'm not having a go at you in particular. But there are plenty of cheats out there, selling hope to the desperate. I don't know what videos you have put out there but my guess is, you are right on the edge this time."

This wasn't the way that Ada wanted this conversation to go, she really needed Maeve's help, but at the same time it raised her hackles.

It was Marianne who stepped in between the two of them.

"I think we need to deal with the issue of the child in the woods, after that you can agree to differ." She was being calm, knowing Maeve needed help to work out the best plan, she went on,

"Ada, I'm not sure if Maeve has already told you the details, but we might be onto something more urgent than we thought. So tell us about the story in your videos?"

Ada's ruffled feathers now somewhat smoothed,

"I said that there was a child looking for help." She wasn't feeling expansive so they had to ask for more detail.

"Okay so. Like that young one Orla just saw, with the 'haunting' in her house. I thought it would be good to put something out that made people listen. Then I discovered that if they 'engage', meaning answer you, your ranking goes up."

The three around the table were silent, fully engrossed in Ada's onscreen presence.

"So, I told them there was an old crime, made a bit of drama with only candle light on my face." She was getting carried away with her own story again, but a quick glance at the serious faces on the other side of the screen, got her back on topic.

"Well then I said I needed their help. I got loads of 'hearts' and messages."

She shifted in her chair, this was the uncomfortable bit.

"So then, TikTok sent me a message saying I could do a 'live-stream' and there's no time limit on them. It's a big deal to be able to do one."

They could see that she was conflicted,

"I didn't stop and think. I was so excited, I put out a message saying who wanted to join a live spirit calling. I was deluged in hearts and messages."

She stopped here, she had been so excited up to this point and now she hung her head deflated.

It was Orla who was first to react,

"So wait, you have said that you will call a spirit to communicate with you 'live', as people are watching?"

Ada nodded, Orla continued.

"But you can't talk to any spirits at the moment. What was your plan? And when is it supposed to be?"

By the time Maeve called Steve to deal with their trip, they had agreed there was nothing for it but to help Ada out. If they didn't then she really would be a charlatan and Maeve hated the idea of that, so had reluctantly agreed.

Maeve had to explain their plan to Steve, because if it worked, then it might help them figure out what had happened in the woods.

Ada, was going to do the 'live' session, which the others would watch, if any spirits got in touch with Maeve or Orla, then they would send the message over to Ada by text. Ada would leave her phone in front of her so she could read out the text as if the spirit was talking to her. It was risky, but at least it was a plan.

While on the phone to Steve, Maeve was unequivocal,

"It's completely insane, totally ridiculous, how can you call a spirit through a screen?" Maeve had to go along with it to help Ada, but was very uncomfortable.

"I mean, I am only just working out how to call a spirit that is connected to the place where I am physically standing. This, is completely beyond me. I have no idea how it will work."

Steve didn't need to be near Maeve to feel the exasperation. He liked Ada, but he also knew that she could cause trouble, usually unintentionally. He was about to say 'she means well', and then thought better of it, he wasn't sure what she was thinking of, or if she really did mean well.

"Is there a time and a date for this event?"

"You won't believe it. She, Ada, the cat's mother, whatever you want to call her, only went and set it up for tonight!" Maeve didn't know whether to laugh or cry.

Steve laughed. "There's no time like the present. And she is impatient." He didn't add, like mother, like daughter, but thought it all the same.

"Anyway, anyway, anyway" Maeve was dismissing her irritation.

"Is there a specific question that would help you? Or Us?" She was using Steve to help her think through any possible positive outcome from this debacle.

Steve, never one to be rushed, took a while.

"If I could ask a question, what would it be? Hmm."

Maeve could almost hear the cogs whirring in his brain as he considered this.

"I want to know if the deaths are linked, hmmm, how would I ask that?" Another pause, "How about, 'Do you know any other spirits who have come from the woods?' Would that work?'"

Steve was pleased with himself.

"I mean, that way if they are linked, they should know each other shouldn't they?"

He was still running through ideas, another thought crossed his mind,

"Can you ask them directly about their death? Like, 'who killed you?'"

"You can ask the question, but so far they don't seem to remember the point of death. Only Anne did, and that had something to do with her dementia." Maeve wasn't certain about anything, so could only go on what she had experienced.

"Well then, if it works, and there is someone you can talk to, try for any links to see if they are connected. You put it whatever way you think best." Steve was still pretty sceptical, so he didn't take it too seriously as a way of getting information.

"Moving on. Cromarty." He was looking forward to having time with Maeve, and being away from the station.

"I have booked us train tickets for first thing tomorrow morning. We may as well take our time on the train. It's too far for the bike. And flights are tricky. Then we pick-up a hire car, in Inverness. "

Maeve was enjoying having someone else sort out all the logistics, she wondered if she should put together a deluxe picnic as her contribution, a treat for both of them.

Steve had more.

"I have spoken to the lady in the B&B, she will sort dinner for us, so that we can have a nice meal when we arrive."

This, really did sound like a holiday, rather than an investigation.

Maeve thought it was a bit like skiving off school, which made it more exciting but she was a little nervous.

"You are sure that this is going to be okay? I mean no one

167

is travelling much because of COVID and I am sure there's going to be a tighter lockdown after Christmas."

"Good thing we are going now then, isn't it?" He had a cheeky tone in his voice.

"Seriously though, I booked us first class from London to Inverness, to make sure we get the space. The trains from Canterbury to London are empty. I get tested regularly." He paused,

"I was thinking, why don't we get a rapid test for you today? We have some in the station, if you can get here before 3pm we'll know within the hour."

Planning for a trip the next day, meant Maeve did a quick dash to the Goods Shed, to pick up some special cheeses, and ended up with the cheese, plus Parma ham, the freshest sour-dough bread, a bottle of Sancerre, and a bottle of St Emilion, (as it was a long journey), plus, they could finish anything left over, at dinner.

Sorting the picnic and packing an overnight bag, required a lot more thought than she had imagined.

Scotland is likely to be cold, and Cromarty is pretty far north even for Scotland, and she didn't trust the tourist information's view of a 'warm microclimate', they might be right, but it was better to be prepared. On the other hand, she didn't want to carry too much. She packed and repacked at least three times, finally deciding that she couldn't carry multiple outfits, so 'comfort and practical' rather than any notion of glamour, would be best. She might not look her best, but she would enjoy it more.

In what seemed like a flash, it was time for the 'live stream'.

CHAPTER 30

THE LIVE STREAM

Marianne and Orla had worked out a system. They could see Ada, the same way that everyone else could. Then, if they had a message, they would text Ada, who would keep her phone hidden from view. Orla was responsible for making notes, and Marianne doing the texts. What the audience couldn't see, was that Ada had put her phone where they thought she had a crystal ball. So in the set up shot you could see Ada and the crystal ball, then Ada moved closer to the camera, pushed the ball to one side, and moved her phone there instead. The trickery of modern technology.

Ada was a great performer. It looked so professional. She had been right about the candle light. The room was pitch black, her crystal ball was in the middle of the table. Between the ball and Ada, hidden from the camera, there were three tea light candles, which made the ball seem to glow. As the candles flickered, the ball appeared to pulse with light. Ada was in full make-up with dark deep purple eyeshadow flecked with gold, black kohl eyeliner and gold earrings. She had gone for muted but dramatic purple lipstick.

She started with the TV presenter style,

"Good-evening and welcome. We are gathered here tonight for a special purpose. As you know I have been receiving messages from the other side."

Dramatic pause.

Ada had wanted some music in the background but Orla had pointed out, that if a spirit appeared they needed to be able to hear them. Instead, Ada had landed on a sound she could make somewhere in between keening and crooning, which came out like a melodic moan, she explained to the audience that this was to call the spirit world, a bit like knocking at the door.

"We are looking for some help. We have a lost child in the woods. Can you help?"

Ada had also told her audience to send love and messages of support, to help call the spirit, "together we will be so much more powerful."

Marianne found herself completely drawn into the performance, and had tears in her eyes, when she saw all the hearts flowing across the screen.

Orla had turned to Maeve, "Who's that?"

Marianne answered, "It's Ada of course, isn't she amazing, I have never seen her like this before."

"No, no, not Ada, the other woman in the summer dress." Maeve had seen her too.

"Text Ada, 'there is a woman behind you. We can't hear what she is saying. Be quiet for a bit.'"

Ada didn't react directly to the information, but got the message. She swayed side to side, then stopped.

"I feel someone coming to talk to us. It is a woman. Shhhh we need some quiet."

Incredibly, Ada who was apparently in a trance was also managing to text them back, 'give me details, anything.'

As Ada went quiet with her newly invented, very low level hum, Maeve and Orla began to hear the woman, who was speaking very quickly, without taking a break, like a stream of consciousness.

"I dunno what I am doing here…..It was such a lovely day out, wasn't it? Mind you, that pub, that garden out back, is far too close to the river, I mean a body could fall in, someone could come to harm there. We was lucky, just far enough away, perfect spot, delicious food. I'd recommend it to anyone I would. The George and Dragon, you know they bake all their own pies on site, that's why they're so tasty…." She carried on as if she was talking to a friend.

They were having difficulty figuring what to text Ada, and how to get her to answer a question. So Ada was just repeating the bits they managed to get across to her,

"Lovely day….The sunshine….. Summer breeze… The George and Dragon, a good place…hmmmm…."

As a result, the woman put her hand to one side of her mouth away from Ada and leant in towards the camera as if she was sharing a secret.

"I don't think she can hear very well, do you? Poor old sod. Never mind, you can hear me and that's all that matters isn't it? I shan't pay her any more attention…"

She seemed to know that Maeve and Orla could see and hear her, so she went on with her story. Ada was still floundering, repeating the bits Marianne managed to text her, but for Marianne, and anyone else who couldn't see the spirit Ada was doing fine,

"This young woman, ….has blond hair, …and she says she has two children one is with her and one is not." Ada does a bit more of the crooning.

Without managing to ask any specific questions the woman was giving them a blow by blow account of a particular afternoon. Maeve guessed that this was the critical day, and she was reliving it.

"….So anyways, as I was saying, Kimberly was right by me holding my hand, and little Jessica kept wandering off the track, and then would come running back to us. You know the way it is with little ones, let them free, I always say. And the woods was beautiful, green, hot in the sunshine and just the right amount of shady under the trees….."

Ada was trying to keep up, mainly concentrating on keeping her audience engaged, so when anything or anywhere was mentioned that she knew, she was filling in her own details.

"...Anyways, they were getting a bit tired, and Kimberly wanted to go to the toilet, you know what kids are like, as soon as they want something they have to have it now…"

The woman was moving around behind Ada, still talking at great speed, as though she had been wanting to tell her side of this story, but this was the first time anyone was listening.

"..so she kept saying 'I want to be a good girl', well of course that was our code for 'I need to go to the toilet'. She got more and more upset….I mean to say, what do you do when you are caught like that?...."

She turned shrugging her shoulders with her hands out to illustrate that she had no choice.

"..I says to her, Kimberly love, just go behind that tree over there, me and Jess, we'll keep watch. Off she goes, like the good girls she is, and we waited."

She had resumed her pacing behind Ada, now she turned to the camera.

"She didn't come back right away." She stopped talking for the first time since she had appeared. Put her hands on the table, and looked straight at Maeve.

"I dunno what she's been telling you. But she is a good girl. She finished her business, but what none of us had seen was,... was there was some bloke behind the tree watching her."

She was having difficulty getting the words out now. She looked down at the table and when she looked back up at the camera there were tears streaming down her cheeks.

"My Kimberly, she'd tried to get away, she'd lost her shoe and was looking on the ground for it, telling me she was a good girl."

She broke down into sobs, and took a few minutes to get herself together enough to talk, before going on.

"I saw the man before she did." Again she shrugged with a 'what was I supposed to do' gesture.

"As soon as I saw him, I knew something was wrong. I wanted to get away from him right away." She was breathing heavily now.

"I told Jess to run, run home I'll get Kimmy."

Her voice had dropped to a whisper.

"Jess ran, she's a good girl. I didn't make it to Kim in time."

Silent tears ran down her cheeks.

"She's such a good girl. Always helping others."

They heard a sigh, and she was gone.

CHAPTER 31

EN ROUTE TO CROMARTY

When it was all over, and the TikTok session had ended, they called Ada back. As she was taking her make-up off, and having a cup of tea, they had a debrief.

Marianne was in awe of Ada, star struck, she had never seen her grandmother perform before and kept saying 'Wow' and 'Amazing, I didn't know you could do that.'

This was a little irritating for Maeve and Orla, who knew that she had put on a good show but without them, it would have been just that, 'a show'.

Maeve was trying to figure out the mechanics of it all,

"Okay so how do we think that actually worked? Who called that woman?"

Ada was exhausted, she really had put on an incredible improvisational show. With very little material she kept her audience engaged, without revealing how she was getting the information. She had done a lot of "ooh,... aah, ...I feel something coming through...' mixed with her humming crooning sounds.

Judging by Marianne it had gone down well with her audience, well that, and all the thousands of hearts and messages she'd received.

Make-up off, back in comfortable clothes, tea in hand, Ada was ready to give her opinion,

"Wasn't I fabulous? We can get on to the plumbing in a minute, but you have to give me that. I was on fire." She was flexing her shoulders, almost preening, plumped up and ready for adoring fans.

'Oh God', thought Maeve, she's going to be unbearable, adding 'who am I kidding, she is unbearable'.

"Glad we could help." Maeve wanted to bring her back to earth without directly crushing her, then she remembered who she was dealing with.

"Actually Ada, you were brilliant. I couldn't have done it, so 'Well done'. You deserve a round of applause." And Maeve raised her hands and gently clapped Ada. Joining in, Orla wolf whistled, then Adam, who had been as quiet as a mouse throughout gave a big 'Hurray!' And Marianne was now clapping her heart out. So what Maeve started a little ironically, turned into the reaction that Ada was craving. On the other hand, Maeve knew that they were also collectively celebrating having achieved something, that none of them really believed was possible.

Smiles all round. Ada in true showbiz fashion said,

"Of course I couldn't have done it without you, the backup team." Maeve winced, Ada didn't notice.

"But I haven't felt so alive in years. I used to think about big live shows, on stage, but I was too afraid that I'd fall flat on my face." Ada looked round at them, this was heartfelt, wistful. A change of tone and she was back to the unstoppable Ada,

"But if I'd known it was this much fun, I'd have started years ago."

Maeve groaned and muttered mostly to herself,

"Thank God you didn't."

Taking a deep breath, and repositioning her smile, Maeve tried to move then on.

"Can we get back to the real issues? How did it work?"

Ada, who didn't really want to know, was still revelling in her performance. So it was Orla who spoke, a little tentatively,

"I think that maybe, Ada hasn't lost her powers, I think that she has shut them out. So Ada could call the woman, but couldn't see her."

Maeve was impressed. "Wow. I never would have thought of that. Well done Orla, that's a very plausible explanation."

Ada was coming down from her moment of glory, and this was a very bright prospect for the future.

"Girl, you are brilliant! That's genius." She was grinning from ear to ear,

"Well, I know which side of the family she got her brains from." As she pointed to herself, just in case anyone might miss it.

After that, they dissolved into general celebrations, talking over each other with how brilliant this or that had been. It was only with the relief they were feeling, did they realise just how anxious each of them had been.

Maeve had a bottle of Prosecco in the fridge, and this seemed like the right occasion to open it. The alcohol went straight to her head so Maeve didn't stay too long, and without Maeve the others called it a day, though Ada was scheduling a future planning session. They had a lot to sleep on.

~

The next day, first thing in the morning, Maeve was up and out, it was so early that she had packed breakfast into her picnic bag. A flask of good coffee and some fresh baked croissant, which she had heated while she was showering. There was enough for Steve too. Better to enjoy it on the train than rush some food down before leaving the house. She wanted to walk down to the train station to stretch her legs, before spending the rest of the day on a train, albeit in good company. Her overnight bag was a backpack and the food was in a neat carrier.

Still dark, she could hear the birds and not much else, breathing in the clean morning air, she felt the rising excitement of heading off on an adventure. The idea of leaving Canterbury, felt exotic; strange how things had changed so profoundly in such a relatively short space of time.

Maeve needed the walk to clear her head, the session on Tik Tok the night before, had taken it out of her. In the quiet of the morning, Maeve could focus on the spirit who appeared, rather than the drama of the event. She had felt the woman's pain. Maeve wondered, had she actually shared any information that was new?

Maeve now had a complete picture of the child's last day, the beautiful, glorious, idyllic start and horrific end. She could imagine the poor woman going round and round those same few hours, stuck in a terrible loop.

She got to the station quicker than she expected, but Steve was already there and waiting. He had the tickets, which was just as well as the ticket office wasn't yet open.

Steve had the same air of 'going on holiday' or 'off on an adventure' that Maeve had. So when they saw each other, they laughed as if sharing a secret joke.

Steve had got used to living on his own long ago. It wasn't that he didn't have girlfriends or the occasional fling, but he had some rules that he lived by. He would never have a relationship with a victim. That was just taking advantage of someone in a difficult situation, and wasn't fair, plus, a grateful shag felt plain wrong.

There had been attractive colleagues who he had considered, but he also lived by the maxim 'don't shit on your own doorstep'. Maeve was no longer, or in fact had never actually been, a 'victim'. And she wasn't in the force, so was fair game.

Steve enjoyed her family too, there was a great atmosphere. He wasn't sure that he wanted to sacrifice his independence, or that he could deal with the proximity of Maeve's family on a daily basis. Maybe he was thinking too far ahead, let's see how this goes and then review.

On the train, Steve was right, they had the whole carriage to themselves. They took a table, one on either side to have enough room to spread out breakfast. Steve had also thought about bringing food for them, and had a bacon butty each, made with delicious fresh white rolls, and a flask of tea. They laughed at each other's priorities.

Maeve said,

"Ooooh that smells sooo good. I had forgotten how good bacon is! This is going to be a culinary holiday. Bacon rolls and tea first, then coffee and croissant as a snack before arriving in London." She rubbed her hands together with glee. The fun of breaking all her own rules for a day, was adding to her pleasure.

It wasn't till later they got the first inkling that something was up.

CHAPTER 32

CROMARTY?

The first leg of their journey had been perfect, watching the waterlogged countryside slide by, glad they were in the train. Maeve had related all of the adventures the night before, both of them laughing with enjoyment at Ada's performance. They went over what they knew about the old murder case.

"The bit I don't get," Steve was going through the photocopied papers from his file, which were spread across the table, "is why the spirit would be getting in touch with you? I mean, this case is old and the murderer, is still behind bars."

"You're right. There are a number of things that don't add up," Maeve was sitting back thinking, "first thing is, why is she getting in touch at all? Anne suggested that she is trying to warn us, meaning, trying to stop something from happening in the future, I guess?"

These were pretty basic questions, to which they didn't have a good answer yet.

Maeve went on, "The next thing is, what's with the missing shoe? Is it important, or is it something she is using to communicate with us?" She was getting out her notebook to write these down, Maeve always felt better, once she had made a list.

"And of course, another critical question; is there any connection between the appearance of this child spirit, who we now know is Kimberly, and the body I found? Or is it some bizarre coincidence?"

Her list of questions was getting longer, rather than shorter.

They both concluded with a 'Hmmm'.

Steve gathered up the paper, tapped them on the table as if to put an end to the conversation for now, and packed up the file, making space for coffee and croissant.

Once the paperwork was out of the way, the atmosphere changed. Moving on to the more personal, Steve was ready to start to open up, somehow he wanted Maeve to know who he was, he thought that the mistake they had made last time, was not getting to know each other better first. They worked well together, and clearly there was some spark there, or he hoped there was. But they didn't really know each other as people. Where to start?

Maeve picked up on the shift, and equally wasn't sure how to do this. She examined her fingernails. It had been a long time since someone was interested in her, as a person, rather than as a mother, or daughter. Then she remembered there was something that she wanted to know.

"When we were talking about Matthew, the guy living out in the woods, and that he might have PTSD, remember?"

Steve nodded this wasn't exactly the direction he had been thinking, but they had lots of time so why not.

"Tell me more. More about you, and PTSD in the police, and what help you get?"

Steve sighed, this really wasn't what he wanted to be talking about.

"There's not much to tell. They started a new program a few years ago, but….. and it's a big but, if you want to be promoted you don't want to look weak, so you don't want to 'volunteer' any information that you don't have to ." He clearly wasn't keen to continue this conversation, but Maeve just waited.

"I mean, the force has been trying. There's a project that Kent Police have been doing with Cambridge University, which says that one in five of us have PTSD." He shifted uncomfortably. "But unless you are a basket case, and bursting into tears every five minutes, no one wants to put their hand up and say help me. We just get on with the job." He spread his hands out on the table, as much to say that's that, end of conversation.

This didn't do much to allay Maeve's concerns about Steve, nor give her any guidance for Matthew.

"So tell me about your life outside the force?"

Silence.

"What do you do when you are not working? What do you enjoy?"

This was clearly not something that Steve thought much about. His life, was his work. Equally, he wasn't feeling in control of the conversation, he was uncomfortable looking vulnerable.

"I like music, I listen to music all the time…..when I'm working…" He was beginning to realise that he hadn't given much, if any, thought to life, in the normal civilian sense of the word.

"I've been doing some subjects at night school to get extra qualifications. And I still volunteer for the Bikesafe course, when I can, teaching advanced motorcycle training. Mostly with the Met now." Silent. He drew a blank, put on the spot he couldn't think of anything else, and most of this was just another form of work. He felt he wasn't coming out of this 'job interview' or interrogation, particularly well, which he resented.

About now, back home, things were starting to wake up,

and not in a particularly good way, but so far Steve and Maeve were oblivious.

They arrived at St Pancras station. The Kent line, lands on the first floor, right beside the Eurostar trains, separated only by a Perspex barrier. The bright sun and blue sky filled the two story glass frontage to the station, as they passed the ticket barrier.

They had about twenty minutes, to get from one train to the other. Maeve had decided that if they moved swiftly, it was long enough to get a coffee refill. At the bottom of the escalators, Starbucks was open. Standing in line to order the coffee, Maeve registered that the station was missing the normal bustle. Even the Pret coffee shop was closed. She wondered how long it would be, before things got back to some sort of normality.

Steve picked up the coffees, from the painfully slow barista. With his bag on his shoulder he managed to balance the cardboard cup holder of coffees as they quick-marched across the road, to Kings Cross. Entering from the Western concourse straight into the impressive sunlit domed expanse, they found their platform, which was further than Maeve remembered, so they ran to get there in time.

Since they had left St Pancras, both of their phones had been pinging, signalling incoming messages. However with hands full of bags, tickets and coffees, they had decided whatever it was, could wait till they were on the express train to Edinburgh.

They just made it, settling into their seats in first class, with bags stashed in the overhead rack, as the train started to move which was a llittle too close for Steve's liking.

Enjoying the luxury, they took a moment to relax, and then took out their phones.

"Shit!" They exclaimed at exactly the same time.

The same urgency, but from different sources.

Steve's from the station, 'Get back here immediately!

People are gathering in Fordwich. To do with the old case you re-opened.'

Maeve's from Marianne, 'Call ASAP! Ada's fans have gone mad.'

They moved to opposite ends of the carriage, to make their calls. The phones lost signal with each tunnel they passed through, and again with each bad 'out of range' patch. It was lucky that the carriage was empty as they were both shouting.

"What, I can't hear you……" then to no one in particular "Shit no signal again."

After a while, with multiple restarts, of "Hello, hello,…. what? I missed that last bit",

they had each begun to form a picture, and returned to their table to share intel. It seemed, that during Ada's performance the audience had picked up some key information, like the car park in Fordwich, and the fact that the missing shoe was important. What they hadn't understood, or Ada hadn't made clear, was that this was an old case. Her fans thought that this was a live case, and somehow they believed, that finding this shoe would contribute to finding a murderer, and possibly saving the life of a child. Urgently.

Maeve had been on FaceTime, with a distraught Ada,

"Oh for God's sake Maeve, how could they think that?" Ada was wringing her hands, Maeve could see that beside Ada was a pile of tissues, she had clearly had a good cry before getting through to Maeve. "Sure, wasn't I crystal clear?.....I think it was just the way I was repeating what that poor woman said, it sounded so real and like it was happening now…." Maeve was nodding in agreement with the occasional "Yes,..... ahum,....yes…..ahum..."

The net result was, that a large number of Ada's TikTok fans had organised themselves via social media and were coming from everywhere, descending on the George and Dragon in Fordwich and walking from there back to Canterbury, through the woods looking for the shoe. They had moved from Tic Tok to a Facebook page and were using Twitter, for instant access to information, with both being shared or retweeted to spread the word. The crowd was growing and growing.

For the police this was a nightmare. There were, by now, more than a hundred, all of them walking in two's 'for exercise' so they couldn't be arrested, but they were flooding the place.

According to the Super, Steve was the cause of all this. Steve had dug up the old case, Steve was on his way to interview an unnecessary witness, when he should have been back at base, and now, all hell had broken loose, QED it was Steve's fault.

Steve was furious, as far as he was concerned this fiasco had nothing to do with him at all. Here he was, policing the old fashioned way, going to interview a witness. He thought that this insanity was all down to Ada and her crazy ideas, it was all her fault. And Maeve. Without Maeve this wouldn't have happened either.

He looked like thunder. This was his promotion down the toilet, to move up the ladder Steve needed to show leadership, good planning, working with a team, this was a disaster.

Maeve was trying to piece together what had happened, what was actually going on, and then trying to figure out what they might do about it. She looked up and saw Steve's face.

"This isn't my fault." She gave him a warning glare. "Don't you dare try to pin this on me." Maeve had to take a deep breath, to calm her own mounting anger, "I'm doing my best to work out a solution. Getting angry with me, won't help anything."

The Super had been clear, Steve had to get his ass back to Canterbury, as fast as he could and sort this mess out. Meanwhile the situation was being 'escalated', the numbers were of the same order as a daylight rave, and growing.

They were now some twenty minutes out of King's Cross station. The train was a non-stop express train. Steve worked out that they had another three and a half hours before arriving in Edinburgh, then he would have to turn around, and go straight back. In total, nearly ten hours. Too long. He needed to do something right now, and he wanted to shout at someone. He was an emotional powder keg.

CHAPTER 33

GOING THEIR OWN WAY

S teve was in no mood to calm down. His feeling of lack of control combined with the injustice of the situation, triggered a complete flip in his demeanour. He was huffing and puffing, whilst gathering all his stuff. Studiously avoiding looking at Maeve, as he tried to keep his temper in check. He was on a very short fuse.

Maeve was in no mood to be generous. She knew, that without Ada this would never have happened, she was fuming, coloured by guilt, her indignation was fiery.

The train went through another tunnel, and suddenly she was faced with their reflection in the window. In surprise she saw their faces, looking at him, she thought, 'this guy needs help or one day he will explode in a dangerous situation'. She knew so little about PTSD, but Steve's fury was excessive.

Controlling her own annoyance, trying to bring things to a more normal level, she said,

"I've been looking it up and if you can get them to stop the train and let you off at Peterborough, you will be able to get a fast train back. It's not worth trying to get off at Stevenage because you will just end up stuck in Stevenage, waiting for some slow train."

Her calm logic was having an effect on Steve, she had moved them away from mentioning anything that might allow for blame, on to useful information and practical help. She could almost see his blood pressure dropping, so she went on.

"I can't do anything in Canterbury, that can't be done via my phone, so I suggest that I carry on, and interview the witness tomorrow morning."

Steve's breathing was slowing to a more regular in and out sound, then as he thought about Maeve on police business on her own, as his responsibility, his breath became shorter with irritation,

"You can't! You are not a police officer. This is official business."

Having made her assessment of the situation, concluding it was likely that his own PTSD was causing Steve to behave irrationally, Maeve didn't immediately take offence. She stayed calm. She could be angry later.

"Well, I can carry out a preliminary investigation. Gather information, and if there is anything important that comes up, then you can call the man and make it official."

Again her voice and measured tones, were having a good effect on Steve, she continued,

"I am not using any police powers. The 'dog walker', our witness, has agreed to have a chat. Although the trip might be official, the conversation can be exploratory. Plus I can cover my own costs." Maeve knew from working with the film festivals that expenses that fell outside of the norm, could be far more trouble than you'd think. This was one more way of making things easier for Steve. And it meant she didn't feel any obligation to Steve, or anyone else.

"Okay, okay. You go." Then thinking about his own situation, he flushed red,

"I've got to get off this bloody train!"

He headed for the guard, driver, or anyone in charge, just

as the ticket inspector walked into their carriage with a normal cheery, "Tickets please."

Steve flashed his badge, as he shouted,

"I need you to stop the train at the next station! Right now!"

Maeve leaning out of her seat to catch his attention, added in a normal explanatory way,

"Peterborough station. He means at Peterborough so that he can get back to London ASAP. Unless there is a quicker route?"

The ticket inspector was not moving, he had his hands on the ticket dispenser hanging in front of him preparing to sell them an upgrade. Steve's shouting, plus his official badge, had frozen the poor man into inaction.

"Out of my way!" Steve headed off in search of the train driver.

Maeve calmed the ticket inspector down, explained the situation and got him to radio the driver before Steve pulled the emergency stop cord.

The next time she saw Steve, was through the window, he was standing on the platform in Peterborough, looking for the London train. The Edinburgh express moved out of the station, he didn't notice her waving at him. 'I hope he catches the express and doesn't take the stopping service', she thought, adding, 'well I did my best for him'.

Getting back to her own problems, Maeve checked in on the girls first, and then Ada.

"Yes, we've been on it ever since we heard what was happening." Marianne and Orla were on speaker phone, so that they could both talk and hear the conversation.

"So Ada has put out messages to her fans explaining the situation?"

"Not exactly. All the fuss moved on to Twitter. She's not on Twitter, so we have been putting out the messages there and on FaceBook." Orla explained.

"Good, good. Sounds like you have things under control at your end anyway."

Silence, the girls didn't respond.

"Okay, what are you not telling me?" Maeve could read the silence.

There was a collective sigh.

"I am not sure that you are going to believe us." Marianne had taken the lead,

"The more we put out the truth, the more it backfires." Marianne paused, and Maeve could hear that she was close to tears,

"The fans, or some of them, react to what we put out, and they say 'fake news'. They think someone is trying to stop them helping to solve the murder. We are getting crazy tweets back, about how we are part of the 'deep state', and are planning to put 'Bill Gates's chip, in the vaccine controlling us'." She was really close to crying now. Orla chipped in,

"We don't know what to do, it just keeps getting worse."

Now Maeve was quiet, thinking 'shit, this could get very nasty'. Not wanting to make them feel worse than they already did, she said.

"Give me some time. And I'll have a chat with Ada. Let's see what we can come up with."

She could hear the relief on the other end of the phone, Marianne and Orla were glad that they were no longer on their own.

Maeve got up and went to the end of the carriage to get a self service cup of tea, more to give herself time to think, than that she needed the tea.

Ready to deal with more drama, she called Ada.

Ada had had a crash course in social media this morning, so was now up to speed on Twitter and FaceBook, as well as Instagram.

"They've taken over, and left me high and dry." Ada was

referring to her followers, or the fan groups that had sprung up on other platforms, to organise the search.

"One minute I am basking in fame, and being sent thousands of 'hearts', the next, they don't give a damn, and no matter what the girls put out, they say it's all 'fake news'. Did you ever in your life see anything like it?"

Ada made Maeve smile. It was still all about Ada. And at the same time, she was taking the entire social media world in her stride, as if she had always known how to play in this arena. That gave Maeve an idea.

"So have you put anything out on Tik Tok?"

"No, why? Sure they were all off on Twitter, why would I go backwards?"

"Your fans followed you on Tik Tok, that's the only place that they are going to believe your side of the story. You have to do another session, telling them the background to the story. I guess, that you are going to have to thank them all, for their support, and maybe set up another 'live' session to call another spirit, so that they don't get too pissed off, and have something to look forward to."

"Oh my God! They have such fragile egos!"

This did make Maeve laugh, to hear Ada talking about other people and fragile egos was funny. But they agreed that this might be the best way to do it, and it gave Ada something to do. Ada was to call the girls and get them to check her script first, to make sure she wasn't inadvertently going to trigger any more crazy reactions.

"Once you are set up, and have put out your TikTok message. Send the link to Marianne and Orla, so that they can spread the word, and put it out everywhere they can."

Earlier, when Steve was getting his bags down, Maeve had picked up the photocopied file and put it in with her stuff. She didn't mention it to Steve, in case he got funny about it, but if this journey was to be of any value at all, then she needed all the information she could get.

Thinking back on how the day had started out with such promise, Maeve was wondering how she had landed herself in this situation. What was she doing, heading up to the north of Scotland on what was likely to be a wild goose chase? She wasn't looking forward to driving to Cromarty on her own. She had looked it up on the map, but only to see where it was, she had left the detailed route planning up to Steve. By the time she sorted the hire car to drive the last leg from Inverness to Cromarty, it was likely to be dark. Hopefully there would be enough signal for her to use her phone for directions.

At least she had sorted some of the issues in Canterbury, it could hardly get any worse, could it?

Now she settled back to read the file from cover to cover with no interruptions. Her indignation returned, would she ever forgive Steve? This wasn't her fault, it wasn't even her idea, it was Steve's!

CHAPTER 34

GETTING WORSE

Back in Canterbury, Marianne and Orla had done a good job on Ada's script. Ada was putting on her make-up, getting ready, and setting up her background for the new TikTok post. Marianne and Orla were organising themselves. They were preparing to watch, when Ada filmed herself, as acting live quality control, focusing on potential bear traps that Ada might fall into. The main concern was to stop the bizarre internet trolls pouncing on or wilfully misunderstanding, anything Ada said.

Adam had been flitting around in the background, making tea, and trying to be supportive. Inside he was worried. This was a family that he cared deeply about, they had saved his life, and they had rescued him a second time, when isolation was really getting him down. He didn't want something bad to happen to them. Adam knew what Marianne and Orla were planning and couldn't see a way that he could help. But he was keen to do his bit. With no one to consult, he decided that the best thing he could do was to go to Fordwich and try to explain the real situation to people directly, and in person. Surely they would understand then.

Not wanting to disturb anyone, Adam left a note by the kettle, and slipped out the door.

Maeve had sent some short messages to Steve, so that he was aware that the fans hadn't accepted the truth of the situation, preferring to believe that there was a conspiracy going on to shut them out. She also updated him, that Ada was doing her best to set the record straight. He didn't reply.

Taking advantage of her first class ticket, Maeve got herself another cup of tea, closed her eyes for a moment and practiced letting go. She wasn't going to let Steve annoy her at a distance. Determined to get into a positive frame of mind before arriving in Edinburgh, she looked up the Black Isle and Cromarty. She found the most important thing as far as she was concerned, an excellent coffee house. It didn't have the most promising name, 'The Slaughterhouse', but pretty much a five star rating from all the customers. Things were looking up. Maybe it was a good time to be away.

Maeve changed trains in Edinburgh, at about the same time that Steve got back to Canterbury. He had jumped on his motorbike and legged it round to the car park opposite the pub in Fordwich.

While he was on the train back to Canterbury, Steve had been in almost constant touch with his team. It was difficult, because he was finding it hard to imagine what exactly was happening on the ground. He had placed a sergeant at each end of the run, so one in Fordwich and one at the most used public exit by the Youth Club in Canterbury, with anyone he could lay his hands on, constables, officers and support staff, joining them.

Steve couldn't imagine how this was going to turn out, it could be like any other sunny Bank Holiday, where some polite but firm nudges would get people to move along and go home. The messages from Maeve suggested otherwise. If it turned into a protest mob, they would be in trouble. He had got as many boots on the ground as he could, hoping he had enough to cover either scenario whilst not 'wasting' resources.

When Steve arrived at the scene, he didn't know what to expect, but what he saw certainly wasn't it.

By now, Maeve was well on her way to Inverness and having checked that the girls were okay, the new TikTok post had gone out, and things were calming down from Ada's perspective. She sat back and embraced the patchy signal. As a last minute thought Maeve had tucked a book in her bag, now with a feeling of the complete luxury of time to herself and absolutely nothing else she could usefully do, she opened her novel, and settled in.

In contrast, as soon as Steve had parked his bike, the sergeant from his team shouted over,

"Good to see you, Governor. It's a right mess."

Steve could see that for himself, "Christ. It's like Piccadilly Circus!"

The car park was full, and cars had been abandoned on footpaths; in people's driveways, blocking the residents into their houses. In fact, everywhere that they could find a square inch to dump a car, they had. The recent rain had made the ground soft, all in all, this was gridlock in a muddy quagmire. Not ideal.

One group of people were milling around in the car park arguing with the officers who were trying to hold them back, and stop them heading off across the fields on their way to the woods.

"Step back, please." The officer was firm but polite.

"This is a public footpath. I have my rights. You can't stop me."

"Yes sir, but during the pandemic we can not allow crowds to gather." The officer was doing his best, but the level of tension was high. This had been going on for some time.

"You are wilfully stopping a community search for vital information."

"Ma'am, with due respect, if there is a search to be carried out then the police are the best people to carry it out." He was managing for the moment.

Steve nodded to the sergeant. "He's doing fine. Been like this all day?"

"Yes Gov, but they haven't always been so polite, we've had quite a bit of argy bargy with pushing and shoving. Earlier, before we had the numbers on our side we let a bunch of them through." He was glad that the boss was here in person.

"Since then we've been doing quite a bit of cat 'n' mouse chasing, as well as holding them off at this end."

"What do you mean?" Steve was struggling to follow, so he sounded sharper than he intended, he needed to be on top of his game, but he wasn't. At the moment he was trying to keep a lid on his rising sense of panic, without letting anyone else pick up on it.

"Well, you can see, they've all got their mobile phones on. They're getting messages from somewhere, and then suddenly they change what they are doing." He shrugged his incomprehension. "So they've worked out there are other ways to get into the woods." He stopped talking, turned and used his eyes to indicate the direction of the old barracks, without actually giving away any specific information to the people hanging around, listening for clues.

"We try to get there before they do. Then they change back. It's a ruddy nightmare."

With that, his radio burst into life,

"Sarg, we've got a problem. A big one."

The sergeant moved away so that no one could overhear what was said next.

Steve had come straight to the site so didn't have the necessary kit, as the sergeant moved off he reached his hand back with a radio in it for Steve. No explanation needed.

Steve moved away from the onlookers milling around before tuning in and hearing,

"....We have a shooter in the woods. Intel suggests them to be plausibly armed with live ammo. We are estimating two hundred civilians in the immediate vicinity..."

CHAPTER 35

MEANWHILE IN SCOTLAND

Maeve found hiring the car much easier than she feared. The office was shut, so they had left a message for her to go and pick up the car, the keys were inside. In less than twenty minutes from getting off the train she was on her way. It's a relatively short drive and her phone worked well enough to get her through the key junctions on the journey.

It was when she logged-in to the guest house WiFi that she got all the news.

Her lovely host Fiona was trying to show her around, when Maeve had to stop her and say,

"Could you give me ten minutes to deal with some urgent messages?"

"Of course, why don't I make us a nice pot of tea? You look like you could do with one."

Maeve was listening to the messages in reverse order, so had to hear them all before she understood what had happened.

Ada's TikTok post had gone out, and was being reasonably effective in stopping the incoming flow of new people into the area. She now had a considerable number of irate followers, but the promise of another live session seemed, if not to get them back on side, then at least to take the sting out of it.

The problem was with the fans who had already arrived, and seemed to be on their own mission. They discovered that some of the loudest voices had never even seen Ada's live stream, they were just there to cause trouble. They had picked up the social media buzz, and added some outrageous comments, fuelling the 'concerned citizens', edging them into an extremist mob.

The crisis point came when people ran out of the woods shouting

"He's got a gun! The man in the trees, he's got a gun, he's going to shoot. Run!"

This had been picked up by the crowd, repeated in all directions, causing mass panic. People fleeing the area, using all possible routes out of the woods, sliding in the mud causing human pile-ups, while those behind walked on, over, or through, those in front.

The police had stepped up their presence, bringing in the tactical firearms unit, with a police helicopter providing eyes overhead.

Officers on the ground were trying to calm the crowd whilst evacuating the area. Initially, the police had wanted all names and addresses, because they knew that everyone here needed to be tested for COVID-19. Once the panic hit, they moved the primary objective to achieving a safe evacuation, only gathering whatever contact information was possible once they were a safe distance from the woods. In what was now a life threatening situation no charges for unlawful gathering were mentioned. That could come later if need be.

In short order the firearms officers were in place, with the estimated location of the armed protester being provided by the helicopter, the officers went into the woods to try to bring him in, without anyone getting hurt. So far, no shots had been fired, but the language reported by the terrified witnesses as they fled the scene, suggested that the suspect had been trained by the military.

Long before she heard the precise information, Maeve had guessed that this was Matthew. The crowds of people must have freaked him out, possibly jolting him into believing that he was in a frontline situation.

Steve had just about managed to keep it together. As soon as a gunman was mentioned, it went above his pay grade. His super arrived on site working with him to manage the crowd. She was directly in contact with the firearms team. They had been lucky that the comms signal was good at all of their base points. Particularly as British Telecom were due to upgrade the telecoms mast which would mean disconnecting the area for a reasonable length of time. The whole area was being upgraded to 5G, without alerting the local community to avoid any mass gathering of anti-5G protesters. If today's debacle was anything to go by, that made sense.

Like Maeve, as soon as the word came through that the 'possible shooter' was in a tree, Steve thought it might be Matthew. Unlike Maeve, who was sure that he wouldn't do any real harm, Steve had grave concerns. He upped the risk level, knowing that this bloke was trained to survive on his own which could mean a Para, SAS or someone with elite skills. His fear, was that Matthew was a trained sniper, invalided out of the military due to battle trauma. He could be in the process of reliving an 'event', where he imagined himself back in a war zone defending a position. Possibly seeing the punters as the enemy. If true, it could be lethal. They couldn't afford to take any risks.

Even to himself, Steve didn't want to use the term PTSD, it was a bit close to the bone.

At some point in the past the police had used these grounds in a firearms training exercise, so a few of the officers were familiar with the internal layout of the woods, and were able to guide their colleagues relatively discreetly, to the spot where they believed the suspect was hiding out.

As they circled round him getting closer, he came down from the tree, and was waiting for them with his hands up, shouting,

"I am not armed, I am a civilian," he kept repeating the words "I am not armed, I am a civilian, I am not resisting arrest."

Whatever had happened earlier, whatever threats he had shouted, he seemed on first contact, to be pretty normal and rational.

It only took a few minutes to establish that it was true, he was not armed. He was wearing what might look like army fatigues to a civilian, but he was not armed. He also made it clear that he did not appreciate the destruction of 'his' woodland by the careless tramping of the 'concerned citizens'.

The officers who first came in contact with Matthew, quickly developed the opinion that he had shouted out using his 'army speak' to frighten the crowd away, because they were destroying his patch, rather than that he meant them any harm. Apart from the limited stretches of path that had a hard surface, a quick look showed that the rest had been churned into a mud bath. He had probably been waving something like a rifle shaped stick. Still it was the equivalent of shouting 'fire in a theatre' and the ensuing chaos, was a public order offence.

The police took him down to the station for questioning.

By the time Maeve had caught up with all of this she felt in need of something stronger than a cup of tea. She had put her overnight bag in her indulgently warm room, and took the remains of her bag of luxury food from the Goods Shed downstairs.

She didn't know her host, but given the day's events, Maeve suggested to Fiona that they put the bottle of white wine in the fridge, to chill, and that they should start on the red right now, if she was up for a glass.

What she didn't know, was that Steve had done an impressive job in sorting out a surprise 'romantic dinner' for them, and had already inveigled Fiona's help. Given the crisis that he was dealing with, he hadn't thought to cancel it. Of course he hadn't discussed any of this with Maeve, so as if by magic as she was discussing the wine, an excellent venison casserole and a flank steak and chips arrived.

Maeve explained that Steve had had to leave urgently, as Fiona showed her the menu he had chosen, to be delivered from their local restaurant, Sutor Creek. Fiona had done her bit, and dressed the dining room with soft lighting from candles, flowers, and a beautifully set table. The room was painted a rich red with a generous wood table, giving an overall effect of one of the more exclusive media type clubs, in Soho.

Maeve looked at the mound of delicious food now being laid out on the table, hesitating for a moment at the quantity of dishes, she asked Fiona if she would like to join her for dinner. Maeve needed someone to talk to, and Fiona was a ready listener and already in thrall with the adventures that Maeve had started to recount, dying to hear the end of the story.

Pushing back her chair Maeve finished with "That was amazing." She sat back extremely satisfied, she hadn't noticed how much she needed a 'girls' night out'. As well as appreciating the good food, and good wine, she enjoyed the good company. Being able to talk to someone who was non judgmental, someone with whom she could be indiscreet, and open up about her feelings and Steve. Someone who might understand and who was already affronted on her behalf with Steve's recent behaviour.

"There's more, we got chocolate cremeux oranges and sticky toffee pudding with butterscotch sauce."

The two women looked at each other, full, but not to be outdone by what looked like fabulous desserts.

"Let's split them and take half each." Maeve thought a taste wouldn't kill them.

By the time they were half way through the second bottle of wine, they had fully bonded and had moved into the more comfortable sitting room, with deep sofas.

"Okay, I don't want to sound too forward, but can I tell you what I think?" Fiona was now fully immersed in Maeve's issues.

"Of course. This is the best fun I've had in weeks."

"Well." She hesitated, but the wine had its effect, so, whereas normally she would have held her council, Fiona was as direct as with her own sister. "I think you need to get out more. Get back in the saddle as they say."

"What? You mean date some men?"

"Yes. But I'm betting the world has changed a lot, since you last had a proper look for someone to suit you."

"Go on." Maeve was definitely outside of her comfort zone, and trying not to be defensive.

"I bet you used to meet people, I mean men, at work or socially and you just don't any more. Is that right?"

"Yes." Fiona was spot on, Maeve hadn't really thought about it before. For years, she had been too busy with work and looking after the girls. On her last birthday she had faced the fact of turning forty and decided it was time to focus on herself. Now or never. However the pandemic, and the shock that she could communicate with the other side, had pushed her emotional needs into the background. Being honest with herself, Maeve had not been ready to face it, yet.

"Right, get your phone out, girl. We have work to do."

Maeve leaned over and lowered her voice to say,

"Before we do whatever you are thinking of, ..and I don't mean to pry, ..but would that lady, ..is it your mother? Would she not like to come over and sit with us?"

Fiona looked puzzled, "My mother?"

"Well, whoever she is, the lady sitting back in the upright chair, by the fire, with the rug on her lap. The one you have been ignoring."

Fiona went pale, "Can you describe her?"

Maeve had seen that look before, 'oh dear', she thought, 'I'm going to have to explain this too'.

CHAPTER 36
COLD WATER

Maeve looked apologetically at Fiona, "Would you mind making us a cup of tea? This may take a while." Fiona was happy to disappear into the kitchen, giving herself some time to recover. Maeve, needed to have some time alone with the spirit in the room.

The elderly woman seemed content, settled by the fire. Not unhappy, not in need. Maeve wondered what the spirit wanted. Maeve hadn't tried to 'call' anyone, or any other kind of spirits on the other side, so she imagined this woman must want something.

"Ach no dear." She had a gentle Scottish accent, and was soft spoken. "I'm here because you have a question that you need answered." She tilted her head slightly, as if waiting for something from Maeve.

After a full bottle of excellent wine, and a wee drop of brandy by the fire, Maeve's brain was running slower than normal.

"I have come here to talk to the dog walker, who is still alive, unless you have bad news for me?"

"No, no, he's not on my side. Your question is about you, girl. No one else. You came all the way here, to have your question answered. The rest is not important to me. This is fundamental. Think."

Maeve was racking her brain, and started thinking aloud.

"Well, I am trying to understand how to control who communicates with me....."

She shook her head.

"...and then I was having those issues with the river...?"

"Yes, go on."

Maeve was on surer ground now, so she took a moment to form the question,

"What is my relationship to water, or rather what is its relationship to me?"

"Well done! That's it. It's at your core, dear." She seemed to think that was enough of an explanation.

"I don't understand. I mean, we are all physically made up mostly of water, but that applies to everyone, doesn't it?"

"Ah, I see. You haven't fully begun your study. You need to prepare yourself, there is much to be done." The fingertips of each hand were touching, pointing towards the ceiling in a gesture of thoughtfulness, selecting her words she began again,

"You are a caring person, that is part of your calling," she paused, considering how to put what she had to say next. She spoke, as if this was the opening thesis of a presentation.

"The elements earth, wind, fire, water, and space or spirit are all important. But everyone has one in particular, that one, being that person's guiding element. In your case it is water."

She stopped, looked at her and addressed Maeve personally.

"You must not be seduced by your element. But you can embrace it. Learn how to read it."

Looking over the top of her glasses, directly into Maeve's eyes.

"You must take control, or you will suffer." She clasped

her hands firmly together indicating that this particular subject was closed.

Smiling she changed the subject,

"And tell Fiona, that she will be happy here. I lived here in the Factor's House for a long time and it gave me great pleasure." Happy memories drifted across her face.

"I spent a lot of my life caring for others less fortunate, in some foreign parts, and in some terrible conditions." She tutted at the shame of what man can do to man in war.

"I watch her and Fiona is like me in many ways. She loves this house, makes it welcoming, and cares for her guests. It's a refuge."

"Should I tell her who you are?"

"She just needs to know that I am keeping an eye out for her. She has made it a happy house again, I'll stay as long as she does." Smiling to herself.

The door opened as Fiona came in with the tea, when Maeve turned back to look by the fireplace she was gone.

The encounter and subsequent chat sobered them.

Fiona was concentrating,

"I did hear tell of a woman living here for a long time, that was back in the eighteen eighties or eighteen nineties but I can't for the life of me remember her name…"

"I don't think that's important. The bit I think is important, is that she has your back. I mean, she is here to help you. If you ever feel uncomfortable about something or someone, go with your feelings. It's likely to be a message from her."

By now it was definitely time to turn in. Maeve had had a wonderful evening, really enjoyed herself, and was happy to have been able to use her gift to help her new friend, as well as herself. Climbing up the stairs, she thought it was strange to come somewhere new and feel so at home.

That night, whether the spirit had a hand in it or not, Maeve had a sound night's sleep.

She wasn't expecting the early morning wake up call.

Fiona knocked on her door, with an urgency,

"You won't want to miss this!"

It was still pitch dark, 'what the hell is going on', thought Maeve as she dragged herself to open the door.

Standing on the landing was Fiona, with some bathing togs in one hand, and neoprene gloves and a woolly bobble hat in the other. Maeve briefly wondered if last night had all been too much for Fiona, and she had gone mad.

"Get this on you. I have special socks too but not till we are down there. The Mermaids are waiting, so get a move on."

Looking back on it, Maeve thought it was the insistence that made her do it. Without really taking on board that Fiona was suggesting they go for a swim, in the sea, in winter, in Scotland. If she had taken a moment to stop and think, Maeve would have known that this was insane. But she didn't. Instead, Maeve did as she was told, and within five minutes found herself, along with a group of women, gathering on the shore. Now, she was awake enough to resist, but the cheery shrieks of laughter as some went in, and the stoical silence of others, plus Fiona's 'go on, go on, you will thank me for it' encouraged her. Plus, she didn't want to be the only one who chickened out, there were plenty in Ada's age group, so age was no excuse.

Thinking 'If you are going to do it, better do it quickly', she braced herself.

Maeve shrieked as she hit the cold water. Now she knew, why they had the hat and gloves and socks. Her body adjusted enough to the cold to allow her to swim a few strokes. Enough to acknowledge the glimmer of dawn as the glorious landscape began emerging from the dark, revealing the hills on the other side of the firth.

This water welcomed her. Once in, it was warmer than the air outside. This strange space affected her senses, the boundaries between the water and the air, were less clear in the dark. At the same time she felt in control. More in control than she ever had before.

As soon as she got out of the water, and the blood flow returned, she felt amazing.

A shock of life. Waking up all of her senses. But something more had happened, she felt in touch with the water, with no fear.

They were all laughing now, shouting about numb toes, and who had the most stylish hat, the one with pink pom poms was the clear winner. Everyone glad to be alive and wrapping up quickly.

Maeve had gained a whole group of crazy new friends.

Walking, dancing, twirling in the sand. Hooting with pleasure, and there to welcome the day.

Now Fiona was hurrying her along,

"Don't get cold. Come on, let's go. A hot shower and I'll have the best breakfast ready for you, when you get down."

Maeve laughed at the idea, that having got her into the icy water, Fiona was now worried that she was going to get cold. She was more than happy to head for a warm shower.

Later, looking at the debris of the most amazing breakfast, where fresh local eggs and bacon, followed delicious fruit compote, and yoghurt with homemade honey granola. Now lingering over the second cup of coffee, Maeve sighed contentedly.

"You could convert me to this cold water swimming. I may have really overeaten but I still feel great. You were right. Thank you for making me do it."

Fiona was beaming. Things had been tough over the last year, generally, activity had dropped off as the oil rigs were being decommissioned. Even though alternative energies were being developed locally, it wasn't happening quickly enough for Fiona, she was watching income disappear. To then be hit, by this pandemic and no tourists, it was really hard.

Regardless, Fiona was optimistic and she was still on a mission.

"Get your phone out. It's probably better that we do this fresh anyway." She hadn't explained her idea to Maeve yet, but the success of the early morning swim had given Fiona the confidence to just do it.

Maeve had left her phone charging in her room, it was only as she picked it up that she saw the message she had missed late last night. It was from Marianne, 'Adam went to talk to the protesters and got picked up by the police. He has been held overnight. I'm sending a message to Steve to see if he can help. Xx'

'Shit', this was not what she needed.

CHAPTER 37

DOG WALKER

Maeve called home to get an update on the situation. It seemed that in the general sweep, after Matthew had been removed, the police had taken a number of people who appeared to be troublemakers for further questioning. Adam, had been trying to explain how Ada's followers were mistaken, which had led to heated exchanges, making him look like the source of the trouble. Once he was being questioned, it became clear that he was here on his Greek passport, and was now being held because he didn't have the right paperwork for the imminent post Brexit Britain.

Marianne had contacted Steve, which was how she knew the situation, but was at a complete loss as to what to do next.

Maeve had an idea. One of her yoga friends worked at the University of Kent, specifically with foreign students, she might be able to help, after all Adam was a PhD student at the University. She would check in as soon as she could reasonably call her. It was still early. But Maeve was almost late for her meeting with the 'dog walker', who she knew from the files was a 'John Graydon'.

She handed Fiona her phone, saying,

"Here, do whatever you think you need to. I will gather

all my stuff together, and get ready to leave. I didn't think I would say this, but I wish I was staying for longer."

"Ach, you'll be back. You'll need your fix of swimming with the Cromarty Mermaids." Phone in hand, Fiona was talking as Maeve's back disappeared up the stairs,

"*You* have to do this, but I'll add something in just to get you started." Now talking to herself, "And I'll put my number in your contacts list so you can give me a call and let me know how you get on."

Somehow Maeve thought Fiona was right, she wouldn't have believed it before she came to Scotland, but now the idea of a summer break in Cromarty was very appealing. As she packed up, she took in the view from the window. The sun was fully up, it was a glorious day, and her room gave onto the back of the house. She could see the walled gardens fall away to the shore and the brilliant blue of the sea, right across to the hills on the other side of the firth. Picture postcard.

For the official meeting, and keeping the 'social distancing' in mind, Maeve had planned on them finding each other at the Slaughterhouse to pick up a coffee, and have a walking meeting along the seafront. It seemed strange now to think that only yesterday she imagined this would be the highlight of her trip.

On her way down, with her newfound fondness for the place, she took in as much as she could. The stone houses were a mix of warm 'red' sandstone and of whitewash trimmed with grey stone. Most of the shops were shut but had tempting local craft, antiques, or delicious food in the windows. They exuded stability, and from her early morning contact with the Mermaids, Maeve projected friendliness.

With the lighthouse at her back, standing by the coffee shop at the water's edge, touching the slipway for the Cromarty to Nigg ferry, Maeve breathed in the sea air. She was conscious that she was standing at the point of the headland, to her right would take her to the open sea and a relatively short distance to Norway, to her left heading inland was the Cromarty Firth. Maybe the tourist information was right and there was a micro climate here, Maeve thought, as she turned to put in her order, it was much the same temperature here, as it was when she left Canterbury.

Back outside, she was enjoying the view across the water, even the waiting oil rigs had some charm, less so now than when she first saw them at dawn, festooned in lights looking like eccentrically decorated Christmas trees.

Miles away, lost in thought, she was surprised by an "Ahem" behind her.

A man with a dog was standing there, he waved, with an awkward gesture replacing the more traditional handshake. He was definitely keeping his two metre distance from her.

"You must be Maeve? I'm John." As they were the only two people there it was a pretty good guess.

Maeve nodded and reciprocated the hand wave. She had already slipped her mask back on. She didn't have much hope of discovering anything new, but it was worth going through whatever John could remember.

Knowing that it had been difficult to get him to agree to talk, Maeve started the conversation trying to put him at ease by recounting the adventures in the woods yesterday. It didn't work.

"Oh dear! Oh dear! I do hope people won't start trying to find me again. I only agreed to this, on the basis that the police had some unfinished business."

He sounded so English and out of place here, Maeve tried a different angle.

"How did you find this place? I love it. And have people accepted you here?"

"Em, yes, well I was looking for somewhere about as far away as I could get. The press kept following me, as if I knew something and was keeping it from them." He let out a breath, perhaps he was beginning to relax.

"Moving here was the best thing I ever did. No one here cares about 'that'." He emphasised 'that' as if he didn't want to say the word murder, in case it would draw attention to him.

"People here welcome all sorts." Now she had him on a subject that he was happy to talk about.

"Once, when I was in the newsagents, I saw a newcomer walking down the High St with the giant head of a duck, I think it was Donald Duck, tucked under her arm. Everyone else saw her too, and one of the other customers said to the newsagent, 'I think she will fit right in, don't you?'" He chuckled to himself at the memory. "Yes, they accept all sorts."

Looking at Maeve, his seriousness returned, he said,

"They are good people here, I hope you are not bringing any trouble?"

Maeve fervently agreed. They talked long enough to finish their coffees but not much longer. Mostly John reiterated the information that was in the files. The only oddity that emerged related to the shoe.

Because she had mentioned all the fuss with the people in the woods. He had 'Tut tutted', and almost as an aside said,

"Why would anyone do that?"

Maeve asked why he said that.

"Because they found the shoe at the time, it's not a mystery." He was very sure of himself.

"It wasn't mentioned because it wasn't important. It had got stuck, caught in some ivy, before the killer had approached the child, and it was just sitting there." He took a pause reflecting on painful images that he couldn't eradicate from his memory.

"It was the other child I felt sorry for. She lost everything that day. Of course she was the one who held onto the shoe.

It seemed she was convinced that, if only she could give it to her sister, it would make things right."

He shook his head, "Wouldn't be parted from it."

Maeve thanked him for his time, and being willing to talk about something he had put behind him for so long.

In turn John said, "You know, I feel better having spoken to you. I think you care. Most people don't. They are just looking for a good story, their mantra is 'never let the truth spoil a good story'." He nodded at the bitter truth of his own statement. As they were saying goodbye he almost shook hands with Maeve in a gesture of friendship and just stopped himself in time.

"Don't take this the wrong way, but I hope we don't meet again."

Maeve countered with,

"If we do, I'll be on holiday, and I promise not to mention, that we have already met." And with that she pulled her hand across her mouth as if closing a zip.

He smiled, and they parted.

Although sad to leave, Maeve had to return the car and catch her various trains; her anxiety over Adam and what she might find in Canterbury was mounting. Back on schedule with the extra twenty minutes she needed to make her calls for Adam. As she went up the hill, glimpsing the last of the town in her rear view mirror, she thought, I am sure I will be back.

She was looking out for the spot, Fiona had suggested, she could park, be private, and get a good phone signal. Once identified, Maeve pulled over, and got her phone out. Offices and hopefully the University were open by now. She didn't look at the app that Fiona had downloaded on her phone, time for that later.

CHAPTER 38

MOVING ON

Maeve knew this might be a tricky situation and didn't want anyone else to call her yoga friend. Doing yoga on Zoom had cut down all the before and after class chat, but Maeve had stayed in touch with Carla on WhatsApp, so that they could occasionally swap messages like 'was she trying to kill us?' Or 'who on earth loves 'downward dog'?' Now they had all got better at the practice, so it had morphed into, 'that was a good session' or 'I needed that stretch', which was less fun, but equally a good sign that they were making progress.

Maeve messaged Carla, 'have you got a minute to spare?' Luckily she hit Carla on a break. Maeve didn't have a job right now, she was furloughed. She might be financially tight but she pitied all those stuck all day in Zoom meetings, especially as at this very moment she was looking out over some beautiful countryside, under a completely clear blue sky.

Knowing Carla's time was precious, Maeve was as concise as possible and put a direct questions to her.

"Do you deal with post graduate students and their visas? If not, who does?"

Carla sighed, this wasn't going to be a quick fix, she needed to know more, "So what's the situation? Surely you don't have a visa problem? I am the 'International Programme Manager', so I do deal with foreign students, but I can't help if I don't understand what you are dealing with."

Maeve didn't really want to go into all of the details but it might be quicker if she did. So she explained that Adam, (everyone knew about Adam because he had been in the press, with his near death rescue), Adam, had two passports. He had entered the UK on his Greek passport, and now that seemed to be a problem.

"Ah, that makes sense. Otherwise, if he only had a Greek passport he would have applied for 'settled status', if he didn't do that then I can see there might be an issue." Looking at the time, Carla wanted to solve this quickly, "Okay, here's my suggestions. Get him to contact the Kent Union, which is the UKC student union, they have a visa department, they should help." Carla was irritated as she was processing the information. "This really shouldn't have happened, though, because the University has a Compliance Team who are very thorough. I'm sure they would have told him what to do."

Maeve was pretty sure that this was a minor error, a mistake on Adam's part. Maybe because he had a British passport he felt secure. Thinking of the lanky young man, Maeve knew he could be an 'airhead' so he probably didn't think when he got off the plane, and showed the first one that came to hand, when coming through passport control. Maeve didn't share her other theory, that maybe someone in the police station was being over zealous, she wasn't sure why someone might do this and didn't want to sound anti the police in general.

"Thinking through Adam's issue, and in reality I don't think it would be an issue...even if he did enter with his Greek passport. He would have applied to the University as a dual national, so there wouldn't have been any concerns from a Compliance perspective. The fact that he entered the country on a Greek passport would be of no real consequence, as he has British citizenship, so he wouldn't even need to apply for settled status. Even if he didn't have his British passport with him, he could leave without consequence, as the UK border system doesn't 'check' people leaving the country."

Carla was silent, clearly it was a massive error that would sort itself out and she didn't have the time to take on problems that weren't hers.

"He might have to leave and then come back in again. But don't quote me on that."

Maeve wasn't so sure, listening to Carla's reasoning she was more certain that someone in the station might have done this on purpose, but saying nothing, she thanked Carla. Relieved to have some suggestions, at least some positive steps that they could follow. She made a quick call to Marianne, who didn't answer, leaving a message to start the process of contacting the student union, and giving her Carla's other thoughts too. If the student's union was alerted to the issue, then at least Adam would have someone else watching out for him. Maeve switched off her phone and headed back to Inverness. Anxiety temporarily relieved, it was a lovely day for a drive.

~

Steve, was dealing with the fall out from the fiasco in the woods. Matthew was indeed ex military, he started out in the Princess of Wales's Royal Regiment in Canterbury, before transferring to Special Forces. He received honours for bravery in Iraq and Afghanistan, and had been invalided out of the army when a rocket propelled grenade hit the vehicle he was in. There had been media attention around the awards for bravery, which was unsurprising, the guy was a hero.

What pulled Steve up short, was the press clipping stating that Matthew had driven himself, at one hundred miles an hour, into a tree. Steve was amazed the man was still alive, but guessed that living out in the woods was his way of getting out of the limelight, while trying to figure things out.

With possible prosecutions for breaking COVID rules an option, the police were concerned they couldn't find a witness who would come forward and confirm that he had threatened to shoot them. All the people they had contacted, when pushed, said that they were further away 'social distancing' and heard someone else shouting it, and they had simply repeated it.

Matthew claimed that he shouted at the people below him to get them to stay on the paths and stop damaging the forest. He couldn't remember the exact words he used.

The police believed that he had shouted authoritative commands, possibly with something 'gun like' in his possession, frightening the onlookers, but with no confirmed witnesses, there were no charges.

Steve made a few calls to see if there was any way he could get Matthew some help, no joy. Catching Lives, would help if he wanted it for practicalities like food, shelter, washing facilities, but they couldn't help with the level of therapy he seemed to need.

Matthew wanted to get out of the station, he was marching up and back in the cell like a caged animal. He wanted everyone to piss off and leave him alone. He had his demons. He was dealing with them in his own way.

Within the force Steve had his own headaches. In every walk of life there are rivalries, creating different teams or tribes, in the workplace. In Steve's world these surfaced as petty acts to irritate, paperwork delayed, applications rejected, but sometimes, it could be more serious. Especially when a promotion was in the air. Whichever way you look at it, police men and women are people too, human with human strengths and very human frailties.

After the fuss over the drama in the Cathedral which had

given Steve's reputation a boost among the powers that be, the animosity between Steve and his colleague Tim Horton, had reached an all time high. Tim had not had an equivalent 'win', so, over time, this resentment had only got deeper.

A little while ago, Tim had been mouthing off about 'bleeding heart liberals' and how people had to take a stand; or saying 'things were better, with a bit of rough justice'. He had been feeling out colleagues who might hold the same views, be on his side, if he ever needed to call on that extra support, he was identifying those who might go 'above and beyond' to be in his tribe.

Since the Brexit debate, there has been a rise in racist activities everywhere, even during the pandemic. Most recently there was a far right march in Dover.

The protestors carried placards with 'We want our country back' as they sang Rule Britannia while they blocked the main route into the port, the A20, in both directions.

On the same day, in the centre of town in Market Square, there was a pro-migrant demonstration. All in all plenty of potential for some nasty confrontation.

The Kent Police were clear about their role, the Chief Superintendent was quoted as saying 'As a force, it is our responsibility to facilitate peaceful protests, however we will not tolerate violence or disorder.'

There were many who held the view that there were a lot of 'grifters' in the far right groups. Meaning that this wasn't primarily coming from the locals, rather Dover was acting as a lightning rod drawing protestors from all over the country as the centre of their attention. The presumed reason being the massive coverage in the media, with endless images of refugees in small boats.

On this particular occasion, the Kent police had over a hundred officers, a mounted unit, and a dozen police vehicles there on the day. They made nine arrests.

Internally, individuals held their own views. In the past,

following tip-offs, the force had more of a role in picking up asylum seekers, who were often dumped in service station car parks on the motorways out of Dover or Folkestone. They would take them to Dover to the screening centre. Since the new systems had come in, this was no longer a police priority. Cuts do that, they mean that priorities have to be set.

However, in the Canterbury station Inspector Tim Horton, had been really pissed off with the shenanigans in the woods, a complete waste of time and resources. He was keen to make sure everyone knew it was Steve's fault. Anything he could do to make matters worse for Steve, without harming his own police work, he was happy to do. Tim happened to be in charge of the team that picked Adam up. They had never officially met, but Tim knew exactly who Adam was, he also knew that Adam was a friend of Steve's, but he didn't share that fact with his colleagues.

Once Adam was in the station, Tim took over the interrogation, and decided this was a good opportunity to cause a bit of trouble. Calling over Constable Clive Richards, a like minded colleague, Tim winked at him as he said,

"This one might be an 'illegal'. Take him over to Border Force in Folkestone, they can deal with him." It was clear that this was not the normal process but it would be a waste of time for Adam, and certainly for Steve, when he found out.

"And bring 'Roge the doge' with you, you can drop him home when you're done."

Tim tipped his head towards Roger, a new Special Constable, who was very keen, but a bit clueless, so unlikely to pick up on anything out of the ordinary and who would appreciate a lift home. Also meaning 'Roge', wouldn't be in the station when Steve got back, so couldn't spill the beans by accident, but equally, official procedure had been followed. Tim smiled to himself, he liked it when a plan worked out.

Tim dealt directly with Adam,

"Well, well. This is a muddle." Feigning helpfulness.

"Your visa is a right problem." Holding Adam's passport in his hand, waving it around as if it would give him the answer, at the same time, making Adam more and more nervous.

"Here's what I think. Why don't we send you straight over to Border Force in Folkestone? They deal with all the visa issues now. And to speed things up Constable Richards here," indicating his colleague who was smiling in the knowledge of this shared joke. "He will take you straight over there."

Adam, not suspecting a thing, thanked him for the help.

When Steve got back to the station, Adam was already being processed as an asylum seeker under Home Office regulations, now out of police hands.

Tim set it up with a few red herrings, so no one had managed to get through to the University to confirm Adam's side of the story, before the end of the working day. So Folkestone handed him over to the accommodation unit for the night. He spent the night in Napier Barracks.

Steve recognised a set up. The "oops sorry" from Tim as he grinned adding, "of course I should have recognised his name. Wasn't he the bloke you, or your wacco ghost talking lady friend, saved in the nick of time?" Turning round to Clive with a wink, and back to Steve, "Sorry mate, my mistake."

Steve was so angry that he couldn't speak, he turned on his heel and headed over to Folkestone to see if he could rescue Adam. As he sped through the Kent countryside, on his motorbike Steve thought this was going to be another day wasted, which he unfairly put down to Maeve and her eccentric family.

CHAPTER 39
SORTING THINGS OUT

Once Marianne picked up the message from Maeve, she set to.

'Shit', thought Marianne, as she googled her way through their website. The Kent Union's emergency immigration advice was closed, only providing a link to the national UK Council for Immigration Affairs.

Marianne had prepared a blank sheet of paper, filling in what she knew about Adam. As soon as she started, she realised exactly what she didn't know. She didn't have any of Adam's official papers, his full address, or his student number. 'Not very promising' she said to herself, as she doodled on the sheet, drawing a string of hearts where the information should be. How could she even explain the situation properly? Never mind making sure that they would take her seriously and deal with him as a priority.

What did she know? She knew she liked Adam, that wouldn't help, and she knew that he was a PhD student in medieval archeology. For now, he didn't have a professor at the University to supervise his work. She knew the name of his old supervisor, but he was the one who had been taken into custody by the police, arrested for murder, and was not likely to be released. Biting the end of her pen, Marianne started over.

Meanwhile, Orla was telling Ada the news. Ada was desperate to help, showing how guilty she felt for causing the situation, she was wildly angry on Adam's part, "Sure isn't he more local than the people who come from here?"

Orla didn't quite follow, "Sorry? He's Greek, with an English father, not really local to Canterbury is he?"

"No, but you know what I mean, who else knows about the ancient water systems? That young man knows every stone in the Cathedral. I mean really!"

Ada was prone to exaggeration. Orla's aim was to make sure that Ada didn't make anything worse, didn't actually do anything at all. Orla got on well with Ada, but she was not at all confident that she could handle her. Deciding 'the less said the better' Orla was wrapping up the call, with a promise to keep Ada up to date with the news. As she was about to say goodbye Ada said almost to herself,

"They wouldn't have taken him down to Napier Barracks, would they?"

Once Ada had finished her call with Orla, and with no evidence at all, she convinced herself that they had taken Adam to the asylum seeker's holding site, at Napier Barracks. She wanted to take action. Ada was trying to be responsible but she was agitated and doing nothing wasn't an option. Thinking to herself, 'Ach, if I try to call, I'll never get through, or they'll keep me for hours hanging-on the phone', so she decided to go there and have a look. What harm would it do, if she went to have a look? It was only a twenty minute walk from Sandgate, up the hill away and from the shore, it would be a good walk for her daily exercise. Within minutes Ada was wrapped up, and had set off.

Steve arrived in Folkestone. The cross country motorbike ride under the archway of trees, now bare of leaves, had brought him back to when he first met Maeve. The roar of the bike, plus focusing on the bends in the road, shut out everyday thoughts, he felt music, the big rock guitar chords of Jimi Hendrix reflected his emotions. He was not calm.

Steve was parking his motorbike at Napier Barracks when he looked up, and saw Ada, making her way towards him wrapped up in a dramatic lime green coat, with a large bright red, floral Russian head scarf swept around her head and shoulders. Hardly discrete, thought Steve, but then she is probably trying to attract attention. He was still furious with Ada, if she hadn't started this ridiculous online nonsense, none of this would have happened. Ada saw Steve, and accosted him first with,

"Aha! If you're here, I was right, Adam must be here too!"

Steve knew that it was partly his fault. It was his colleague Tim, who was playing internal politics, who had caused this particular issue. This only added fuel to his ire. Anger building, he didn't even try to control himself,

"You are a selfish, self centred, self important woman." He was drawing breath to let rip, building up to a full on explosion, when Ada hooted with laughter.

The stress and anger in Steve had reached boiling point. He had turned bright red. He wanted to smash something.

"Is that the best you can do? Oh my gawd! You need to get out more."

Once Ada had started laughing, it triggered a release, she was now convulsed with laughter.

"I thought you fellas dealt with the rough side of life," almost hiccuping "haven't you got any better swear words than that?"

She had been feeling very guilty, but Steve, heading in for an attack before she had time to grovel her apology, absolved her.

Steve wanted to be angry, but at the same time there was nowhere for the anger to go. Looking at this little Irish woman, killing herself laughing, suddenly seemed ridiculous. Seemed funny. They say 'laughter is infectious', and without meaning to, he joined in. Like it was with Ada, it was a release for Steve, so he too started a deep belly laugh. The two of them looked at each other and started again. It was a good ten minutes before some semblance of calm returned.

"God Almighty, how did we get here?", Ada with tears still running down her face. "We are some pair." Trying to control her breath, Ada was talking in short bursts, "I never meant that to happen. You know, in the woods." Pause. "But what happened at your end to let Adam end up here?"

In a considerably better emotional state Steve began to see the two sides of the situation. "If only Adam......"

"...Hadn't been Adam?" Ada was laughing again, "He's such a nice boy, but he's not really with it, is he?"

Steve shrugged, smiling, and exasperated,

"Yes! Exactly." He didn't mean to agree with Ada but she was right, thinking of the well meaning, kind young man, Adam, he was far too trusting.

Ada sighed, she was now fully recovered.

"So what do we do now? I was ready for a fight. Do I need to go and make placards and 'man the barricades'?"

Steve gave himself a mental shake, back to the professional Steve, "Hopefully not." He could just see Ada on the barricades in Paris and it was an image that he did not want to see here.

"Right now it would be better if there was no fuss, no media. Ada, I mean that. No media. Understand?"

Ada was a little shamefaced, "I hear you. But you have to tell me what's going on, or I might have to do something….."

She was still a bit uncomfortable about all the trouble she had caused, but she was also aware of the pressure that the media can bring to bear on a situation. For now, she was a hot property, and that meant power. This time she had no intention of doing anything, until she fully understood the situation. If she caused a media storm it would be on purpose, not by accident. She could drum up a crowd if need be, and she knew it. She waited for Steve to explain.

"Look, I don't know the full extent of the situation yet. I know there have been a series of cock-ups." He looked up at Ada, she wasn't buying that these were errors, "Well, whatever the reason, it may be simple to resolve, or it may already have gone too far in the system." He looked at her again and added, "I may be able to do something. If, there is no outside pressure!"

He didn't trust her not to act impulsively, sighing at the idea that he was making a deal with Ada said,

"Give me an hour, if he's not out by then……well, then you do whatever you have to, but I don't want to know anything."

Ada nodded acceptance, "You'd better go in then. It's bloody freezing out here, so hurry up!"

She had a grim smile, it wasn't a threat, but it left Steve in no doubt that if he didn't find a solution, she would. Steve left her on the pavement, as he made his way to the central admin block.

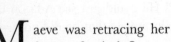

Maeve was retracing her journey in a very different frame of mind. It was only yesterday morning that she had set off thinking this was a romantic tryst, how wrong could she be. 'Steve really needs some help', she thought, and 'I don't think I am the right person to give it'. She was pretty sure that the biggest step for Steve was for him to admit that he wasn't in control and that he needed to act. His concerns over how it might affect his career were real, and probably valid, but she was equally sure that there were other routes he could take. Maeve appreciated how Steve had been there for her when she was dealing with Ada, now it was her turn, if she couldn't be the professional that he needed at least she could point him in the right direction.

Reflecting on the day, and all the events, she had discovered a fabulous hideaway with a like minded community, who already felt like old friends. Sitting on the train, she was still smiling at the insanity of going swimming in the sea, in winter. Maybe she should get Ada started on it, after all her house opened onto the shore. If it didn't kill her it would probably keep her heart going for years. She couldn't quite imagine Ada with neoprene extremities and a bobble hat, still the image made her laugh to herself

On the train, Maeve was enjoying the time to think things through. Fiona had returned the bag Maeve had used for indulgent food for the journey but had repacked it with fresh scones, butter pats, and homemade jam as a delicious surprise, which it was. Maeve had already picked up some good coffee at the train station in Inverness, and was enjoying laying out a spread for herself, as she went through the issues. The business with the shoe was confusing.

Maeve was coming to the conclusion that the only way to resolve this, would be to manage her way through the spirit world. She thought back to her experience in the river, how could she control that? The pull from the water spirit had taken her over completely. In all the fuss, the scrambling up the river bank, and the sorting out of wet clothes, she had buried her panic, her fear. Maeve wasn't good at sharing emotions so the others didn't know. If Steve hadn't been there, would she have drowned?

She needed to take another walk through the woods, maybe starting close to the river, to see what emerged. Was she ready to face her fear directly?

If she could address the water spirit first, it might work, but what if it pulled her into the water and she was alone?

CHAPTER 40

PROGRESS

M aeve arrived home late that night, feeling like she had just had a holiday. Tired from the travel, but she enjoyed the time to herself that she needed. Time to finish her book, time to think out the next steps.

Maeve re-lived their alcohol-fuelled late night bonding session, mulling over everything Fiona said. It started with Maeve's story about how at forty she was determined to take stock and not let life drift by. Fiona brought a fresh perspective, but first she had let Maeve talk herself out. This was when they had moved on to 'a wee drop of whisky' in your tea.

Fiona began in earnest with,

"I don't think you have given yourself a proper chance."

"What do you mean?"

"Well, you probably haven't taken a good hard look at yourself in some time, have you?"

If it hadn't been for the whisky Maeve would have shut the conversation down, it made her uncomfortable. But talking to a stranger can be liberating, add a warm fire, and a glass or two, and maybe this was the best time to open up. For whatever reason, Maeve did.

"You're right. I've spent the last ten years focusing on work, and money, to provide the best home I can for the girls." Maeve was reviewing it in her mind as she spoke. "It's been head down, and get on." She nodded to herself.

"So, I'm guessing that when you accidentally met up with Steve, it woke up feelings that you had ignored for a long time? And you were flattered that he found you attractive, am I right?"

Maeve nodded again, she didn't want to say anything out loud, and was glad that Fiona was doing the talking, because part of her felt that she had been a failure. Once she had parted ways with her ex, Pascal, she found that she liked having the children to herself and she didn't want to bring anyone else into the home. She had created an environment that worked for her, and was not prepared to risk it, or have to start all over again.

"I'm guessing again here, but maybe you didn't want to get back into the dating game?"

Fiona was right, again, Maeve had told herself that she was doing this for the children, but part of her knew she wasn't brave enough to face rejection, or be disappointed.

"Okay, so here's the radical part."

Maeve straightened up, radical was not a word she was easy with, but she wanted to find a future that worked for her, knowing that her children wouldn't be in the house for much longer. It was becoming time for her to act, or to decide to give up. Either way, she wanted it to be her choice, and sooner was better than later.

"I think you need more experience."

That didn't sound radical, nor a solution, so Maeve melted, a little underwhelmed.

"Ah, I can see, I am not making myself clear. What I mean is, it's time to start over, and go looking. Without any expectations."

Maeve was now frowning at her, "How?"

"As I said before, the world has moved on. The lonely hearts section of the Guardian, is not where it's at. Actually, it closed down over the summer."

Maeve was smiling, she hadn't even got to the point of considering the Guardian ads, and Fiona was telling her that it was already out of date.

"Stop thinking of this person as a partner for life. That makes everything far too serious, before you have had any fun." Fiona was really getting into her stride now.

"I'm going to tell you about a friend who lives in Copenhagen, Denmark. She was in the same quandary as you, and she spent a long time thinking about it, finally coming to a decision." Pausing, as Fiona warmed to her story. "She decided that she was trying to fit too much into one person, really she wanted not one man but three. One for sex, one for practical handyman jobs around the house, and one for company."

Maeve was smiling, this definitely wasn't her, but it was good to think differently.

"She went ahead and did it. This is a while ago now, so she put an ad in the paper and described the three roles, and said she would interview candidates, but beforehand they would have to choose the role that they wanted. And they couldn't change."

By now Maeve was laughing incredulously, "I don't believe you."

"It's true, she wrote a book about it, 'Three men, one woman.'"

"So how did it work out? Did she end up with three men in her life."

"No, actually, in the end it worked out differently. But, and this is the key point, she found herself. She regained her confidence. Understood her value, and stopped trying to be someone else, to please whoever she was with."

Maeve had stopped laughing and was now taking this

very seriously. It was true, at work she was confident, but in terms of personal relationships she had never even thought of herself like that. As far back as she could remember it was always about 'them' first. About making yourself as attractive as possible, so that 'they' would choose you. Not the other way around.

She looked at Fiona, eyes wide open, "Really? I don't think I could do that."

Now it was Fiona's turn to laugh, "I wasn't suggesting that you launch straight into her extreme version. I was thinking that there are a few steps to this." She put another log on the fire before going on.

"Step one. Do a make-over for yourself. Dress yourself in a way that you feel good, confident, sexy, strong, this is all about you. Try out any style that you like, until you are happy. No preconceived ideas of 'I'm too old for that'. Rubbish. Oh, and don't consider what anyone else might say, not your children, not your mother. This is the new you. Then take a photo."

Maeve started to look at Fiona in a different light, she was strong and confident.

"Next, decide what you want, and what you like doing. Don't think about them, just what you want, what you like. Write it down. This is step two, your new bio."

Mentally ticking off her list, Fiona finished with, "Step three, sign up to Tinder, or Bumble or Hinge, and get out and do it."

That's where they had left off the conversation.

On the train she had looked at what Fiona had put on her phone. It was the Tinder App. She had also sent Maeve an email with instructions. 'I thought you might lose courage so I have set up a profile for you, that way you have an idea, and I used a photo I took this morning. Have a look at the men who want to meet you already! Go for it, it will give you the confidence you need to decide if Steve is the right person or just the person right in front of you. PS - Tinder for confidence. You might prefer Bumble or Hinge, but have a look before you decide!'

As Maeve was reading, a text came through on her phone from Fiona, 'Be extreme. It's only by going to the edges, do we find out where the middle is.'

When Maeve opened the app, she was taken by surprise.

CHAPTER 41
BRAVING IT

The next morning over breakfast, they were all able to catch up.

A very relieved Adam was at the breakfast table, tucking into two perfectly poached eggs on toast.

Steve had acted as guarantor, or guardian, for Adam and the asylum seekers centre, had enough problems of their own so were delighted to get rid of him, handing him back to the police, (as far as they were concerned Steve was there in an official capacity), seemed reasonable.

Adam had been held in isolation, which turned out to be a good thing as it meant he hadn't come into direct contact with any COVID-19, so he didn't have to go into self isolation.

Marianne and Orla, were delighted to have both Maeve and Adam back. Talking over each other with blow by blow accounts.

Adam had arrived back long before Maeve, so had to a large extent recovered and was adding to the list of things that he was grateful to this family for. He credited Marianne and Orla, they had managed everything perfectly, along with Steve. Now the two young women were fussing over food, and refilling the big pot of plunger coffee, taking no offence as Maeve regaled them with descriptions of Fiona's breakfast feast.

Ada was having her own cup of coffee, appearing at the table, via the now familiar propped up iPad.

"Who'd have thought that you could cram that much food into twenty-four hours!", she wanted to move on to her part in Adam's rescue mission, so was getting sniffy.

"Wait till I tell you all about Steve."

That brought Maeve back down to earth. Steve, she would have to deal with him today, best hear Ada's side before catching up with him.

Of course in Ada's version nothing would have happened if she hadn't turned up and pressured Steve.

"Ada, tell me the truth, did you actually threaten him?" Maeve was cringing at the thought of having to apologise again for Ada's behaviour, it was clouding the real issue that she had to deal with.

"I suppose I didn't use the language of an actual threat. But he knew I meant it alright."

Ada was purse lipped, thinking that she wasn't getting the credit she thought she was due.

"And I'll tell you something else for free. I don't know if something is up with him, but that man has some anger management issues. Though he could do with some lessons in colourful language." Smiling to herself.

Maeve hadn't shared the full story.

"He's probably mad at you." She said quietly. This was tricky, Maeve knew that Ada didn't actually incite the mass gathering, but equally if she hadn't started down that path there would never have been any trouble.

Ada was becoming defensive, then she changed, something had occurred to her, "I don't think it's that at all." You could almost see the idea dawn on her face. "I think it's something completely different." Pointing at Maeve, "Remember when we had that trouble with the press and Anne?" Maeve nodded. "He wasn't a bit like this, that time, he was professional. This time he looked like a child having a tantrum." Ada looked at Maeve as her eyes narrowed, "Did you two have a bust up on the train?"

Maeve felt herself turning red, and fidgeting with crumbs on her plate. "Well..Not really," she managed to mumble, they hadn't actually shouted at each other and this wasn't a subject that she wanted a family discussion on. To change the subject Maeve took the lead,

"Actually, I haven't been in touch with Steve since I got back and I have news for him about the shoe."

Now, everyone around the table was paying attention. "Go on. What news?" They clamoured.

"Apparently there is no drama about the missing shoe. The other sister wouldn't be parted from it and it didn't form part of the evidence, so they let her have it." Maeve shrugged, aware that this was more of an absence of news. "Which means….." recapturing her audience, "which means, that it is likely that Kimberly is using it to communicate with us. It's important but not in the practical, physical evidence way that we thought before." Maeve was confident that she had moved the conversation on, but just in case, she added "which is why I have decided to go back to the woods on my own."

This time it was Adam who interrupted with a loud guffaw. "I don't think so."

Everyone turned to him, "Why not?"

"Oh, you really don't know."

He didn't like the attention and felt under pressure, so gabbled his way through the explanation,

"they have cordoned it all off. At least they were doing that yesterday and I doubt they will have opened it up already." Pouring himself more coffee to end his contribution.

Maeve sighed, "Well, that's another reason to talk to

Steve this morning." With a more businesslike demeanour, to chivvy them along, "Right, more toast, fresh coffee anyone?" Silence. "I guess that's a 'no'?" Gathering up the plates, "Time to start the day then."

Maeve decided to take her morning's exercise by walking into town and getting a takeaway coffee. There were a couple of new places, 'Fringe + Ginge', and one of those miniature trailers on the High Street in the style of an old french 2CV or 'deux chevaux', but where the side opened up revealing a full barista station. However, Maeve already knew she was heading for Fonds, she texted Steve and they had agreed to get their coffees at the same time. She had to face Steve.

This was going to be awkward, Maeve had spent time on the train thinking this over too. His behaviour was out of order, pretty unforgivable. She didn't like confrontations, but if she said nothing that meant it was okay to behave like that. On the other hand, they had been through some major dramas together. Letting go of her hurt, Maeve remembered that Steve had supported her as a friend, when she really needed it with no questions asked. It hadn't always been like that in terms of police business, but as a straightforward human being, he had been there for her. PTSD would have to be mentioned at some point, but right now, she knew that things were closing in on him and that he needed help. She would be supportive but distant, so was planning to make this meeting just business.

Maeve was a little early, so that she could get her coffee and wait outside. All tables and chairs had been removed as lockdown had been tightened. Maeve didn't think that easing up for Christmas was a good idea. Official plans were to allow family gatherings but that might change, in the family they had already had the discussion. Marianne and Orla said they wanted more Christmases with Ada in the future, so could manage this one without her. Ada was less sure, final decisions could wait a few weeks.

When he arrived, Maeve could see that Steve was not at ease. She smiled, saying,

"It's fine. We are fine. I want to tell you all about John Graydon, the 'Dog Walker'."

He visibly relaxed. "Go on in, and get your coffee, we can talk and walk."

The walked straight down Stour Street, past one side of RockPaperScissors and towards St Margaret's Church, then on round by Canterbury Castle. They ambled rather than walked, giving them enough time to talk.

Maeve retold her conversation, giving her opinion that she now wanted to try again to communicate with Kimberly, the child,

"I believe that she has been trying to give us a message that we haven't been able to understand. Just like her saying 'I want to be a good girl', really meant 'I need to go to the toilet'."

Steve was being measured, he was nodding, to show that he was listening more than that he agreed. "On your own?"

"Yes, I think so. I want to focus." She clenched her fist but didn't mention the courage this was going to take.

Adam was right. They had cordoned off the woods. They were now out of bounds for normal walkers, or people taking exercise. The police had decided that it was safer to close down access completely, until they were sure it was safe, and things had returned to normal.

In police world, Steve hadn't shared the whole background reason for the mass murder hunt, with his colleagues. If he had started talking about seances and TikTok, things would only get worse. So he hadn't said anything. Just that 'some mistaken information' had been put out on the internet and had gone viral, like those kitten videos, and now it was over. Steve was sure that Tim was still sniffing around to see what he could dig out, to use against Steve when the time was right.

"Alright, but this has to be managed. I will organise for you to enter the woods from the Fordwich end tomorrow morning. The official reason that you are going, is because you know Matthew and you are checking up on him, with the possibility of getting some additional information from him. Okay?"

"No pressure then. Not ideal. But fine. Yes, okay."

Nothing to do but wait.

CHAPTER 42
GOING ALONE

The next morning, early, Maeve had the conversation with Oral while Ada was on screen, telling them she was planning to go into the woods on her own. As far as Maeve was concerned this was her business, her choice and she didn't want to bring Orla into it right now. When the time came, Orla would have to face her own calling. Today, it was Maeve who needed to dig deep and find herself.

"What if you can't handle it? That last time, if Steve hadn't been there you might have drowned."

Ada wasn't pro this line of action, she was genuinely worried. Just as Maeve wanted to protect Orla, so she wanted to protect Maeve, but Ada couldn't. This left her feeling both helpless and useless.

Orla was more positive, almost aggressive, "Why can't I come too?"

Maeve smiled at both of them, she read the concern behind Ada's comments. Turning to Orla,

"I'd love you to be there, but I think I need to do one session on my own. Plus, I had enough trouble getting Steve to let me go past their barrier."

The three women looked at each other without speaking, holding a steady gaze full of understanding.

Ada broke the silence,

"Well then, we need a plan. If you enter the woods by Fordwich have Orla, and Marianne, waiting for you at the other end by the youth centre. Let's give you an hour, then if you don't show, Orla can go looking for you and Marianne can raise the alarm."

"Wow, Ada, that's a really practical plan." Orla was impressed that Ada could be so 'real world'.

Maeve was amused, "I think Steve will be waiting at that end too. So I'll be in good hands."

Ada snorted, "Well, you will with Orla and Marianne there, Steve's a bit moody for my liking."

The atmosphere was serious.

Marianne stuck her head round the door, "It's almost time, so I'm off to put on some warm clothes."

Marianne was the designated driver this morning, reflecting on all the previous adventures that Maeve and Orla had on that walk, she had prepared the car. The boot was now full of extra towels, blankets, and she had even found a length of rope, just in case. Plus a bag with the obligatory flask of coffee, she had added a packet of biscuits, enough for her and Orla, to have some while waiting, and a separate serving specially for Maeve.

Upstairs, while she was getting ready, Maeve took a moment to prepare herself, both mentally and physically. Wrapping up in warm old clothes she kept coming back to what she hadn't done. She hadn't told the others about her Tinder profile, she knew this was her problem, she was embarrassed. She just had to get over herself, but not today, as soon as she was ready.

The surprise when she had opened up the app and had a look was twofold, the obvious was that despite Fiona's pretty flimsy bio for her, and photo taken that morning as she was laughing over breakfast, there were a number of handsome, interesting men waiting. The real shock was that one of them was Matthew.

Maeve knew that she should talk to Steve about it, but at the moment that was definitely a step too far. She would have to explain why she was on a dating app at all, which sounded like she was cheating on Steve, before they had even had a chance to try a relationship. He had his own issues at the moment.

She had other things to deal with, the principal one being the water spirit. When Maeve had inadvertently 'tuned in' to the gory event in Butcherly Lane it had really shaken her. The water spirit dragging her down in the water, was both calm and potentially deadly. If the Scottish message was right, then she might, or should, be able to control the spirit. Sometimes things sound easy, but doing them is hard.

What did she actually need to do? Was she strong enough to do whatever was needed?

She was about to find out.

Steve had agreed to meet them in the pub car park, and get Maeve through the cordon. He wasn't confident, but he didn't want Maeve to feel that he didn't trust her.

He took Marianne aside and said,

"You take Orla and drive round to the youth centre, I'll meet you there. But I'll hang around this end, till she has made it safely to the edge of the woods." And he indicated that this was just between them. Orla understood.

There was one officer on duty, the police presence was being downgraded as the interest in the area diminished. Should there be any trouble, he was in radio contact with his colleague stationed at the other car parking area, by the youth centre, only minutes away by car. The blue and white tape marked 'police, do not cross' was stretching across the gateway between the car park and the ramblers path. The stile to the left of the gateway was also cordoned off.

Steve spoke to Maeve before she moved off,

"Are you sure about this?"

Maeve nodded, she wanted to get going and keep herself in the zone, mentally prepared; she didn't welcome the conversation.

Steve wasn't letting up,

"Do you have your phone with you? Just in case, you know that I can get to most places in there" pointing across the field to the woods "..on my bike, in minutes."

Maeve tapped her pocket to indicate that she had her blackberry with her.

"Okay, let's go." Steve escorted her past his colleague.

Maeve didn't head straight down to the riverbank where she had that disturbing encounter with the water spirit. She was pretty sure that Steve would be waiting to see that she was okay and she didn't want to feel watched. And anyway the policeman was on duty, and the sense of someone else being there, would pull her in two directions. She changed her plan to head for the reed lake in the middle of the woods where she would be completely alone.

Steve stayed until Maeve had crossed the meadow and disappeared into the woodland. Before moving off Steve turned back to the speak to the officer on duty,

"Are we one hundred percent sure that the suspect has returned to the woods?"

They still thought of Matthew as a 'person of interest', it was easier to call him a 'suspect'.

"Well Guv, I didn't see him arriving, but then I imagine if he didn't want us to see him, then we wouldn't. He did say he was 'going home' when he left the station."

"Thanks Dave, if you see or hear anything, I'll be waiting at the other car park." Steve said as he strapped on his helmet, and left.

As soon as Maeve entered the shelter of the wood proper, she saw the devastation caused by the mass exodus. The trees were fine, but the ground was destroyed, it had been turned into a sea of mud and was now struggling to dry out. You could just make out the bits of path that had once had a hard surface. But the multiple tracks crisscrossing between the trees, from the off road bikes, or other possible animal tracks had all disappeared, melding into a new homogenous surface of mud and debris.

There were signs where people had been pushing, shoving, slipping and sliding and had gouged new tracks. There were points where the drama was obvious, one where they had been funnelled into a narrower, deeper section round a fallen willow tree and another where you could see they had been taken by surprise by a waterlogged ditch, and there was more than one wellie left behind.

Taking a moment, to orientate herself by the trees she could recognise along with the shapes of the ridges and hollows of the terrain, Maeve moved on, heading in the direction she hoped would lead to the reed pond.

It must have been insane, she thought, and pretty frightening, to have been caught up in the mad dash of people who thought they were fleeing for their life.

This wasn't how she had planned her trip this morning, and she was having difficulty focusing on her own priorities as each new change in the landscape presented itself.

However, she managed to settle once on the hard track, passing under the giant buzzing power cables, with the row of large poplar trees to her right, it felt more familiar. Soon she was striding with confidence, happy to be out in nature, albeit an altered nature. Coming back under the canopy of branches, down towards the pond, bringing her mind into focus, she moved too quickly and slipped.

Recovering her balance, a voice that was unpleasantly familiar, whispered in her ear, sending shivers down her spine.

CHAPTER 43

THINGS ARE NOT WHAT
THEY SEEM

Maeve couldn't move out of the way, her foot was stuck in the mud, he was uncomfortably close and she felt the smell from his rotten teeth as he spoke.

"I knew you'd come back."

His tone was slimy, but also indicating that he was talking from a position of power. She was on his turf.

"I was waiting for you. Bring me food, did ye?" Thomas didn't step back, he was enjoying the proximity.

He had taken Maeve completely by surprise, she thought she had seen the end of him, so he definitely wasn't in her plan. Racking her brain for ideas, anything to distract him and get him further away from her, was her immediate desire.

"So you didn't come over to see Edward did you? I bet you can't move from here, can you?" Maeve said, pointing a finger towards him, as if accusing him of something. "Something keeps you anchored here, doesn't it?"

For a moment it worked, he backed away seemingly having lost his edge, and shrugged, "So? I can wait. You come to me didn't you?"

Maeve was desperately trying to think. She was very close to the pond, would the water spirit be any help, or would it overwhelm her. Was he connected to the water? Was there some link? He had been close to the water every time they met. Had she been seeing this the wrong way around? Did he have some information for her, maybe from the water spirit, if so, how should she get it?

Maeve remembered something Ada had told her, plus, what the woman in Cromarty had said. She needed to take control and she could demand an answer, demand information.

Speaking with a level of confidence that she didn't feel,

"I am not here for you. I am here for the child. What do you know about it? Do *you* have something to tell *me*?" Pointing at him again, Maeve was almost shouting. It gave her courage.

He wasn't happy with her questions.

"I know's there's bad people round here." He tapped his nose indicating that this was insider knowledge, "I seen things. Maybe I have something to tell ye", leaning in towards her. "You take care, or you'll end up like the others." As he drew his finger across his throat, like a knife, indicating 'dead'.

But as she watched him. he seemed to merge with the woodland and was gone. This gave Maeve confidence, the control had worked. The message however was not pleasant. Was he referring to the spirit world or the real world? Time to find out.

Before she could lose her self confidence, she took the last few steps down towards the reed pond. It wasn't appetising. There was a green scum growing on the surface. Maeve moved around the edge, away from the bulrushes towards the clearer water. She could see some reeds swaying under the surface and felt a strong desire to touch them. She had heard of people who are afraid of heights because when they get close to the edge they want to jump. It was like that. She wanted to get into the water, but this time she was prepared.

Maeve let herself go, "Nooooooo!" Bellowing with all she had, another full bodied roar. "Nooooooo!". Silence.

She breathed in, puffing her chest out and leaning back. The desire to throw herself into the water receded. She felt strong. Confident.

Moving backwards, Maeve didn't shift her feet quickly enough, landing on her backside sitting in the mud. She sat there smiling.

A hand reached out, she looked up, it was Matthew.

"Again!" Matthew was laughing. "I heard a voice shouting and thought it was more of those awful people."

Having pulled her up, he had run his hand through his hair with a Hugh Grant kind of mannerism, and went on.

"I'm so glad it's not them, and it is you." He had a charismatic one sided smile, that made you think spending time with him would be a pleasure. He looked away,

"I'm sorry I shouted the other day. I have some dark days." When he looked back, he had a pleading look, like a puppy, wanting forgivenesses for having made a mess where they shouldn't have.

"And I'm so glad it's you." Matthew was easy to forgive, for a moment she forgot that Matthew was a suspect, that his moods could flip in an instant.

Maeve remembered that the others were waiting for her in the car park, so having regained her balance, she started to walk as they talked.

"So tell me all about it, what really happened?"

Matthew moved beside her. They went on back into the woods proper. Some of the trails of ivy that hung down from the trees were still there, but most had been pulled off, or were much shorter, and dragged into the mud creating a mesh of debris to walk on.

"It all started pretty early, it's a time of day that I often get about thirty minutes of deep sleep, when night is over but the day hasn't properly started." He was moving around

Maeve as they made their way, clearing any major obstacles out of her path. Ready to catch her if she slipped again.

"Then I heard a wave of noise. People were shouting out to each other, shrieking, squealing." He shrugged with his hands out gesturing 'what was I supposed to do?'.

"It was a shock. I reacted in my own way." He looked down at his feet. "Training and brainwashing are more alike than people think." Now looking up at Maeve to see if she understood.

"I shouted a warning, to get them to move back. I needed time to assess the situation."

Maeve asked the one question that she really didn't want to hear the answer to, "Did you have a gun?"

Matthew looked down at the ground, weighing up his answer. Turning back to Maeve, he tipped his head to one side and looked at her, "what do you think?"

Maeve was afraid of the answer,

"I don't think you are the sort of man to make idle threats."

His face was no longer animated, it was cold, professional, he answered. "Correct."

Maeve felt her body go cold. The confidence she had gained in the spirit world, evaporated. Here she was in the middle of an isolated wood with a trained killer, who could suddenly have an 'episode' and mistake her for the enemy. Was this what Thomas was warning her about? This line of thinking was not destined to make her feel at ease. Taking a breath, she decided to lighten the mood. Keep it light and avoid anything that might be a trigger.

"So how did you get back into the woods, I saw police stopping people."

He laughed, clearly assessing that Maeve had accepted that he was armed and that she had not panicked, good.

"I wouldn't be much good at undercover ops if I couldn't

slip past them." He had picked up a stick and was using it to flick any small debris left in their way.

"Anyway the telecoms guys have been around today, and no one is paying any attention to them." He snorted with derision,

"The police are just out there to stop stupid 'Lookie-Loos' coming to see where it all happened. They are not after me."

As Matthew seemed normal, Maeve wanted to know how dangerous the situation was, "Do you want to talk about it?"

His head whipped round, "What do you mean?"

"You are here for a reason, I'm guessing that something bad happened. Do you want to talk about it?"

His mannerisms changed, the movements with the stick in his hand became fidgety, on edge.

Maeve recognised the signs of stress and anxiety so channeling Saskia, her yoga teacher, said,

"Take a slow, deep breath, full inhale and slow exhale."

Matthew didn't react, but Maeve could see the movements becoming less jerky.

"Taste the air you breathe in, cool. Fill up your belly, your chest right up to the top, and gently, slowly let it out, noticing the warmth as you exhale." She could see that he was calming down.

"That's it, notice your breath, slowly in, full deep breath, and gently, slowly exhale." The hand holding the stick was now still. "Let the breath return to normal, listen to the sounds, the birds, the gentle wind in the branches."

And he was back, like waking up from a nap.

Happy that the breathing exercises had worked for the moment, Maeve was frustrated that she didn't know more about how to handle the situation. She had seen that he was really on the edge. But what triggered it, and how would she know if he had gone too far. She needed to know more.

"That was good. That's why I like to be in the open air. I can breathe." He was smiling. "Okay, I'm going to say this quickly, don't ask questions." Following Maeve's previous guidance he took a deep breath before starting, "In Afghanistan, I was on a week long training mission off base, we were doing the training. It should have been fine but it wasn't. We were attacked."

He paused to get his breathing back to normal, "It had been my turn to kip, so I was in a deep sleep. Noise, general commotion, and high pitched female shouting woke me." Another pause to lower his heartbeat. "The Taliban were using some local women as human shields in front of them." He stopped here. He wasn't ready to say any more, he had said enough for now. His breathing was short and shallow again.

Maeve immediately started, "Breathe in slowly, fill your belly, chest, right up to the back of your throat, hold it, slowly let it out." After a few more breaths he was calm.

CHAPTER 44

GETTING INTO MORE TROUBLE

They looked at each other. "That was good, you really helped." Matthew was impressed, "I didn't think it could work like that."

Maeve smiled, "we were lucky." They had moved further through the woods, and Maeve was wondering if she could get him to talk to Steve. Maybe not yet, she didn't want to betray Matthew's trust in her. She changed the subject.

"So, what's with Tinder…? That's not very undercover.."

Now he was right back in the present, and looked sheepish,

"Actually it is. I train to keep myself in shape out of habit. It's not just physical training, so I decided to check you out. Practice. Dating apps are revealing, a good source of intel. Use an untraceable IP address and..." He shifted hopping from foot to foot avoiding the worst patches on the ground, "Anyway, to cut a long story short, I found you, … " Head down, eyes glancing up at Maeve, checking her reaction. "And it was nice, you are nice, so I swiped right."

Maeve's turn to look embarrassed, "I'm not really there," which sounded pathetic even to Maeve, so she launched into,

"A friend posted my details…I," she paused not sure what she wanted, or what she wanted to reveal,

"..I haven't decided yet." She didn't dare look up, his physicality disturbed her.

They had been walking on a slight incline steadily upwards, the floor of the woods here was normally leaf mould in between ground ivy, mixed with twigs and light windfall branches. Now, all of that was mushed together with the mud, so they were picking their way carefully, aiming for the driest patches, like stepping stones. Although the trees were bare of leaves, there was no uninterrupted vista. The clinging ivy bushed out, and the random spread of the trees, meant that it was easy to see for fifteen or twenty feet, but any further was only by making an effort and peering through gaps in the trees.

As a result, they were taken by surprise by a woman shouting. At first it wasn't clear where it was coming from, or what she was saying, but it spooked Matthew.

Just what we don't need, thought Maeve as she made her way ahead, to see if she could make the woman stop the noise. As she got closer, Maeve saw that it was the same woman that she had seen, in what seemed like an age ago, near where she had found the body. And thinking about it, she was the same woman who was nearby when Maeve and Orla had seen the child. She wasn't sitting on the fallen tree trunk this time, she was standing waving, and getting louder.

"Get away from me!" She shouted, apparently addressing Matthew. She was waving a large walking stick up over her head, like a distress signal. Her voice was loud and turning into panicked shrieks "Get away. Don't come any closer. I will scream."

Then she did. A piercing high pitched scream.

Maeve turned back to see if Matthew was okay. He wasn't.

He moved his hands behind him, in a second he was holding a gun between both hands, pointing at the screaming woman. Maeve knew he was in a different place right now, his body posture had changed. He was standing, back straight, arms stretched in front, both hands holding the gun steady. He was working on autopilot and he was very capable of pulling the trigger, she didn't have much time to think.

Maeve realised that she didn't know how to address him officially, he was clearly back in Afghanistan or wherever, but not here.

Using as much force as she could, in as deep a voice as she could manage, "Stand down soldier." Matthew lowered his hands so that the gun was now pointing at the ground.

Avoiding anything that might be close to a female shout, she barked at Matthew,

"Innocent bystander. Don't shoot."

Maeve was using any military terms she could remember from the movies, to stop him actually firing the gun. She had no idea if it made any sense, but it seemed to be having some effect.

She needed to get him away from this woman. Then she could deal with the woman. So far, the woman had stayed silent.

This time in an urgent conversational tone, "We need reinforcements."

Trying to get him to focus on her, "Matthew, I need you calm, go down to the Youth Centre, help is there." She was trying to send him towards Steve, who she hoped would know how to handle him.

Matthew still held the lowered gun. He began to walk backwards. When he had put some distance between them, he turned, put the gun away and started jogging in the right direction.

Maeve was shaking, now to deal with the other issue, what was wrong with this person?

As Matthew moved further away, the woman's shouting resumed this time at a lowered volume. His very presence did seem to be the cause of her problem.

After a little while she sounded like she was talking to herself but out loud. "You get away, I know you. Get away, or else." She carried on repeating herself.

Maeve got her phone out to warn Steve that Matthew was heading his way and armed.

"Shit, and double shit." No signal. The telecom guys must have done something. There was absolutely no signal. Maeve sent a text on the basis that if any signal drifted by then he would get it. As soon as she had pressed send, she became conscious that her legs had turned to jelly.

Recovering from the adrenaline high, Maeve was also furious with this woman who set Matthew off. Especially now she knew why female high pitched shrieks were a critical trigger for Matthew.

The woman had retreated to the fallen tree trunk, and wiped a spot beside her indicating that Maeve should sit there.

As she began walking towards the woman, Maeve became aware of someone else.

The child spirit, Kimberly, was standing just behind her, almost trying to catch on to Maeve's coat to get her attention. Maeve moved round to face her and squatted down to be at the same level. Gently she asked, "What do you want, Kimberly?"

The child was pointing down to her dirty sock, the foot where the shoe was missing, "My shoe."

Maeve was thinking, not right now, but she managed to smile at her, "Yes, I know, you lost your shoe. But you are a good girl. Everyone knows what a good girl you are. And they found your shoe."

Kimberly was shaking her head, indicating that Maeve had misunderstood. She pointed to her sock and then she raised her hand and pointed straight at the woman sitting on the log, insistent, almost shouting "My shoe!"

CHAPTER 45

HELP

As a reason for turning away and squatting down like that, Maeve pretended to fix the laces on her walking boots.

She needn't have bothered, when Maeve looked at the woman, she wasn't paying any attention; she was rocking herself backwards and forwards, mumbling something Maeve couldn't quite catch. Every so often, she would pat the wood beside her, as if to say 'sit here, it's nice and dry'.

Maeve turned her full attention to the woman now. She looked about thirty-five or forty. From previous encounters Maeve recognised the platform boots and the dyed hair. Nothing gave her any clues as to the state of her mental health. She had an open, parka style jacket, with a fake fur trim around the hood. She was overweight, heavy, with skinny legs, mushroom shaped. She needed a walking stick, so probably some health issue. Otherwise she looked like any number of people Maeve had come across walking the woods.

Maeve made her way over to the fallen tree, thinking, 'what is the connection between Kimberly and this woman?'

'Nothing for it', Maeve decided, 'I will just have to wing it and see what I can find out.' The closer she got the clearer she could hear everything, it was like a stream of consciousness.

"Get away, get away, he has no business here." Her voice was alternating between shouting and almost whispering, "I have a right to be here, I have business here."

Then looking at Maeve her voice changed, now she had a child's voice, "Lady sit here."

It was very disconcerting. Maeve wasn't sure if she was pretending, or changing personalities, either way this was not a normal situation. Maeve was struggling to keep her mind in the present, she was going to have to concentrate if she was going to get any sense out of this woman. She took a moment, suppressing any thoughts about what had just happened and bringing herself to right now.

"You like coming here?" Maeve started with something she hoped was a neutral phrase which didn't really need an answer.

The woman nodded, and then sucked her lower lip, like a child who is a little shy.

"You come here often." The woman nodded again. Maeve noticed that she had one hand in a fist, which she was clenching and unclenching. A sign that she was not yet comfortable.

Maeve tried again, "I like to walk in these woods." Keeping fairly neutral for the moment.

The reaction was more animated than Maeve was expecting.

"Don't go on your own! There is a bad man in the woods." She exclaimed, banging her stick on the ground like a staff. "I am okay, but you don't know anything."

Maeve didn't want to look directly at her, so looked at her walking stick properly, for the first time. It was a beautiful smooth dark wood, and the top was silver, but not the normal round knob, it was shaped to fit the heel of her palm, with a perfect indent. She must have some issue with her hand, this was specially made to support her weight.

Funny, Maeve thought, when you looked at it quickly it looked like an upside down golf club. That thought, rang some distant bell in Maeve's head, she couldn't quite catch the fleeting significance.

"You are okay now. I come to make it okay." The woman sounded calm now. And If she thought men were bad news, it explained why she reacted to Matthew.

Turning to look at Maeve, she still had the movements of a child,

"I've seen you before." She seemed to be weighing something in her mind before speaking. "You found the man."

She was swinging her stick, again like a child playing with a new toy. She was holding it upside down, using the handle to flick the few leaves nearby that were lying on the surface.

Maeve looked at her puzzled, "The man.....?"

As Maeve spoke, the thought clarified in her head, that's where a golf club had been mentioned. When they did the autopsy on the body Maeve had found, someone made the remark that, it was as if he had been hit by a golf club on the back of his head. Or something like a golf club.

"Yes, yes!" The childish voice was adamant.

As the penny dropped, Maeve realised that she was absolutely alone in the woods, this time with the person who was possibly the real killer.

In that instant, time slowed down, she could hear every sound separated out. The light breeze through some branches, a robin trilling his heart out, the rustle and jump of a squirrel. No other sounds. No traffic. No sound of the occasional train. No twigs cracking. She was rooted to the spot, her legs wouldn't move.

Thoughts were racing through her head now. 'Humour this woman' was at the front of her mind. Should she pull her phone out of her pocket to see if it was working? She didn't want to provoke her. On balance better not. Maeve tried to pocket dial Steve.

"Did you see him too?" Maeve asked.

"Yes, I helped him." She sighed as though it was a lot of work, "I have to keep the woods safe. Safe for children." Still like a child sorting the logic of the situation. "Bad people in the woods. They hurt people."

Maeve's mind was running through random thoughts. Kimberly's murder took place about twenty-five years ago, this woman might have been around ten years old then.

What was the linking factor? Aware that her heart was thumping, Maeve began doing her own breathing exercise. As she slowed down, counting through her inhale, and exhale, her mind opened to a new idea. Could this be Kimberly's sister? It was a risk, but Maeve needed to know.

"I bet you have a pretty name, is it Jessica?"

The woman's hand involuntarily reached up and clutched the 'J' hanging from her necklace,

"How do you know my name?" Her voice had a note of panic. A child caught doing something wrong.

"I don't, it was just a guess. You look nice, a good girl, like a 'Jessica'."

"No, no, no. You don't know me!" She was sounding more agitated, verging on angry.

She stood up. "What's that?" She was pointing to the spot where Matthew had been standing. "Is that man coming back?"

Maeve got up to take a step in that direction, "No, I.." Then she began turning back towards Jessica, just in time to see the glint on the silver before it hit.

The force of the blow knocked Maeve flat out on the ground. Jessica was a lot stronger than she looked.

Maeve opened her eyes in time to see the next blow coming, she rolled over on her front in time to hear the thud, as it hit the earth. Maeve was disorientated, warm blood was streaming down her face into her eyes. Pulling herself up on her hands and knees as quickly as she could she didn't know which was the right direction to move to get away.

Trying to move, staggering like she was paralytically drunk, disconnected sounds were coming at her, some close, some far away. She could hear spirits, they were crowding in on her.

She wanted to stop the world from spinning, it was making her feel ill. Maeve's one solid thought was to avoid another blow.

She made out one spirit standing in front of her. Weakly she called out,

"Jessica!" Panting, "Don't you want to talk to your sister?"

Her voice now getting stronger, "Jessica. Kimberly is here. She's here and she wants to talk to you."

It was like someone had poured cold water over Jessica's head.

CHAPTER 46

SAVING THE DAY

Still in shock, Maeve caught her breath, thinking, this woman is going to kill me. What am I doing here? Why can't I just, run? She was almost squatting with her hands on her knees, as she looked down, Maeve saw blood dripping onto her hands, which must be from her own head.

Now she heard Kimberly, beside her, shouting "I want to be a good girl!"

Through the blur, Maeve suddenly got it, "You want to be a good girl, you want to stop Jessica?"

"Yes!" The child jumped up and down, "Yes, yes, yes!"

Keeping her distance, Maeve called out,

"Jessica."

Jessica had moved back to the tree trunk and was sitting up straight now like a child in school waiting for a story.

"Kimberly wants her shoe back." It was difficult, but slowly Maeve was piecing things together. "She's waiting for you.

"And I spoke to your mother, who said what a good girl you were that day."

Jessica spoke,

"Kimberly didn't come quick, because she couldn't get her shoe."

Exhausted, Maeve tried to nod, but her head hurt too much.

"Yes."

Then as if reassuring herself Jessica said. "I got it for her."

Maeve hadn't noticed that she had a bag, dumped on the ground. Jessica leaned down, opened it and took out Kimberly's shoe.

Kimberly had gone over to Jessica, and was now sitting beside her, seeming to pat her on the back as if to comfort her big sister.

"She knows you did that for her. And now she wants you to stop. She is safe, and you are safe, so no need for you to help anymore, in the woods." Maeve was about to ask Kimberly what else she wanted to say, when she heard noises behind her.

Jessica switched personalities, and had become the woman again. She had pulled herself together, seemed taller and slimmer. Just another walker out for exercise in the woods. Looking down at her muddy clothes, Jessica remarked,

"I never even noticed that. This mud is everywhere. It'll soon dry out though."

Maeve was struggling and couldn't believe her ears, "Who are you?"

Jessica replied "Jay" as she turned round to face Maeve,

"Oh my God, what happened to you?" The look of shock on her face was real. "We have to get you some help."

Struggling to get up, the shoe fell unnoticed to the ground. This Jessica, needed the walking stick for support to move.

Maeve was about to answer when she heard a friendly voice behind her.

It was Steve, as Maeve turned towards him, she briefly heard, "Ooooh! That's going to hurt." She fainted.

Coming round seconds later, she found herself awkwardly in Steve's arms, as he was on his phone giving the ambulance directions.

Marianne and Orla, had been given instructions to wait, so they gave Steve a few minutes head start, before following him, as Orla said, "what would he do if she needs help dealing with the other side?"

Arriving, they both chorused "Oh My God! Mum! What happened to you?"

Maeve looked a sight. The head wound wasn't that serious, but the blood had run down half of her face, so she looked like someone out of 'Carrie' the movie.

Maeve needed to sit down, she was sure she didn't need an ambulance, she reacted with the automatic

"I'm fine, don't worry about me."

It didn't wash, Steve was his professional self,

"You need to get checked out. Frankly that's a lot quicker if you arrive in an ambulance." There was no argument.

Trying to tell Maeve what had happened Steve added, "By the way you didn't manage to send me a text, but you did pocket dial me, so I heard most of what happened."

Between them, they got Maeve over to the fallen tree trunk, and Marianne and Orla each took a side in case she fainted again.

Steve turned to Jessica, or 'Jay' as she called herself now. In a calm and friendly manner he asked her what she knew.

"I often sit here. And my mind drifts, you know." Nodding while looking from face to face, seeking confirmation that others did this too.

"It's so peaceful." She spoke slowly, taking her time, she didn't seem phased by Maeve's bloody appearance. More like she was emerging from a trance.

"The birds sing. Sometimes, people go by. I don't pay

them much attention." Now she was trying to work it out herself. "Sometimes, it's like, I wake up after a sleep." Then she looked down at her clothes,

"Like today, I don't remember falling or getting dirty, but look." She gestured at her trousers and hands. "I don't know how this poor woman hurt herself, I didn't see anything till just before you got here."

It was all Steve needed to know for now. "Thank you for that." Steve's voice suggested that he believed her.

"However a crime has been committed. As soon as the ambulance arrives and the injured party is taken care of, I suggest that you come with me to the station. A statement from you will be needed. Best to do it now, right?" Steve was firm and positive.

"Of course. I can't imagine that I can help. How did that happen? It looks terrible." Jay pointed at Maeve's head.

Steve called for a police car to come and pick them up. He also took Jessica's walking stick holding it discreetly in the middle with a paper tissue. He could still see some blood on the handle as he looked closely.

Maeve was having difficulty grasping that Jessica really didn't know that she had done it. Steve caught Maeve's eye and winked, to indicate that he knew Jessica had, even if she couldn't remember it herself.

The ambulance arrived just before the police car. Marianne and Orla took Maeve, one each side. Steve supported Jessica, because he was holding onto the stick, so what looked like a gesture of kindness tucking her arm under his was also a firm grip.

Before they all parted ways, Steve said, "I'll come over for an update at say, seven or seven thirty this evening. I'll bring food."

Orla stayed with Maeve in the ambulance, while Marianne went round to pick up the car and meet them at the hospital.

Maeve felt a bit of a sham, but the paramedic warned her about concussion and said

"That needs a proper clean out and some steri-strips. I don't think you'll be up for stitches on this one. And you were only out for a few seconds so they probably won't keep you in overnight. Lucky escape that one."

Maeve thought, 'you have no idea just how lucky!'

Once they were on their own, Orla said, "I saw Kimberly there too. She seemed happy. She was skipping around Jessica."

Maeve was lying down holding a cold compress on her head, "Yes, I saw her before I fainted. I am not sure what else we are supposed to do, but I'd like to know what's going on with Jessica. I don't think we are finished with her yet."

CHAPTER 47

FISH AND CHIPS

As good as his word, Steve arrived just after seven o'clock. Like a Deliveroo driver he had come straight from Marino's at St Dunstan's, which in his view was the best chipper in Canterbury, there may be those who disagree, but best not say so to Steve. Freshly cooked, smelling of salt and vinegar, he had personally watched them dip the fish in batter. No fish came out of the freezer here!

Maeve had a dramatic bandage across her forehead but was in good form, the table was set, chilled beers at the ready and Ada was on screen.

Ada had been fussing over Maeve at a distance, wringing her hands, "If it wasn't for this bloody lockdown I'd have been there."

Maeve was too tired to argue.

Orla piped up, "Of course it would have been great to have you there too, Kimberly wasn't talking and Jessica has other problems. Plus, you are still not talking to spirits, are you?" Deathly silence, no one knew where to look.

Ada sniffed, took a look at Maeve's white, bandaged head, and softened,

"I suppose you're right. Still, I could have pushed her over, I'm not as weak as I look!"

The others smiled, tension relieved, just as Steve's motorbike could be heard roaring up to the hill. The neighbours wouldn't love that

Steve's arrival was welcomed with the normal kerfuffle of people changing places, getting in each other's way, at the same time all of them wanting to hear the news. The aroma of fresh fish and chips, tinged with vinegar, filled the room. Everyone remembered that they were hungry. Orla brought in the quorn 'chicken' goujons for the vegans. As she heaped her plate with the tempting chips, Ada was watching

"Go easy girl, you'll be fat as a pig after all that! Anyway, have you never heard of FHB?"

"Ada!" They shouted in unison.

"Well," a clearly miffed Ada replied, "I'm like Orla, a plain speaker, not good at all this pussyfooting around."

She was making faces and with air quotes she added in a terrible mock American accent, "oops, a'sensitivity infraction', whatever that really means"

They had agreed to eat first, share news over pudding and coffee. By now everyone had been served and a silence of contented eating and drinking was descending on the group, when Adam asked,

"What does FHB mean?"

Maeve glanced at Ada with a look which said 'now see what you've done', as both of them spoke,

"Nothing really, just an old family saying." Maeve

"It means Family Hold Back, leave enough food for the guests." Ada

Adam smiled, "Thank you for being so direct, Ada. Many times I make mistakes. When you all come to Greece, I will be honest with you too." Here he beamed, and the thought of a holiday on a Greek island lifted everyone's spirits.

Maeve made a mental note to have that 'let's be friends' conversation with Steve, sooner rather than later.

While Maeve had been resting that afternoon, Marianne had made a 'Carluccio's' recipe Tiramisu with plenty of alcohol. Orla had been dismissive because it wasn't vegan, but when Marianne presented it, followed by 'ooh's' and 'ah's' and "That's the best dessert I have ever had!", she regretted not being able to eat it.

"I take that back Orla, all of the rest of you, will be fat as pigs." Ada was drooling. At her end she had managed a boiled egg on toast, some dark chocolate, and a glass of red wine, which was not quite the same.

Marianne turned pink with pleasure,

"I wanted to do something Italian for Adam. Adam hasn't been to Italy.."

Adam had just been indulging in an extra slice,

"Oh, you will have to bring the recipe and make it for my boyfriend Nik, he loves everything with cream, and coffee, so this is perfect for him."

Adam was burbling on, lost in his thoughts of back home so happily, he didn't see the looks that passed around the table, disappointment on Marianne's and Orla's faces, raised eyebrows on Maeve's, as Ada mouthed 'we never thought to ask...'

Steve with no reaction asked "How does Nik feel about you spending so much time over here?"

Adam hung his head, "Not so good. We are on a break actually."

Deciding this was the moment to change the subject, Maeve intervened,

"I am sure we are all looking forward to meeting your friends, and especially your mother. I for one, can't wait."

Looking round the table with a 'now let's move on attitude', Orla, Marianne, and Adam, got up to clear the table.

They moved into the kitchen, Maeve heard the kettle going on, so asked Steve,

"Coffee, tea, or a glass of something ? Then we can get down to business."

Maeve could also hear Edward, complaining about the mess in the kitchen, she didn't say anything but was hugely relieved to have him back. She had missed the feeling of Edward fussing in the background. So far she was still the only one who he appeared to, those in the kitchen were unaware of his irritation, which made her smile.

As they regrouped accompanied with alcohol, or hot drinks, Maeve said,

"There's nothing like thinking someone is going to kill you, for appreciating what you've got!"

This was greeted with laughter and conversational hubbub, as they all talked over each other. Maeve's comment seemed to be the signal for general expressions of relief.

Calling them to order, it was time to pool all their knowledge, Steve went first,

"When Matthew got to us, at the youth centre exit he didn't have a gun. I guess he dropped it in the woods somewhere near the exit. He had come out of his episode, and seemed normal to us. He was a bit vague but adamant that you needed some back-up."

Steve had taken out his notebook, "Later on he shared a description of his internal experience." He looked at Maeve, "I think you need to hear this."

Flicking through the pages as he found the right spot, he read out,

"I feel like I'm straddling a timeline, where the past is pulling me in one direction and the present another. I see flashes of images, and noises burst through, fear comes out of nowhere. My heart races, my breathing is loud, and I no longer know where I am."

They were silent for a moment. "That helps," said Maeve

who started to nod but regretted it as the egg developing on her head suggested nodding was not a good idea for the moment.

"And Jessica?" She promoted Steve.

"To finish with Matthew first. You made him realise that he could do something, so he has asked for help. The Council and Jan at SAFFA, got him some accommodation and he asked us to give you his contact info."

Steve looked up at Maeve, unasked questions in his expression,

"He said, he trusted you. And he wants to continue some private conversation…"

Maeve was glad that the colour in her cheeks could be put down to good food and a warm room. At the same time it reinforced the mental promise to have that conversation with Steve.

Steve flipped the pages back, "Jessica. Or should we call her 'Jay'? She has absolutely no recollection of the events leading up to her attempt on your life." He stopped to check that everyone was okay. The atmosphere was sombre.

"We took a sample of your blood from the handle of her walking stick, as proof. Now it's up to you, if you want to press charges." Again he scanned his audience for reactions, each was lost in their own thoughts, so he went on.

"I checked in with one of the 'psych's, who gave me a possible cause. If someone suffers extreme trauma they can create a new personality to deal with the trauma."

Steve stopped to take a mouthful of his beer, there was silence as they waited for him to finish.

"It's still not proven, but in some cases they believe that people can switch personalities without being aware of the other persona, or its actions. Think 'Dr Jekyll and Mr Hyde'." He closed his notebook and put it away. "We are keeping her under observation until she has had a full psych evaluation."

Steve was serious, "There's still a lot to do to confirm it, and at the moment, we have no known evidence, but as Maeve suggested, she may well be the one who killed the rough sleeper."

He rubbed his eyes, thinking back on cold cases, "...and God know's how many others."

Orla spoke first, "Well, Kimberly seemed to think that we'd resolved something major."

Fatigue was beginning to overwhelm Maeve. Marianne glanced at her mother and saw that she had turned completely white, this wasn't the time to be polite, so she spoke up

" That's all brilliant. Now I think we should call it a day, everyone needs to process this. And we need to get Maeve off to bed."

CHAPTER 48

MORNING COFFEE

M aeve took the next few days easy, giving herself some time to recover physically and mentally.

She enjoyed having young people in the house again, and listening to Edward buzzing around, which before had been irritating at times, now it was comforting. He knew all about Thomas and that he couldn't get to them. Edward whispered, "I felt him passing, I think he is at peace." Maybe this was just Edward telling himself that everything was okay. Maeve didn't reply. She knew there were other things to be resolved, nothing urgent, but anomalies unanswered.

At one point Orla admitted to Maeve

"I can see Edward, but don't tell him, in case he might stop cleaning my room." Maeve laughed wondering how long Orla could stop herself from talking directly to Edward. Imagining the 'could you do that corner too?'comment slipping out when Orla wasn't thinking.

Maeve had a growing feeling of apprehension. And she knew what it was. She was going to have to talk to Steve, putting it off wasn't helping anyone.

She texted him and they agreed to meet for an early morning coffee.

'Coffees at dawn' she thought to herself, 'well better when less people are around to watch'.

Maeve had been in touch with Matthew too. It turned out that he didn't need help with accommodation or resources, he was fine, but he did need help with trusting people and addressing his PTSD. He was relying on Maeve as a guide. Her ad hoc moment had offered a chink of light for Matthew. So Maeve was on a crash course to learn more about trauma as fast as possible.

Maeve hadn't mentioned meeting Steve to anyone else. That morning she got up early, it was that gloomy pre-dawn winter darkness. As she headed into town, Maeve reflected on Christmas. Over the ages people have needed something to look forward to. Even if it's bringing some greenery in the house as decorations, and nice food, and good company to take our minds off the short days. Once the New Year's celebrations were over, the days would start getting longer again, that was something to look forward to. If the government cancelled Christmas this year, that would be hard for so many people. Still it would make it a Christmas to remember.

She barely noticed the walk and was the first customer at Fond's.

Coffee in hand, she stood outside, anxiety building. Within minutes Steve was standing there beside her.

"You don't need to say anything." He started straight in, "I have come to a decision." He was looking at the ground, no eye contact yet, "Since that shitty train journey, I have been analysing myself." Pause. "I need help."

He stopped, Maeve could see that he wasn't finished yet.

"I'm nowhere near as bad as Matthew, but something happened and this time the past is catching up with me. It's affecting my work, and I see that now."

He glanced up, still not prepared to look her straight in the eye,

"So what I'm saying is. Let's be friends for now." Steve was looking at the ground in front of him,

"We work well together and I trust you. Let's keep that."

When he looked up, Maeve had a big grin, "That's exactly what I would like."

Tension relieved, they both laughed.

Steve had a bit more of the twinkle in his eye as he said, "There is something there, between us, but best not act on it right now." Maeve smiled in agreement.

There was nothing else to say.

Kieran popped his head out, to say Steve's coffee was ready and waiting.

Maeve took the remains of her cup, and slowly walked past RockPaperScissors, and saw the last of Ada's prints in the window. She went on, turning down Water Lane towards Greyfriars gardens.

She stopped on the bridge, looking down at the water running under Greyfriars Chapel. The morning mist was 'wisping' up from the surface of the water, the slight fog of early morning air, had not yet burnt off, it was lingering in the background. This time she was not afraid, she was just looking at the water, listening to the gurgling as it flowed past the stone pier in the middle of the river. She became aware of a presence beside her, turning to have a good look, she recognised the woman she had almost drowned trying to 'save'.

Not quite sure how to proceed, Maeve asked, "Have you come to talk to me?"

"Yes. To answer your questions."

She was standing there beside Maeve, both of them leaning on the top rail of the bridge. Maeve with the dregs of her coffee in her hands. If anyone else could actually see both of them they would look like friends.

Maeve had difficulty expressing herself, "You are not just

the woman who committed suicide are you? And did you, or did she, kill herself?"

"Yes and no. Yes, I took my own life, I fell asleep at the water's edge, then 'Ophelia' like, floated down the river. Yes, I am 'that woman'. Also I am not." Her voice took on the different roles as she spoke.

"Are you also the water spirit?"

"Yes. You know that. You were right, when you thought that I was talking to you in the woods. You know me. You did well. You are strong enough."

"Are you always here to help me?"

She laughed, "What a question!"

Maeve remembered Ada's first overreaction to Maeve's feelings in the woods. Ada had said these spirits could lead you astray, like a 'will-o-the-wisp' leading unsuspecting travellers to their doom. She also remembered the spirit in Scotland warning her to be careful, to take control, or else...

Right now Maeve was feeling emotionally strong.

"To be clear, we have solved Jessica and Kimberly's problems. Haven't we?" Maeve wanted to know something for certain.

"Yes. *We* have. We have helped Kimberly. Jessica's, is your world's problem now." There was an emphasis on the word 'we', from which Maeve understood, that one way or another they were linked.

Maeve finished the last mouthful of her coffee, moved to put the takeaway cup into the bin. Turning back, she was on her own. Maeve was aware that this was only the beginning. The first step on a new journey.

Later that day, the whole family were working from the one functional table in the 'breakfast-cum-dining-cum-office' room, including Adam. Having taken a side of the table each, they were sharing a lot more than usual. Maeve's drama brought them closer together, appreciating what they had. Maeve had no intention of sharing the outcome of her meeting with Steve, his problems were his own, personal, and not to be shared.

Orla had been helping Maeve with her trauma research, "Mum, I've been thinking."

Everyone stopped to listen, this sounded momentus.

"The experience of saving the trees and then coming home, meeting these people, I mean Matthew, and actually Jessica too, has taught me something. Well, really it has shown me how much I don't know."

Maeve knew that if Orla was ready to talk, then she had already spent some time thinking it through.

"I think I would like to study something useful. I am not sure exactly what. But let's take this as a year out?"

"So you mean, back to school in September?" Maeve smiled at her, with an eyebrow raised.

"Yes, maybe not back to the same school. My aim is to do some more research, until I know exactly what I want to do. I need to help the world, and want to help the people in it. I am giving myself until the spring, so that I can choose the right courses."

Her sister was smiling too, "Good plan!" Marianne had always believed that Orla needed time to understand herself, then she would make the right choice.

They grinned at each other.

Maeve agreed, "Yep, that sounds like a good plan."

Much relieved, it sounded to Maeve like she might have Orla at home, at least for a few more years. Rubbing her hands together, she moved into family mode,

"So now we have to make some really important decisions. What do we want for Christmas dinner?"